The Meet Cute Café

by

NICOLE PYLAND

The Meet Cute Café

Years ago, two women met outside a café. Later, they would buy that café together and make it part of their community. People met there for a cup of great coffee or a fresh pastry, and they'd strike up conversations, make new friends, check in on the hot gossip, and in some cases, meet the loves of their lives.

In *The Meet Cute Café*, you'll find eight love stories. Some women went there with a purpose in mind. Others were just grabbing a cup of coffee and met someone they could fall in love with.

Join all of these women as they discover a bit of themselves, find a home at a café, and have a little meet-cute of their own.

To contact the author or for any additional information, visit: **https://nicolepyland.com**

BY THE AUTHOR

Stand-alone books:

- The Fire
- The Moments
- The Disappeared
- Reality Check
- Love Forged
- The Show Must Go On
- The Meet Cute Café

Chicago Series:

- Introduction – Fresh Start
- Book #1 – The Best Lines
- Book #2 – Just Tell Her
- Book #3 – Love Walked into The Lantern
- Series Finale – What Happened After

San Francisco Series:

- Book #1 – Checking the Right Box
- Book #2 – Macon's Heart
- Book #3 – This Above All
- Series Finale – What Happened After

Tahoe Series:

- Book #1 – Keep Tahoe Blue
- Book #2 – Time of Day
- Book #3 – The Perfect View
- Book #4 – Begin Again
- Series Finale – What Happened After

Sports Series:

- Book #1 – Always More
- Book #2 – A Shot at Gold
- Book #3 – The Unexpected Dream
- Book #4 – Finding a Keeper

CONTENTS

PROLOGUE

People don't often stop to think about being overheard. They just walk down the streets with their cell phones stuck to the sides of their faces or their Bluetooth headphones in their ears, talking about their days to the person on the other end of the phone. They stand in lines, and as they wait, they talk about their spouses, their children, or that cousin that's the black sheep in the family. They sit in restaurants and pay no attention to the waiter who approaches to take their order as they talk or fight with each other about who forgot to pick up the dry-cleaning or why they haven't had sex in a month. They stand at water coolers and relay their thoughts on politics, sports, and the woman who works in accounting that has gained a lot of weight since Christmas, never stopping to think that the woman they're talking about is standing just on the other side of the wall listening in, lowering her head and walking back to her desk.

People pretend as if they're in this bubble that only they're a part of; that only the person or people they're talking to can participate in. It's an odd phenomenon, but it happens millions of times a day. And it happens a lot where I work.

I see and hear things I probably shouldn't, and not because I'm trying to listen, but because people forget I'm even there. I don't work for some clandestine government organization – I can't use any information I overhear for any real purpose, and I wouldn't even if I could – I work at *The Meet Cute Café* and spend my days making coffee, baking fresh pastries in the back every morning, and taking care of my customers. I love my job. I've been at it for over five years now, and I can no longer count the number of conversations I've heard. This isn't about me, though. This is *about* those conversations; the things I've seen and heard ever since I made my first cappuccino. *The Meet Cute Café* was named because of the meet-cute between two people at this very location, and it has become a well-known place for people to bring their dates for the view of the beach out the back patio, for the good service, and great coffee.

Now, not to sound too much like an episode of *Law & Order*, but these are their stories.

BROWN EYES

"She's so dreamy," Chelsea said, standing in the doorway but keeping herself just behind it a bit so as not to be seen.

"Aren't you supposed to be counting down your drawer?" Makayla asked.

"Everyone pays with credit cards or their phones; it takes less than two minutes to count the cash," Chelsea replied, still staring.

"Who are you looking at?"

"Brown Eyes."

"Who?"

"She's looking at Brown Eyes," Aunt Shelby said, walking out from the employee bathroom in the back. "She's *always* looking at Brown Eyes, aren't you, Chels?"

"I am not," Chelsea argued, turning around to face her aunt, who was walking toward the back office.

"Who's Brown Eyes?" Makayla asked, looking out at all of the customers.

"Don't stare at her," Chelsea scolded, pulling Makayla back. "She'll see you."

"She?" Makayla asked.

Chelsea looked at Makayla, who was four years younger than her and hadn't ever been in love with a complete stranger, so she obviously didn't get it. At nineteen, Chelsea knew not only that she was gay but that she was in love with someone she'd never even spoken to.

"Yes, *she*," Chelsea replied to the younger girl. "And she's out there studying and looking all studious." She wished she'd thought of a better word, but *math* was Chelsea's thing, not English.

"You like a girl out there?" Makayla asked.

"Ask her out," her aunt said in a sing-song voice from her desk.

"Aunt Shelby, she's a customer. I can't just ask her out," Chelsea argued. "And my shift's over, so I think I'll just go home. Can I have one of the leftover blueberry scones?"

"Of course," Aunt Shelby said. "And take a few for your Mom and Dad, too."

"Thanks," Chelsea replied, taking off her burgundy *Meet Cute Café* hat and matching apron, hanging them both on the hook, and then walking out to the display case to grab a few scones they'd have to throw out tonight anyway.

That was when she saw her. The woman who looked about Chelsea's age approached Brown Eyes, leaned down, and kissed her. She just kissed her right there on the lips, claiming her like Chelsea wasn't standing twenty feet away, making goo-goo eyes at the woman who'd been coming in for the last few weeks. Chelsea sighed and stacked scones into a brown paper bag. This was the third woman Chelsea had seen Brown Eyes with, but this was the first woman to just walk in and kiss her.

The first one had walked in, looked around for a minute, found her, and sat down. They talked for a bit, and then they left together. The second time, Brown Eyes and the other woman walked in holding hands. That had only been two weeks ago. This one was different; she'd kissed her. Chelsea put the tongs back on the side of the display case, then crinkled up her bag, which made a much louder sound than she'd expected, and looked up. Brown Eyes was looking at her. No, she wasn't just looking. She was staring, and she was smirking.

"Are you ready?" the woman asked Brown Eyes.

"Did you grab enough?" Aunt Shelby asked Chelsea.

"What?" Chelsea said, turning to her aunt.

"Do you want some of the coffee cake, too?"

"No, I'm okay," she replied, turning back, but Brown Eyes wasn't staring at her anymore.

She was leaving the café with her hand on the small of the other woman's back.

"You know, you'll never know unless you go for it," Aunt Shelby said.

"I can't."

"Why not?"

"Because look at her…" Chelsea motioned to the now-closed glass door. "She's perfect."

"How do you know that?" Aunt Shelby laughed.

"She's beautiful."

"Beauty doesn't mean perfection. Chels, you can at least try to strike up a conversation with the girl."

"What's the point? She has a different girl in here each time. I don't want that."

"She's in here studying a lot, too."

"She is," Chelsea said.

"Maybe you could study with her."

"I can't just sit down and study with her," Chelsea argued. "Aunt Shelby, I don't know how to ask a girl out."

A customer approached the counter, and they were looking at the menu board, so Chelsea knew they needed a minute. She was technically off, but this was her aunt's café, so she never minded staying to help out when needed.

"I've got them," Aunt Shelby told her with a squeeze to her shoulder. "And I know it seems intimidating, but if you think you could really like her, you should at least try to talk to her. Maybe she only speaks Greek or has three wives or something."

Chelsea laughed and said, "I think she's about my age, so if she has three wives already, she's a big overachiever." Then, she looked at the glass door again, adding. "She's also gone, so I think I'll just head out."

***

"Can I get a latte?"

Chelsea's eyes went wide.

"Sure," she said eventually. "What size?"

"Large," Brown Eyes replied simply. "And maybe a cinnamon scone."

"Maybe?"

"Sorry?" Brown Eyes asked back.

"Do you want a cinnamon scone or not? You said *maybe.*"

"Oh," Brown Eyes laughed a little. "Yes, I'd like a cinnamon scone. Sorry about that. And yeah, thanks."

"No problem. We're not busy. If you want to sit, I can bring it to you."

"How did you know I was staying?"

Shit… Chelsea swallowed as soon as she realized her mistake. She needed to backtrack now. She needed to make sure Brown Eyes didn't think she was constantly being stared at by an employee of *The Meet Cute Café* every time she came in.

"You didn't say to-go," she replied in explanation, and in her mind, she was dramatically wiping imaginary sweat off her brow.

"Right. Okay. Thanks."

Chelsea rang her up, and Brown Eyes placed her phone against the reader, paying for her coffee and scone.

"Do you want a rewards card?"

"What?" Brown Eyes asked just as she turned back to the counter.

"We have cards." Chelsea held one up. "We're not cool enough to have an app, but I'm thinking about making one for us. Anyway, we have these cards. Every ten drinks, you get a free one. Or, you can get a free pastry; whatever. You know, super chill."

"Sure," Brown Eyes replied.

Chelsea stamped the card three times and passed it to her, regretting the fact that she'd just said *'super chill'* for absolutely no reason.

"I gave you a little head start," she added.

"Thanks," Brown Eyes said, sounding surprised.

There was that smirk and stare again, and Chelsea wondered if someone could live off of a smirk as Brown Eyes walked over to her usual table. She was blonde and with shoulder-length hair that she usually tossed around a bunch as she sat and studied. Chelsea hadn't been able to check out the books she was reading and highlighting yet, but maybe today she could bring Brown Eyes her coffee and get a glimpse.

"Calculus?" she said when she dropped off the latte and scone.

"Yeah, I hate it," Brown Eyes replied. "But I've got to pass it this semester. I've put it off for two years."

"I like calculus." Chelsea set the coffee and pastry down on the other side of the small table.

"You do? God, why?" Brown Eyes asked, looking up at Chelsea.

"I like math. It's logical. It just makes sense."

"Are you in school?"

"Beach State," Chelsea said. "Freshman."

"Junior," Brown Eyes shared, smiling at her.

"Chels, the dishwasher is making those sounds," Makayla half-yelled from behind the counter. "The ones it makes when it's about to start leaking soapy water."

"Shit. Oh, sorry," Chelsea apologized for her outburst. "I've got to go."

"No problem," Brown Eyes replied.

Chelsea went to the back room and found her aunt already opening the dishwasher and inspecting it.

"Why did you call *me* if she's here?" Chelsea asked.

"She wasn't here when I called you," Makayla stated.

"I came in the front and heard it going crazy," Aunt Shelby added. "Chels, can you find me the number of the guy?"

"It's on your desk. I already pulled it out for you because it did this with the last round of dishes, too. You just have to shake the thing, and it stops."

"Let's wash dishes by hand tonight, and I'll call to see

if we can have someone take a look at it tomorrow. Maybe it's still under warranty."

"Great. Shake the thing. I've got to get back to the counter; customers waiting and all that."

When Chelsea walked back out, there was a woman sitting across from Brown Eyes. The woman was laughing as Brown Eyes did that sexy hair-toss thing. Then, the woman gave Brown Eyes the wiggling-eyebrows thing that made her intentions for the evening all too clear to Chelsea.

"Another one?"

"What?" Chelsea asked.

"Another woman?" Aunt Shelby said as she stood next to Chelsea.

"I guess so," Chelsea replied with a sigh as two customers approached the counter. "I'll close up tonight, Aunt Shelby. It's not like I have anything else to do on a Friday night."

***

"Now is your chance," Makayla said.

"Huh?" Chelsea asked, leaning over the counter on her elbow, with her hand on her chin.

"She's here again."

"Who?"

"Your girl."

"I don't have a girl," Chelsea replied.

"Brown Eyes is sitting on the patio."

"I assume she has a girl with her," Chelsea said.

"No, she's alone."

Chelsea shrugged a shoulder and said, "For now."

"We're about to close, Chels," Makayla reasoned. "I don't think anyone's joining her."

"Can you go close down the patio, Chels?" Aunt Shelby told her, coming out from the back room. "I'm going to take the deposit to the bank drop box, and I'll be back to help. Makayla, you were supposed to be off the clock an hour ago."

"I was. I've just been hanging out," she said.

"It's late. Do you need a ride home?" Aunt Shelby asked.

While they worked that out, Chelsea stared out the floor-to-ceiling back windows that gave their customers the view of the patio and the beach. She hadn't seen Brown Eyes come in tonight, but she'd been doing schoolwork for the past hour in the back, so she must have come in during that time. From what Chelsea could see, Brown Eyes was the only customer on the patio that had enough lights on it to allow customers to hang out there until closing and still see.

"Hi," Chelsea said, looking around the patio to make sure there weren't any more customers.

"Hi," Brown Eyes replied, looking up at her.

"Can I get you anything else?" Chelsea asked.

"No, I'm okay. Thanks, though," she replied.

"We're closing up," Chelsea blurted.

"Oh, shit," Brown Eyes replied, checking the time on her phone. "I didn't realize how late it was."

Chelsea walked to the table and saw the calculus textbook open and a notebook next to it. Then, she noticed Brown Eyes had a near-empty coffee cup.

"I'll be right back," Chelsea told her.

She walked inside and grabbed the coffee pot, carrying it out to the patio and pouring coffee into the woman's mug.

"I thought you were closing," Brown Eyes remarked.

"We are, but it's barely hot anyway, so you can probably finish it while you work out that equation."

Brown Eyes smiled up at her and asked, "You really like this stuff?"

Chelsea smiled back because she'd remembered their one and only conversation.

"I'm an applied mathematics major, so yeah," she replied.

"Really?"

"Yes," she said. "I haven't figured out exactly what I

want to do yet, but I know it's something to do with math."

"I'm just hoping to pass calculus," Brown Eyes said. Then, she held out her hand for Chelsea. "Taylor."

"Chelsea," she replied, shaking Taylor's hand.

"Nice to meet you," Taylor replied.

Brown Eyes had a name. Her name was Taylor.

"Am I keeping you here?" Taylor asked.

"No," Chelsea lied.

"I am, aren't I," Taylor said, laughing a little. "I have three roommates, and I can't study at home."

"You don't like the university library?"

"I like *some* noise, just not *so much*. One of my roommates, for example, has a new girlfriend, so it's not just sounds of the TV or music I get to hear – they go at it like bunnies." Taylor laughed. "We share a wall."

"Oh, wow," Chelsea replied. "I live at home with my parents, and thankfully, I'm upstairs, and they're downstairs, so I never have to hear that."

"The library just kind of drains all my energy; I don't know how to explain it."

"Well, you can't have coffee there, so the lack of caffeine might have something to do with it," Chelsea said.

"Maybe," Taylor replied. "What do I owe you for this?" she asked, motioning to the coffee cup.

"Nothing. I would just be throwing it out anyway."

"Thanks," Taylor replied.

"Sure," Chelsea said. "I have to go clean up now."

"I'll just finish up," Taylor said.

"Take your time," Chelsea replied, giving her a shy smile.

Taylor smiled back.

"I'm going to take Makayla home before I hit the bank," Aunt Shelby told her, putting on her jacket. "How did *that* go?"

"I just refilled her coffee," Chelsea replied.

"I see," Aunt Shelby said. "Feel free to refill it again if you want. I can take the long way home."

"Aunt Shelby!"

***

"Hi."

Chelsea looked up from the display case and said, "Oh, hi." Then, she promptly dropped the tongs and the bagel she'd been pulling out of the case. "Crap."

Taylor laughed a little and asked, "One of those days?"

"No, I–" Chelsea stopped herself from telling this woman that she made her nervous and, thus, the dropping. "Yeah, I guess. Latte?"

"Yeah, that'd be great."

"Bagel?"

"Well, *not* the one on the floor," Taylor joked.

"I can discount it for you." Chelsea picked up the bagel and dropped the tongs into a dirty dish bin to carry into the back.

"I'll just have a–"

"Cinnamon scone? Yeah, I know."

Chelsea rang her up and planned to take it out to her, but she was the only one behind the counter, with her aunt on the phone in the back, and the other barista calling in sick today. When the line got crazy, she had to resort to yelling out Taylor's order instead. She managed to get the line down to the last two people when she looked up from the milk she was steaming, blew her brown hair that had fallen from her hat out of her eyes, and watched as Taylor picked up dirty dishes off of a table and put them into the bus bin on top of the trash can, allowing two other customers to sit down at the empty table.

"*She's* helpful," Aunt Shelby commented. "Sorry, I couldn't get off the phone until now. How can I help?"

"Take their order for me?" Chelsea asked, nodding to the other customers.

"I will. You should take her a free coffee or something for helping out just now. She's alone again, by the way,"

Aunt Shelby noted.

It was true; the last three times Taylor had been in the café, she'd been alone. She'd had no more study dates or girls walking in kissing her or holding her hand on the way out. They hadn't been able to talk much because Chelsea was always working, but according to Makayla, Taylor only seemed to come in on the nights Chelsea was there now. Chelsea smiled at the naïve thought of the fifteen-year-old Makayla, who wasn't even old enough to work the espresso machine, but knew Taylor's visits to *The Meet Cute* likely only had to do with when she needed to study while her roommate was getting laid next to her bedroom.

"Hey," Taylor said as she approached the counter.

"Hey. Do you need a refill?" Chelsea asked. "It's on the house. I saw you helping out earlier. Thank you for that."

"No problem," Taylor said. "And no, I don't need a refill."

"Oh, okay," Chelsea replied. "Need any help with calculus?"

Taylor laughed and said, "No, I'm heading out. I brought contemporary social and political philosophy tonight."

"That's a mouthful," Chelsea noted, laughing a little.

"I only took it because my girlfriend was taking it," Taylor said.

"Ah," Chelsea replied, swallowing.

"And then we broke up right after the add/drop deadline, so now I'm stuck with it until the end of the semester."

"Awkward?"

"The class is about eighty people, so we just sit on opposite sides and ignore each other like mature adults." Taylor smiled at her and shifted her bag on her shoulder.

"I'm lucky I don't have any exes, I guess," Chelsea said for some reason and then instantly blushed.

"None?"

Chelsea shook her head.

"You have a *current*, though, right? Some high-school sweetheart you're making it work with while you go to separate colleges or something? He was a varsity football player; you were the cheerleader."

Chelsea laughed so hard, one of the remaining customers in the place looked up at her like he thought she was crazy.

"Not even close," she said.

"No?"

Chelsea shook her head. Then, someone walked through the front door and toward the counter.

"I should let you get back to work," Taylor said.

"Oh. Yeah, okay," Chelsea replied.

"Have a good night," Taylor said, shifting her bag again.

Chelsea watched her leave the café.

"Can I get a cappuccino and a hazelnut biscotti?" the man said without waiting for Chelsea to greet him.

***

"I think I have a free drink," Taylor said, holding up her card.

"You do," Aunt Shelby replied. "What would you like?"

Chelsea pretended not to be interested in Taylor's conversation with her aunt as she made a drink for another customer, but she started the espresso for a large latte just as Taylor ordered it. When she then walked to the display case to grab the cinnamon scone, Taylor caught her eye and nodded. Chelsea put it on a plate for her and finished making the drink for the other customer and Taylor's, putting hers in a mug and his in a to-go cup.

"Thanks," Taylor said. "I think I need a new card now."

"Did Aunt Shelby not give you one?" Chelsea asked.

"No," Taylor replied, taking her coffee and scone off

the counter.

"I'll grab one for you and walk it over. Just give me a minute?"

"Sure," Taylor said with a smile.

A few minutes later, Chelsea headed toward the table on the patio with a new card that she'd punched a few times.

"Does your boss know you're giving out all these head starts?" Taylor asked, taking the card.

"Yes. She doesn't care," Chelsea replied. "Well, good luck with your studying."

"Any chance you're on a break soon?"

"We usually get busy with the night owls right before closing, so I'll be behind the counter until that last rush dies down," she replied, wondering at the question.

"I can wait," Taylor said.

"Do you need something?"

"Help with calculus," Taylor said, smiling. "I have a test tomorrow."

"Oh," Chelsea uttered, hoping she didn't sound too disappointed.

"I'm kidding. You're working, and it'll be late when you close. I–"

"No, it's fine. I can take a look at your study guide or something and see if I can help."

"I have practice equations you could take a look at and tell me how wrong I got them." Taylor smiled up at her.

"Sure," Chelsea told her. "Just give me twenty minutes."

She walked back to the counter feeling defeated. When Taylor had asked if she was going on break, Chelsea had thought for one fleeting moment that Taylor might want her to sit down and join her for a coffee, but of course not. That wouldn't make any sense. She just needed help with calculus and, apparently, none of her three roommates could make the time, Taylor couldn't make the professor's office hours, and the test was tomorrow. Of course, she just wanted help with math from probably the only math major she knew.

***

"You did pretty well," Chelsea said as she finished looking over the practice test Taylor had shared with her. "You only missed two."

"Really?" Taylor asked, looking down at the paper in Chelsea's hands.

"And on this one," Chelsea added, "you just didn't put the negative sign, is my guess, because you got the answer right. It's -7/4, not 7/4, though."

"Oh, right," Taylor replied, leaning over a little to add the negative symbol before the fraction.

Chelsea didn't mean to, but she breathed her in. Taylor smelled of coffee, cinnamon, and perfume. Chelsea didn't wear perfume herself, so she wasn't familiar with the specific brand or scent, but it smelled really, really good. She pulled back a little and took a drink of the coffee she'd brought to the table that was already starting to cool.

"Well, you seem like you should be good for your test tomorrow. I should probably get moving."

"I should get going," Taylor replied as she started packing up her stuff. "Thank you for this."

"You didn't need me," Chelsea told her, standing up and taking both of their mugs as she walked toward the counter. "Good luck tomorrow."

"Thanks. I guess I'll see you around," Taylor said, following Chelsea.

"I'm pretty much always here or in class."

"Why don't I ever see you on campus? It's a big university, but I'm around a lot. Do you not go to the union or hang out on the quad?"

"No, I don't live near campus, so I just go to class and leave. Sometimes, I'm at the library."

"Which explains why I don't see you because I'm *never* in the library," Taylor replied.

Then, Taylor's phone chimed, and Chelsea watched her pull it out of the front pocket of her jeans.

"Sorry," she said. "That's my roommate. *One* of them, anyway. She's just texting to let me know she and her girlfriend just got there, which is my cue to either stay away or put on noise-canceling headphones when I get home."

"They really go at it, huh?" Chelsea asked, moving behind the counter.

"Chels, can you drop the money at the bank for me tonight?" Aunt Shelby asked. "I've got a headache, and I think I'd rather just go home and get some sleep."

"I guess, yeah," Chelsea replied as her aunt emerged from the back.

"Oh, sorry," Aunt Shelby said when she noticed there was still a customer inside the café. "Did I forget to lock the door? The machines are clean, but–"

"No, I was just leaving," Taylor said.

"I didn't drive tonight; Dad dropped me off. My car was being funky earlier," Chelsea told her Aunt.

"*I* could take you," Taylor offered.

Chelsea turned to the older girl and gave her an expression that likely showed both confusion and surprise.

"I can't go home just yet anyway," Taylor added. "Maybe if I take you there and drop you at home, they'll be done by the time I get back – or on break, at least."

"Chels?" Aunt Shelby checked.

"I promise, I'm not crazy. My roommate is having loud sex in her room, which is right next to *my* room," Taylor said. "This place is closed, and so is just about everywhere else in town, so *you'd* actually be helping *me* out."

"You can take my car," Aunt Shelby offered.

"No, it's okay," Chelsea told her aunt and then turned to ask Taylor, "Are you sure?"

Her heart pounded happily that she'd get a few more minutes with her, despite the fact that Taylor was only trying to delay going home and wasn't actually interested in more time with Chelsea.

"Yeah, I'm sure," Taylor replied with a smile.

"Okay. Just give me a minute to grab my stuff."

"You're not trying to get Chelsea and the money alone so that you can ditch her on the side of the road and run off with the cash, are you?" Aunt Shelby asked, only somewhat jokingly.

"Oh, my God!" Chelsea yelled in exasperation. "Can you wait outside so she doesn't say anything else like that?"

Taylor laughed and nodded.

"To be clear," she added seriously, "that nod was to the waiting outside thing, not the other thing."

***

Taylor's car was nicer than hers, but not by much, and, Chelsea guessed, it was at least a few years old. It smelled like Taylor, though, which made her smile as she put on her seat belt. She was in Taylor's car, and she couldn't believe it. This was the girl she'd been staring at from afar, and now she was in her car.

"So," Taylor said when she turned on the ignition.

"So," Chelsea replied.

Taylor smiled over at her and added, "The bank? I need directions."

"Oh, right," Chelsea replied. "Straight for two blocks. Then, take a right."

"Got it."

"You're a safe driver, right?" Chelsea asked.

"Well, I've never killed anyone in my car, if that's what you're asking." Taylor laughed.

"That's an interesting qualifier."

"What?" Taylor asked, pulling onto the street.

"You said you've never killed anyone *in your car*," Chelsea said.

"Oh." Taylor laughed in response. "I've never killed anyone, period. Is that better?"

"Yes," Chelsea said.

"I've had two speeding tickets in my life. One wasn't my fault; the cop was just an asshole – I was going two miles over the limit."

"And the other one?"

"My fault," Taylor replied. "I was running late to pick up a girlfriend. Well, she's my ex now, obviously, but I was already on thin ice with her as it was, and I was trying to make up time. I got pulled over instead, and she dumped me about two weeks later."

"Same girlfriend you're in that class with now?"

"No, a different one. I was a freshman when she and I were together." Taylor stopped the car at a light. "Is that a problem for you?"

"Is *what* a problem?" Chelsea asked, turning to Taylor just as Taylor turned to look at her.

"The girl thing? I assumed that you'd be okay with it given that *Meet Cute* is kind of known as a lesbian hangout."

"Oh, yeah." Chelsea nodded. "Totally okay with me. No problem with girlfriends. Never had one myself, but I don't–"

The way Taylor's eyebrow lifted at that last part both embarrassed Chelsea because *she'd* been the idiot who had just rambled about how much she didn't have a problem with girlfriends and that she was a loser who'd never had one, but also really, really turned her on. She could write love poems about that eyebrow lift. She wished Taylor's roommate was the one who needed to use noise-canceling headphones tonight because Taylor and Chelsea were in the room next door going at it like rabbits.

"We're here," she announced thankfully a minute later, despite them being a block away from the bank. "You can just park here."

"No way. I'm driving you all the way there," Taylor replied.

Chelsea climbed out of the car as soon as it was parked in order to get some fresh air and space away from Taylor, who really did smell that good, and in the car, Chelsea was so close, she couldn't avoid it. At least, in the café, she could walk away. Taylor often sat outside, and the breeze and saltwater often helped Chelsea take her mind off the fact that she wanted to pull Taylor against her just to breathe her in. Well, and kiss her. She also wanted to kiss her.

"I'm walking with you. Hold on," Taylor said, climbing out of the car.

"It's just right here," Chelsea replied. "I'll be right back. I just need to drop it in the box, and I'm good."

"I've seen enough true crime shows to know that a pretty woman walking by herself at night can disappear in a second. You're also carrying money. So, I'll just walk with you to be careful. I have pepper spray on my key chain," Taylor told her as she appeared on her right side.

Chelsea didn't say anything about the pretty woman comment. She didn't want to draw attention to it because Taylor might want to take it back. So, she just walked up to the box, dropped the bag into it, and turned around.

"Okay. Done. Keep the pepper spray capped, and let's go."

Taylor laughed and asked, "Where do you live?"

"You can just drop me back at the café. I can text my dad and have him pick me up."

"I promised I'd take you home, and I'm taking you home," Taylor replied.

"Right; we've only killed, like, five minutes. You still think they're… you know?"

"If my roommate were with a guy, I'd make some comment about stamina here and say they're probably done." Taylor laughed a little at her own joke as they climbed back into the car. "But two women… It's a lot longer than five minutes."

Chelsea swallowed as she turned, blushing, toward the passenger window to avoid Taylor's sexy smirk. They drove for another ten minutes, with the only words between them being the directions Chelsea gave Taylor to her house. Taylor pulled into the driveway and turned off the car.

"I'm sorry if I said something that made you uncomfortable," she said.

Chelsea turned to her and said, "What? You didn't."

"The sex comments?" Taylor asked, looking unsure in that moment.

"I can handle comments about sex, Taylor."

"And the girl part. I mean, the two girls together part – you stopped talking to me after that."

Chelsea opened her mouth to say something but didn't.

"Right. Sorry, again." Taylor nodded once. "My bad."

"No, it's not. My aunt is gay," she said louder than she'd intended.

Taylor nodded again, and there was this expression that Chelsea couldn't read on her face. Chelsea closed her lips tightly. She couldn't believe she'd just said that. She had a lesbian aunt? Where had that even come from?

"I didn't mean it like that. I–"

"No, it's cool," Taylor replied, starting the car up again.

"No, it's not. I don't even know why I just said that." Chelsea sighed. "That's not true. Yes, I do." She looked down at her hands clasped together in her lap. "I said that because I don't know how to say that I've never…" She twiddled her thumbs. "I like girls."

"You do?" Taylor asked.

Chelsea nodded.

"Are you not out?"

"No, it's worse than that. I've been out since I was sixteen. My parents are completely supportive. My mom baked me a rainbow cake for my seventeenth birthday, and my dad waved the flag at Pride last year. My aunt is gay and married to my other aunt. They're both crazy supportive, obviously. Everyone in my life knows, and they've all been there for me."

"How exactly is that worse?" Taylor asked. "That's the dream, Chelsea."

"It's worse because I've never had a girlfriend. I've never even been on a single date with a woman."

"What? Why?"

"I told you I wasn't the cheerleader with the football-playing boyfriend. I'm a math major. That didn't give away that I was a big nerd in high school? I got my braces off junior year and finally switched to contacts before college, but if there's a nerd stereotype, I would have fit it easily."

"Why did you switch to contacts?"

"Huh?"

"What's so wrong with glasses?"

"Nothing. I love my glasses. I just wanted a fresh start. And since I was going to college in my hometown, I thought a new look would help with that; maybe the people I'd gone to high school with would finally see me differently. I would have gotten them sooner, but it took me years to get over the whole touching my eyes thing. I hate it."

"Do you still have your glasses?"

"Yeah, I bring them with me everywhere in case my contacts irritate my eyes, or one falls out. Wait. Why are we talking about contacts?"

"Are they in your purse?" Taylor asked.

"Yeah."

"Can I see them?"

"You want to see my glasses?"

"Yeah. Can I?"

"O-k-a-y." Chelsea dragged out the word, wondering how they'd got here, picked her purse up off the floor, and pulled out her glasses case. "Here."

Taylor took it and opened the case. She pulled out the glasses with the dark rims that Chelsea had picked out the previous year.

"Can you take your contacts out?"

"I'm not supposed to do that with dirty hands."

"Okay. Close your eyes, then," Taylor said.

"Why?" Chelsea asked, laughing.

"Just for a second. Humor me." She shrugged a shoulder.

"Okay."

Chelsea closed her eyes, and a second later, she felt Taylor moving closer as her glasses were placed on her ears. Then, Taylor's warmth moved away again while Chelsea kept her eyes closed.

"Perfect," Taylor said softly.

Chelsea opened her eyes then, forgetting the now-double prescription, and instantly regretted it.

"Shit," she said.

Taylor laughed but helped take her glasses off. Chelsea opened her eyes again, and Taylor held out her case.

"You should wear these more often."

"I just ordered a six-month supply of contacts," Chelsea told her, tucking her glasses back into her purse.

"Well, that was a waste," Taylor replied. "Glasses make those baby blues of yours really pop."

Chelsea risked a look over at Taylor, who was looking back. She knew her cheeks were bright red, but she could do nothing to cover her blush.

"I should go. My dad's probably sitting on the couch waiting for me to call him to have him pick me up. Good luck with your oversexed roommate."

"No such thing," Taylor said, winking at her.

"Right. Bye." Chelsea pushed the door open and tried climbing out without undoing her seat belt. "Ow!"

"Hold on," Taylor said, leaning over. "I've got you." She unbuckled the belt, paused for a second as if she was going to say or maybe do something else, and then she moved away. "Good night, Chelsea."

"Chels."

"Taylor," she said. "Are we saying our own names now?" She laughed.

"No. I mean, you can call me *Chels*. Most people do." She climbed out of the car. "Night."

***

"So, how did it go?" Aunt Shelby asked.

"How did *what* go?" Chelsea lifted two gallons of milk

out of the small fridge behind the counter.

"Brown Eyes Taylor dropped you off at home, didn't she?"

"Yes, she did. So what?"

"Chels, I'm looking for some details here," Aunt Shelby said.

"There *are* no details. She took me to the bank, *didn't* try to steal the money, and then took me home."

"You didn't talk at all on the way? That's at least twenty minutes of prime talking time."

"You set the whole thing up, didn't you?" Chelsea asked, placing the milk on the counter. "You didn't have a headache?"

"I *had* a headache, but I could've still taken the money to the bank. When I saw Taylor standing there, though, I thought there might be an opportunity. And I was right – she took it."

"She took what?"

"The opportunity," Aunt Shelby replied as she placed more of her freshly baked chocolate croissants into the display case.

"You guilted the girl into taking me to the bank."

"No, I didn't. She could have said goodnight and left the café. She *chose* to offer her services. You had no car, but you could have easily driven mine or called your dad. She offered, and you accepted – opportunity." Her aunt nodded proudly.

"Well, nothing came of it, so opportunity wasted, I guess."

"Chels, did you really not even talk to the girl?"

"No, I did. We talked," she said, moving to refill the espresso beans in the machine while they were in a lull. "But you might have noticed she hasn't been in all week. She probably had five dates with five different women, taking them home to have marathon girl-on-girl sex that is, apparently, amazing, but I wouldn't know because I've never even kissed a girl."

"Chelsea, I love you, but you've got to stop imagining things that you don't know to be true. Besides, women are allowed to go on dates with different women; there's nothing wrong with dating around. You're both young. You said she's a junior, right?"

"Yeah."

"So, she's about twenty-one. She *should* be dating around. You should be, too. There's nothing wrong with going out with another woman just to see if there's anything there. Don't fault her for that because you have a crush, okay?"

"No, I know," Chelsea replied. "I'm a feminist. I'm also basically her stalker."

"Have you followed her outside of the café, and I don't know?"

"What? No," Chelsea said.

"Then, you're not a stalker." Her aunt wrapped an arm around Chelsea's shoulders. "You just like a girl, Chels. That's an amazing thing. I hope you get the courage to tell her one day, but even if you don't, you will when the time is right. And I promise, it'll be worth it, okay?"

"You say that because you're happily married."

"We all have to start somewhere."

She knew her aunt was right. Chelsea was just so ready to get this part of her life started. She'd had a crush after crush in high school, and now she was crushing on Taylor, who at least knew she existed, so that was something to celebrate, right? None of the girls in high school had even known Chelsea's name. Taylor knew her name, though, and she knew she could call her Chels. She'd also told Chelsea she looked perfect in her glasses. Chelsea smiled as she poured steamed milk into a to-go cup.

"What has *you* smiling?"

Chelsea looked up with wide eyes to see Taylor standing there with her bag slung over her shoulder.

"I didn't see you come in," she replied.

"Because you were smiling at that cup," Taylor noted,

pointing at the cup Chelsea was holding.

"Oh, sorry. Can I get you something? Makayla's on the register right now, but I can get something started for you. Latte?"

"I just wanted to say hi," Taylor said. "My study group is meeting here today. We're going to grab a couple of tables out on the patio if that's okay. I'll wait until they're all here before I order."

"Sure. No problem," Chelsea replied.

Taylor nodded and asked, "How have you been?"

Chelsea placed the cup on the counter and said, "Medium vanilla cappuccino; extra dry." Then, she turned back to Taylor and asked, "What? Sorry."

"Nothing," Taylor replied. "I'll let you work."

Later, Chelsea looked out at the patio where a group of people sat with Taylor. There were two girls and three guys. Was one of them her newest girlfriend or potential date? They all had their noses in their books or seemed to be discussing something seriously. Once, Chelsea looked over and saw Taylor looking up at the same time. Caught, Chelsea turned toward the ocean and pretended like she was just taking in the view, which technically, she *had* been. Taylor had been doing that hair-toss thing a lot today, and Chelsea wanted to run her hand through it after she did it as a way of saying to everyone watching that this beautiful girl was hers. Yeah, right. She rolled her eyes at her own ridiculous thoughts and got back to work.

"I'm heading out," Taylor said.

"Oh. Okay. How was studying?"

"Good. We're all in the philosophy class I mentioned I took with my ex. Since it's not really my thing, I joined a study group."

"Cool," Chelsea replied, having nothing else to say.

She couldn't exactly ask Taylor why she hadn't been into the café all week or if any of those girls were next up on her dance card.

"I left something on the table," Taylor told her.

"Oh, I'll clean it up," Chelsea said, grabbing her rag.

"I just wanted *you* to know since other people work here, too, and…"

"Taylor, are you coming?"

Chelsea turned to see a girl standing at the front door, holding it open for Taylor.

"We're going to class now," Taylor said. "She's just waiting on me because we're all going to the same place." She shifted her bag.

"Okay. I'll take care of the table. Part of the job," Chelsea replied.

"I'll see ya?"

"Sure," Chelsea said.

"You should go out there," Taylor added, pointing to the patio. "Soon. Just in case."

Chelsea looked at her, confused, and said, "Yeah, okay."

Taylor nodded and then followed her study group out of the café. Intrigued, Chelsea walked to the patio and saw the two tables they'd pushed together. There wasn't any trash on the table, so she was confused. All the mugs and plates were in the bus bin they always placed on the patio for easy transport of dishes. The only thing on the table, besides the sugar caddy, was a flower. Not just any flower, though. It was a red rose, and it looked like it had something underneath it. Chelsea stared, even more confused now. This couldn't be what Taylor meant. She got closer and looked down. There was a note on a napkin.

Chels,

No glasses today? Maybe next time.

Taylor

"What's that?" Makayla asked, looking over Chelsea's shoulder.

"A flower."

"Someone left it here?" she asked.

"Yeah," Chelsea said, smiling. "I guess so."

***

Chelsea stared. She couldn't help herself. Taylor was sitting on the patio again, but this time, she was sitting with someone. It was a girl, and they were looking at one of their phones. So, Taylor was just a flirt. Or, maybe she hadn't been flirting – she'd just found a rose somewhere or pulled it from someone's garden like a psycho, probably, and wanted to get rid of it. That was it, right?

When Taylor looked up at her and gave her a smile, Chelsea looked away. Taylor wasn't hers; she could do whatever she wanted. It was just hard to watch. Chelsea knew she wasn't *actually* in love with Taylor. She knew it was only a crush. It was still hard, though, watching the girl she was crushing on crush on someone else, and repeatedly at that.

"Hey, that table asked if you could come over," Tina said.

"What table?" Chelsea asked.

"The one on the patio, with the two girls," she replied.

Tina was another barista. She was sixteen and only worked part-time. She'd only started a few weeks ago, and Chelsea wasn't all that impressed with her aunt's most recent hire, but it wasn't Chelsea's café, so she let it go and looked up to see Taylor *and* the girl she was with looking at her this time. What the hell was going on? She walked over there reluctantly, hoping to God that Taylor wasn't going to introduce Chelsea to her date while asking her to bring them lattes and cinnamon scones.

"Hey," Taylor greeted when she arrived at the table.

"Hey," she said. "Can I get you something?" she asked right after, wanting to move this along as quickly as possible.

"Oh," Taylor said, looking confused. "No, I just noticed the line had died down, and I thought you could maybe meet my sister."

Chelsea's eyes widened, and she said, "Sister?"

"Yeah, this is Tanner. She's in town for the week, visiting home. This is Chelsea," she said to the woman sitting next to her.

Now, Chelsea could see it – they looked a lot alike. They had the same nose, the same brown eyes, and ash-blonde hair. Tanner looked to be a few years older, but that was almost the only difference between them.

"Nice to meet you," Tanner said.

"You too," Chelsea replied. "So, you live out of town?"

"Out of state," Tanner replied. "I moved away for college and never came back. I live in Portland now and work in environmental law."

"That's pretty cool," Chelsea said.

"She's the overachieving older sister, and I'm the underachieving baby of the family," Taylor said, smiling at her sister.

"You are *not* an underachiever," Tanner told her, slugging her shoulder playfully.

"Do you have siblings? Do they beat you, too?" Taylor asked Chelsea while laughing.

"I have a little brother, but he's fourteen and spends most of his time in his room playing video games," Chelsea replied.

"Taylor is going into criminal law," Tanner said, bragging about her sister.

"You *are*?" Chelsea asked, realizing they'd not yet talked about what Taylor wanted to do after college.

"That's the plan, anyway. I'm pre-law right now."

Chelsea smiled a little and said, "You have to take calculus for pre-law?"

"I needed a math class," Taylor replied.

"So, she chose the easy one," Tanner commented. "Well, easy one for her. *I* chose algebra because I couldn't handle even pre-calculus."

Chelsea met Taylor's eyes and asked, "Easy one?"

"Not exactly," Taylor said.

"You aced pre-calculus in high school, and Mom said you're getting an A in that class now," Tanner argued.

Chelsea smiled at Taylor and said, "So, you didn't need help, after all?"

"Help?" Tanner asked. "She hates math, but she's good at it. Why would you need help?"

"Chels, can you help out?" Makayla asked as she walked out to the table. "I can ring them up, but Tina can't keep up with the drinks."

Chelsea turned around and saw the line of five people and the struggling Tina trying to steam milk and pour the espresso into cups at the same time.

"I've got to go. It was nice to meet you, though," she said, giving them both a wave and walking to the counter.

She didn't have time to consider what all that had meant because the line of five turned into ten, and Tina couldn't handle doing even one thing at a time, so Chelsea put her on the register, sent Makayla out to clean the tables, and handled making the drinks until their other part-timer showed up to handle closing the place down. It was only then that Chelsea could finally go into the back, count down her drawer, and head home. She was exhausted. There had been a non-stop rush of customers for most of the day, and Tina had created more problems than she'd solved. When Chelsea put her cash in the safe and started the dishes, she clocked out and left through the back door, which led to the beach and the small parking lot where she'd parked her car.

"Hi."

She turned around to see Taylor standing there next to the patio.

"Hi," Chelsea replied.

"I didn't lie to you," Taylor said.

"Sorry?"

"About calculus; I don't like it."

"But you didn't need my help, did you? Did you miss those two questions on purpose?"

"I may not have needed your help with the math, but I wanted to talk to you, and I thought it was a good excuse," Taylor told her, taking a few steps toward her. "These are for you."

Chelsea watched as she pulled a bouquet of mixed flowers from behind her back and held them in front of her.

"Flowers?"

"You got the rose, right?" Taylor asked.

"Yeah, but then you…" Chelsea inhaled and exhaled deeply. "I saw you with another girl, and I figured you were just being nice."

"Tanner was here because I wanted her to meet you," Taylor said.

"Me? Why?"

"Because she always gives me a hard time about the women I like," Taylor replied. "I've not always made the best decisions where women were concerned, so I thought that if she could see you and talk to you for a few minutes, she'd, I don't know, see what I see and think that maybe I'd met…" Taylor paused. "She liked you, by the way."

"She did?" Chelsea asked with a soft smile.

"I was wondering if you'd maybe want to go out with me sometime," Taylor said.

"Me?" she asked.

Taylor laughed and said, "Yes, you. Chels, I'm literally holding out flowers for you right now, and I left you one on the table the other day."

"But you have dates in here all the time," Chelsea said.

"I *used* to, yeah," Taylor replied, shrugging a shoulder. "I haven't in a while, though. Have you not noticed?"

"No, I've noticed," she said.

Taylor moved a step closer and said, "Will you take these, please?"

"Oh, sure." Chelsea took the flowers from her. "No one's ever given me flowers before, and now you've done it twice."

"I like you," Taylor said. "Will you let me take you to dinner and a movie or something?"

"You like me?"

"Yes. And I think you like me, too," Taylor replied.

"Not to sound like an egomaniac or anything, but I just have this feeling."

Chelsea blushed and nodded.

"So, can I pick you up at seven?"

"When?"

"Tomorrow."

"Tomorrow?" Chelsea asked, wondering how the hell she could get ready for a date that quickly.

"Well, I've been working up the courage to ask you out for a while now, so I'm kind of really ready," Taylor said.

"You've been…"

"If I don't see you in the café when I pass by, I don't come in. I stopped bringing dates a while ago. I stay until closing only on the nights when you close, and I stare at you constantly. You really haven't noticed any of this?" Taylor laughed. "My sister called me pathetic."

"You're not pathetic," Chelsea told her, not liking that someone would say that to Taylor, even jokingly.

"She's my big sister; she doesn't mean it," Taylor said, biting her lower lip.

Holy shit! Taylor was nervous. She was holding her hands in front of her, twiddling her thumbs just like Chelsea did when *she* was nervous.

"You still haven't answered my question. Does that mean it's a no?"

"No," Chelsea said quickly. "No, I mean… It's not a no. It's a yes."

Taylor laughed a little and said, "Yes?"

"Yes," Chelsea confirmed.

"Tomorrow?"

"Yes."

"I'll pick you up," Taylor said, smiling at her. "Is your car parked back here, or should I wait with you until your dad picks you up?"

Chelsea smiled wide and said, "It's right here. My dad got it to work."

"So, I'll see you tomorrow?"

"Yeah, I guess you will."

"You look really cute in the apron and hat, by the way," Taylor said as she backed away. "But I'm looking forward to seeing you *not* in your uniform."

***

"I'm running out of places to put these," Chelsea said as Taylor handed her another rose.

"Who's there?" Chelsea's dad said from behind her.

"No one, Dad. I'll see you later. I'm going out now. Bye." She closed the door after rambling all that off quickly.

Taylor laughed and said, "I thought you were going to put that in water."

"Trust me, you don't want to go in there," Chelsea replied, still standing in front of Taylor on the front porch.

"Why not?"

"Remember the part about how I've never been on a date and my parents are really supportive? Well, if they see me dressed up like this and you looking like…" Chelsea faded out as she took Taylor in. "They'll know this is a date, and they'll invite you inside, and we'll never get out of here."

"I don't mind a little parental inquisition," Taylor said. "And what exactly do I look like?" She smirked.

"Oh, don't do that," Chelsea said.

"Don't do what?"

"That smirk thing you do. And don't do that eyebrow thing, either. When you do, I blush."

Taylor took a step closer to her and asked, "Why do you blush, Chels?"

God, her voice was deeper and huskier somehow, and Chelsea couldn't stop the heat creeping up her cheeks.

"Yeah, don't do that, either."

Taylor laughed. Then, she took Chelsea's hand and entwined their fingers.

"Are you ready?"

"Yes," she said, looking down at their joined hands.

Then, she heard a sound and turned her head to find her parents staring at them out the window. "Oh, my God! Please get me out of here."

Taylor followed her glance and gave her parents a wave with her free hand. Chelsea just pulled her down to the driveway as Taylor continued to laugh.

"You look great," Chelsea told her finally. "You look…" She stared at Taylor's jeans that were dressier than the usual ones she wore in the café, and her eyes traveled up to the evergreen-colored sweater she'd worn. "Really good."

Taylor pulled Chelsea a little closer to her and said, "You look beautiful."

Then, Taylor glanced back at the window.

"Are they still–"

"Yeah," Taylor confirmed.

"Mortifying," Chelsea said.

***

"Why do you look upset?" Aunt Shelby asked her. "Wasn't your big date last night?"

"My first *and* last date," Chelsea mumbled as she put cash into the drawer she'd then take out to the register.

"What happened?"

"Nothing," Chelsea replied.

"Nothing? Did you not have a good time?"

"No, I had a great time. She showed up with another flower for me. She dressed up. She took me to a nice dinner, and we talked about pretty much everything. Then, we went to a movie, and she held my hand. She actually put it in her lap, and I just sat there frozen like an idiot because I've never held anyone's hand in a movie before, and I didn't know what to do, so I just let it sit there and get all sweaty. I wanted to, you know, make a move or something; maybe put my arm around her or put my head on her shoulder – but no, I just sat there and let our hands sweat all over each other. Oh, and that was *after* my parents embarrassed the crap out of me by staring out the window when she picked me up. They *waved* at her, Aunt Shelby. They waved at my older, much cooler, and much more experienced date like we were going off to junior prom. I'm surprised they didn't ask us to come in and take a picture by the fireplace."

"Okay. Hold on. I'm trying to keep up here," Aunt Shelby said, tossing the rag onto the counter.

"She dropped me off after the movie and didn't even make a move to kiss me," Chelsea added. "She was probably so grossed out by my sweaty hands that she didn't even want to have her mouth touch mine."

"Calm down," Aunt Shelby told her. "She might have just wanted to take things slow."

"Yeah, because she knows I'm a nineteen-year-old who's never kissed a girl. She's had sex, Aunt Shelby. Probably a lot of it. She's had two serious girlfriends, and I'd never even had a date until last night. I think I'll just be done with them from now on. My father – your brother, by the way – actually turned the porch light on when she walked me to the door. She probably thinks I'm a kid now."

"You're two years younger than her; that's nothing. Did she say anything about it?"

"No, but she's nice like that. God, Aunt Shelby, I was so nervous, but she was so great. She opened the doors for me. She even pulled out my chair at the restaurant. We talked about what she wants to do after school, and I told her I was still trying to figure things out but that I was considering changing my major to mechanical engineering." Chelsea paused. "She likes when I wear my glasses, Aunt Shelby."

Shelby rubbed Chelsea's back and said, "Has she called or texted you?"

"No," Chelsea said on a sigh. "I think I messed it up."

"No, you didn't," Taylor stated, coming from around the corner of the counter. "Sorry, there's no one out here, and I wasn't eaves-dropping, but I–"

"Hey, Taylor," Aunt Shelby said. "Why don't you

come back here? I'll take the counter. Do you want a coffee or something?"

"No, thank you," Taylor replied, entering the back room. "I just came to see her." She smiled at Chelsea. "Do you have a minute?"

"I'm on the clock."

"No, you're not," Aunt Shelby winked at her. "Take your time."

Chelsea quickly gave her aunt a *'don't leave me here'* expression, but the woman just winked at her and walked to the counter with Chelsea's drawer.

"Can we go outside, maybe?" Taylor asked.

"Uh, sure. I mean, yeah," Chelsea said.

Taylor was here to tell her she didn't want to see her anymore and, apparently, wanted an ocean view to break the news. Taylor held the door open for Chelsea, though, and smiled as Chelsea walked past her. Then, she offered her hand to Chelsea, who took it. Taylor entwined their fingers like she'd done the previous night, and they walked to the sidewalk and then up into the sand. There, they stared out at the water for a moment, and Chelsea just waited. Either Taylor would start talking, or the sweat from Chelsea's hand would start to mingle with Taylor's, and they'd pull apart.

"You didn't mess anything up," Taylor said as the waves crashed to the shore.

"What?"

"Last night," she said, turning her face to Chelsea's. "I had a great time."

"I was a mess."

"No, you weren't," Taylor said.

"I am one-hundred-percent certain you have been on dates with women who don't act like nervous idiots, with parents who aren't quite ready to let their kid be an adult."

Taylor dropped her hand, and thank God! Chelsea was starting to sweat. Next thing she knew, Taylor was behind her, her arms were coming around Chelsea's waist, and she was pulling Chelsea back against her. Taylor's chin was on her shoulder now, and she'd never done this before. She'd seen other people hold each other like this, and she'd always wanted it for herself, too, but she never thought *Brown Eyes* would be the one to hold her this way.

"I like you," Taylor said. "A lot. I like that you always try to tuck those flyaways back under your cute hat. I like that you're a math genius. I like that you get embarrassed by your parents." She laughed. "Who doesn't?"

"*You* don't seem to," Chelsea argued.

"You haven't met them yet," Taylor replied.

She said *yet.*

"My dad still has a baseball bat he keeps specifically for any guy or girl taking his daughters out on dates," Taylor continued. "Tanner is twenty-six; I'm twenty-one. Neither of us lives at home." Taylor's hand moved to Chelsea's, which had been at her side, and she placed it on top of her arm on Chelsea's waist.

Chelsea swallowed and moved her other arm on top of Taylor's as she looked out at the water, hoping Taylor couldn't feel her heart pounding.

"I wanted to kiss you last night," Taylor admitted.

"Why didn't you?"

"Your dad gave me the signal," Taylor replied, laughing. "When the light went on, I knew they were probably watching us. I didn't want our first kiss, even a chaste goodnight kiss after a first date, to be with your parents watching us."

"So, it wasn't because I have, you know, no experience?"

"No," Taylor replied, moving her hand a little under Chelsea's T-shirt to rest just above her hip. "And I was going to call and ask you out again, but I thought I could just do it in person. So, here I am."

"You want to go on another date?"

Taylor nuzzled at Chelsea's neck and said, "Yes. You smell really good."

"I smell like coffee," Chelsea replied, laughing, but

leaning into the touch.

"And cinnamon," Taylor added.

"I may have helped make the cinnamon scones this morning."

Taylor pressed a kiss just below Chelsea's earlobe and asked, "Can I come in and hang out for a while?"

"You want a scone, don't you?"

"I just like watching you work," she replied. "Maybe you could take a break, and we can plan another date."

"I'd like that," Chelsea said, closing her eyes and smiling at the same time.

"You're working the morning shift, so does that mean you're off tonight?"

"Yes," she said.

"Only one of my roommates will be home tonight. One's staying with her girlfriend, and the other plays volleyball and is at a tournament for the next few days. Do you want to come over to my place and watch a movie? We could order in."

"The roommate that's home isn't the one that's–"

"No," Taylor said, laughing against Chelsea's neck. "My quiet, keeps-to-himself roommate is the one that will be home tonight."

"Okay," Chelsea said.

Taylor was moving her arms, and Chelsea wanted them to stay there. She tried to hold them in place, but Taylor spun her around slowly instead until they were staring at one another, and Taylor's hand moved to cup Chelsea's cheek.

"You could stay," Taylor offered.

"Stay?"

"Tonight," Taylor added. "We could just sleep. And before you say something about your lack of experience – it's not because of that that I'm suggesting sleep. I just…" She bit that lip again, and Chelsea saw that nervousness she'd seen before. "I don't want to make the same mistakes I've made before with you, Chels."

Chelsea nodded and said, "Okay."

Taylor let go of her lip, and Chelsea watched what happened next as if it was happening to someone else, like she was floating above the two of them as they stood on the sand – Taylor leaned in and connected their lips. It was like she was watching them as they kissed but was experiencing it for herself at the same time. Chelsea wrapped her arms around Taylor's neck as the other girl moved her own to Chelsea's waist and pulled them closer together, connecting their bodies. Then, Taylor's tongue slipped into Chelsea's mouth. When they finally pulled back, Chelsea was short of breath and had no words.

"You *taste* like cinnamon," Taylor noted, kissing her again quickly.

"I may have also sampled the scones," Chelsea said breathlessly, with her eyes still half-closed.

Taylor leaned in once more and took Chelsea's bottom lip between her own.

"Come on. I want to see you in that cute hat-apron combo," Taylor said, kissing her forehead.

"I hate that I have to wear that stupid hat," Chelsea replied.

"I don't," Taylor stated, taking Chelsea's hands in her own. "Do you know how many times I've pictured taking that hat off you and then everything else?"

"What?" Chelsea asked. "Everything else?"

Taylor kissed her again, long and slow, and said, "Everything."

LEZCONNECT

"I cannot believe you talked me into this," Erica said. "Why do I even listen to you?"

"I have no idea, honestly, because you never listened to me when we were together," Shelby replied.

"Low blow, Shell," Erica replied.

Erica and Shelby had ended their five-year-long relationship a dozen years prior, and they hadn't seen one another for years until about two years ago when Erica walked into *The Meet Cute Café* not expecting to find her ex-girlfriend behind the counter. Finding out that the woman she'd thought to be the love of her life was actually now happily married to someone else was hard. That was especially so because Erica had been the one to end their relationship. They'd loved one another very much, but Shelby hadn't wanted kids, and Erica had been ready to start a family.

She supposed they both assumed the other would change their mind over the course of their relationship, and that had been how they'd stayed together for so long. Erica had avoided bringing up having a baby until year two. They couldn't get married officially back then, and they hadn't had any kind of ceremony, but they *felt* married, and that was all they'd needed. By year two, though, Erica had asked Shelby, and Shelby had told her she didn't see herself with kids and didn't think that would change.

So, Erica waited until they'd been together for three years and brought it up again, getting the same exact result in response. By four years, Shelby had assumed Erica had given up, but she hadn't. She'd started looking into donors, presenting Shelby with a list to try to get her excited about the prospect of being parents together, but Shelby hadn't gotten excited, and they'd stayed together until just after a last-ditch trip to try to save their relationship, which failed.

Erica had moved into a two-bedroom apartment on her own then, starting the process to become a mom shortly after. She had never planned on doing it alone, but when Deacon came along, she knew she'd made the right decision for herself. Her son was now ten years old, and while she was still single, she'd given up on trying to find someone until after Deacon went off to college or, at least, hit his teen years.

That was until she'd let Shelby, of all people, convince her to try a new dating app for women who loved women. It was called LezConnect, and despite the ridiculous name, she also hadn't wanted to do this on principle. Erica was only thirty-eight. She managed to hit the gym three times a week even though she was a single parent of an active kid. She owned her own home, had a very nice job that paid her well enough to send that active kid to a private school, and she was attractive enough – at least, the women she'd dated here and there had always told her she was beautiful. She'd managed to keep her son out of her dating life all but once, and that had been a mistake.

She'd met Rosa through Deacon's school. The woman was a parent of a girl in Deacon's class, and despite Erica's better judgment, she'd gone out with her. They'd been together for a year before Rosa proposed, and they moved in together after Erica said yes. Three months into their engagement, though, Rosa admitted she'd been having an affair with someone from work. Erica had been beyond hurt, but Deacon had been heartbroken. He'd had a second mom and a sister for a bit there, and moving out and leaving them behind had been harder on him than it had been on Erica.

"When was the last time you went on a date?" Shelby asked, placing a coffee in front of Erica.

"A while ago."

"Exactly," Shelby added, sitting down at the table with her.

"You know why."

"I know Rosa did a number on you, and I know you're worried about Deacon, but he's ten years old now – he gets at least how some of this works. You're a catch, Erica."

"You threw me back," Erica said with a lifted eyebrow.

"You were supposed to be a mom, and I never wanted to be one. It doesn't mean I didn't love you," Shelby told her.

"Yeah, I know," Erica replied. "And I'd never regret Deacon, but I do sometimes wish things could have been different. I know you don't – you found your person. But it's different for those who spend their whole lives looking."

"You're not even forty," Shelby reasoned. "You still have at least more than half your life." She grabbed Erica's phone then. "Now, did you connect with anyone on the app?"

"No, I just set up my profile." Erica took a drink of her coffee.

"Did you at least scroll through to see some of the eligible ladies? This is a hopping lesbian beach town – I'm sure there are many attractive, intelligent women who would be lucky to match with you."

"I don't think I'm looking for anything serious. I could use *something else*," Erica stated, taking another drink.

"Something else?" Shelby asked, putting the phone down on the table.

"Yeah, I could use *something*," Erica said. "Deacon is at a baseball tournament with his travel team, and I'll have the house to myself Thursday night. I'm going to drive to the tournament Friday after work."

"You're just doing this for a one-night stand?"

"I think the kids call them hookups now," Erica said, smiling at her ex.

"I thought you wanted a relationship."

"Yeah, in a few years maybe, when Deacon is in high school or even better, out of the house. You didn't see what losing Rosa and her little girl did to him. It was like I'd finally given him a whole family and then took it away."

"Hey, you *are* a whole family," Shelby told her. "A family isn't a mom and a dad or two moms or two dads or anything else – it's what you make it. And you've made a perfect family for Deacon."

"Well, while I'm not looking for anything serious, I could definitely use that *something else*," Erica replied. "It's been a while, and my…" She leaned over the table toward Shelby. "My vibrator just isn't doing it for me anymore."

"Time to get some new batteries?" Shelby teased.

"I'm keeping batteries in business," she said. "So, no. I could just use someone else's hands and… other things instead."

Shelby laughed and said, "I think you're looking for Tinder, then."

"Eligible lesbians in their mid-to-late-thirties hang out on Tinder?"

"Probably not. Then again, I wouldn't really know," Shelby replied. "I've got to get back to work. Good luck."

"Thanks," Erica said, not feeling all that confident.

Nevertheless, she picked up her phone and opened the app to scroll through a few profiles, finding the women attractive and feeling hopeful, at least. Suddenly, her phone dinged with a notification, but it wasn't a text or a work email; it was from the app. Someone had messaged her.

Hi,

I never do this, and I should warn you that I'm new to this whole thing, but I saw your picture and read your profile. We can talk on this thing, I guess, but I'm still getting used to the idea of being on a dating app. Would you want to maybe have coffee sometime instead?

Melissa

***

"You cannot embarrass me," Erica told her friend.

"How would I embarrass you?" Shelby asked.

"Stay behind the counter. Don't make any mentions of being my ex. I don't want her to think I still have a thing for you or something. Don't walk over here with a fake reason like refilling her coffee. I'm only here because she said she liked *The Meet Cute* – I would have gone somewhere else."

"Well, I'm offended," Shelby said playfully. "I like to think our coffee is the best in town."

"Well, this Melissa seems to think so, and it's Wednesday afternoon, so if I have any chance of…"

"Having that *something else* tomorrow night while Deacon is away?" Shelby finished.

"Yes. Don't worry; if it goes well, I'm going to be honest with her. I'm not going to lead her on."

"You're assuming she'd be into you at all," Shelby joked. "I'll stay out of your way. Wait until she gets here, though. Then, ask what she wants and come to the counter for your drink and hers. I'll give you a chocolate croissant to split on the house."

"What if she doesn't like those?"

"Then, she's not human." Shelby winked.

As she walked away, Erica remembered how easy it was to love that woman. It had been instant when they'd met, but she'd thought then that it was chemistry more than anything else. The sex had been great, but there had been so much more between them than that. With Rosa, the sex had been good – not great, but it was good enough – Erica came more often than not. They just weren't usually the explosive orgasms that Shelby had given her nearly every time they'd been together, though. Rosa seemed happy with their sex life, or so Erica thought. Of course, Rosa had been getting it elsewhere, so that was likely why she seemed fine with the once every week or two adequate and often short sex they'd had.

"Hello?"

Erica's thoughts were interrupted when she looked up from her phone to see the woman from the app staring down at her. She was even more beautiful in person. Melissa was older; Erica knew that from the app, but at forty-five, she didn't look a day over *thirty*-five. Her long red hair was pulled back into some kind of hold Erica couldn't see. Her hazel eyes, which had looked amazing in her profile photo, were popping thanks to the light in the café. She'd worn a pencil skirt and heels along with a black silk blouse, indicating that she'd likely just come from work. Erica swallowed and looked over at Shelby, who was behind the counter staring at her.

"Stand up, you idiot," Shelby mouthed silently.

"Oh, sorry," Erica said, standing up and straightening her pants as she did. "Hi. Melissa?"

"Yes. Erica, I presume?"

"That's me," Erica said.

She didn't know what to do now. They didn't know each other. They'd exchanged a few messages on the app after Melissa's initial one, but they hadn't talked about how to greet one another in person for the first time. And now, Erica wasn't sure if she should go for a handshake, a kiss on the cheek, or just a hug.

"Have you ordered?" Melissa asked.

"No, I was waiting for you. What can I get you?"

"I've got it," Melissa replied, hooking her thumb to the counter.

"Oh, no. I can get it," Erica said, feeling flummoxed by the attractive and assertive woman.

"Really, it's fine. I come here a lot. I can recommend something if you'd like. They have a great Columbian blend, and their cappuccinos are really good, too."

"Okay. Sure," Erica said.

"Which one?" Melissa asked.

"Surprise me," she replied.

Was she crazy, or had Melissa just smiled for a split second at that?

"I'll be right back."

Erica sat down, watching Melissa walk to the counter.

The café wasn't all that busy, and with the lack of customer conversations and the low music, she could hear the woman place the order with Shelby.

"Can I get a large cappuccino and a large Columbian blend?" Melissa asked.

"No problem. Anything to eat?" Shelby asked.

"No, thank you."

"I have fresh-made chocolate croissants."

Erica was going to kill her. She glared at Shelby, who pretended like she didn't notice.

"No, thank you," Melissa replied, handing over her credit card.

"I'll have your drinks right up for you," Shelby told her.

Melissa walked over to the coffee bar without turning to Erica and waited for their drinks. Shelby made the cappuccino and shrugged at Erica, who just sat there, waiting.

When Melissa came back over, she placed both to-go cups on the table, smiled, and said, "Take your pick. I like both, so I'll drink whichever you don't want."

"I'll take this one," Erica said, not knowing which drink she was picking up.

"So, how long have you been on LezConnect?" Melissa asked, getting right to the point.

"Honestly, I put my profile up the day before you messaged me," Erica admitted. "What about you?"

"About a week before you, I suppose," she replied. "Not that I want to spend this whole time talking about my ex, but I got divorced about a year and a half ago, and this is my attempt at putting myself back out there again. What had you joining?"

"Oh, a friend of mine suggested it. I haven't been dating much, and my last relationship ended when she cheated on me *after* she proposed, so I wasn't exactly thinking about diving back into the whole thing."

"Damn," Melissa said. "Sorry."

"I'm over it. But you did see the kind of big thing on

my profile, right?"

"Your son? Yeah, I saw that," Melissa replied. "It's actually the thing that made me want to reach out to you."

Erica wasn't sure how to take that.

"Oh, not in a weird way," Melissa added, taking in her confusion. "Your profile mentioned that he played travel baseball, and you spend a lot of time at games."

"Oh, yeah. He's ten, but his coaches say he's pretty good. So, he plays travel ball whenever The Little League season ends."

"My brother plays for the Mariners, and my dad used to play, too."

"Really? Wow! Well, Deacon is, apparently, a very good pitcher. I guess; I don't know much about it. I mainly just sit in the bleachers and close my eyes whenever he's up to bat."

"I played myself when I was young," Melissa shared. "And then I switched to softball in high school and played in college."

"Your whole family is talented," Erica commented. "I'm just impressed when he asks me to play catcher for him, and I manage to actually catch the ball."

"I don't have any kids," Melissa said. "And I'm not saying I'm looking to become a stepmother or anything – I think that would be a little much on a first date – but I *do* like kids, and it's not going to keep me from pursuing someone I like, if that's why you were asking if I saw it on your profile."

"I tried to be pretty blatant about it. I have a hobby or two, but not much to really list in that section in the app. My life revolves around my son and my job, and I'm good with that."

"I think that's how it should be," Melissa replied. "Well, I don't know about the work part – I agree with the son part, though. So… Is the woman you were with, the one who cheated, his other mother?"

"No, he doesn't have another mother. I had him on

my own; anonymous donor. I was with someone for about five years, and I thought we'd have kids together, but she didn't want them, and I really did. So, I became a single mom, and it's been Deacon and I ever since. Then, I was with my ex for over a year, but when I found out she'd been having an affair, Deacon and I left."

"Rightfully, so," Melissa remarked.

She crossed her legs, and Erica watched. Then, she licked her lips. Melissa was sexy in a skirt. She had a feeling the woman was sexy *out* of it, too, and the way she carried herself was a total turn-on for Erica. She liked strong, assertive types, which was true in all things, but especially in the bedroom. Shelby had been assertive in bed, but not overly so. Rosa had been fine with Erica topping her, but Erica had always had a desire for Rosa to just get on top of her and take her. She had tried to make that known by attempting to roll them over or making comments in bed, but Rosa never took the lead. And by now, Erica had been so sick of her own hand and her vibrator that she'd bought three new toys for herself just the other day. She knew they'd help, but she wanted a woman's body pressed to her own. She wanted hot, sweaty sex that didn't have to mean anything. It could just be about the moment and the two of them enjoying one another.

They talked about their jobs, and Melissa talked just enough about her ex-wife without it becoming a problem for a first date. Erica offered to get them refills when they'd both run out of coffee, but Melissa declined.

"I should probably be going," she said.

"Oh. Really?" Erica asked.

"I left work early, and I need to get some stuff done before a meeting tomorrow."

Erica nodded and said, "Speaking of tomorrow… Are you busy?"

Melissa lifted a curious eyebrow at her as she reached for her purse hanging on her chair.

"Tomorrow?"

"We could grab dinner," Erica suggested.

"We could," Melissa said.

"Or, we could just have dinner at my place. I could cook for us," she said, licking her lips as Melissa's intense gaze met her own.

Melissa's eyes lowered to Erica's mouth and seemed to follow the movement of her tongue.

"I can't tomorrow night," she said.

"Ah. Okay," Erica replied.

"What about Friday?" Melissa suggested.

"I'm on the road with my son's team this weekend," she replied.

"But you'd be cooking for me tomorrow night at your place?"

"The team is leaving tomorrow; I just can't join him until Friday."

"So, you have the house to yourself," Melissa noted.

Erica leaned in and said, "We'd have it to *our*selves if you come over."

"I see," Melissa said. "So, you're thinking about dinner and something else."

Erica turned to look at Shelby behind the counter when she heard her laugh. Erica gave her an expression that told her to knock it off.

"Only if that's something you'd be interested in, obviously," she told Melissa.

"Is that *all* you're interested in?" The woman asked. "Your profile led me to believe you were looking for something more."

"No, I am. I don't know," Erica sighed. "I wasn't looking for anything, but then my friend, who I might *un*friend after this, suggested I join the app to find someone. I did, but then I started to think about Deacon and what happened last time I was in a relationship. I don't want to risk putting him through that again, so I thought–"

"That you and I could have fun?" Melissa interrupted. "Am I right?"

48

"I've enjoyed having coffee with you, and I thought we could have dinner," Erica told her. "We could see what happens; no pressure. I can even take the whole thing off the table. We could try coffee again next week if you want."

"I think I'll pass," Melissa replied. "Not that I wouldn't be interested in…" She looked Erica up and down. "But I'm not looking for sex. I've had plenty of that since my divorce. I'm in a place where I want to meet someone for more than that."

"I get it." Erica nodded. "I wasn't trying to insinuate that was all we could have."

"I better be going. A lot of work to get caught up on," Melissa said, standing.

"Sure," Erica replied, looking down at the table now. "Good luck with that."

"It was nice meeting you, Erica."

"I promise, I'm not a bad person," she said.

"I don't think you're a bad person," Melissa replied. "You seem like a really nice person, actually. I just think we might be looking for two different things."

"Yeah, I *definitely* get that," she said, looking over at Shelby.

"How did it go?" Shelby asked after Melissa left the café.

"Don't pretend like you didn't hear most of it."

"I'm sorry, Erica," she replied.

"No, it's fine. I should have just asked her out on a date and not mentioned my place."

"But then you would have been lying about your intentions, which isn't you," Shelby reminded her.

"I like her. She's gorgeous, and I could definitely see us having some fun, but I also just like her."

"Did you tell *her* that?"

"Kind of hard to do that when she couldn't escape from me fast enough. I think she would've just run away had she been wearing other shoes."

"Give her a few days. Then, message her in the app.

Apologize for the confusion. Hell, tell her you're just really horny or something, but that you'd like to take her out on a date that doesn't end in sex."

"I think I'm good," Erica replied. "Can I have a coffee for the road? I need to pick up Deacon from practice soon anyway and then help him pack. If I don't, he'll forget underwear *and* socks. He'll manage to remember to pack his phone, tablet, and Nintendo Switch, though."

***

"I heard you won the tournament," Shelby said.

"I did," Deacon replied when she handed him his hot chocolate.

"*We* did," Erica corrected. "Your *team* won, so you say *we*, Deacon."

"Yeah, we won," he said. "I pitched. I had a bunch of strikeouts."

Erica ruffled her son's blonde hair that nearly matched her own. He hadn't gotten her green eyes, though; he'd gotten the brown eyes of the anonymous donor. Deacon had gotten her nose, her ears, and her stubbornness, though.

"Congratulations," Shelby said.

"Deac, can you go sit at that table? I need to talk to Shelby for a minute."

"Okay," he mumbled, caring only about getting at the extra whipped cream Shelby had given him before it melted.

"Everything okay?" Shelby asked, putting the milk back in the refrigerator.

"His coach had a heart attack after their last game," Erica sighed. "The kids don't know yet."

"What? Is he okay?"

"His wife told me he'll recover but that he needs to take it easy for a while. So, no more coaching. Travel season is over, but Little League starts soon, and he coaches that team, too, so I've got to find a way to tell Deacon the team will have a new coach. I thought hot chocolate would be best for delivering the news."

"He's close to the coach?" Shelby asked.

"He's had the same coach since T-ball. It's why he and his team are so good."

"I'm sure he'll be okay. Maybe once his coach gets out of the hospital, Deacon can go visit him or something."

"Yeah," Erica replied. "It's more about the coaching for the season. This is the first time he's eligible for the Little League World Series, which is a big deal to him and all the kids on the team. He's going to get chosen for the all-star team even though he's younger than most of the other players, and his coach would've been coaching the team."

"Isn't there an assistant? I don't know baseball."

"For the regular team, yes. For the all-star team, they'll find someone Deacon doesn't know from the Little League. I'm sure it'll be fine for the team. I just hate to see him disappointed, and I think I'm about to."

"Hi."

Erica turned and saw Melissa standing there.

"Oh, hi," she replied to her.

"I should go to the register," Shelby said.

"Mom, can I have a cupcake?" Deacon yelled from the table.

"Deacon, don't yell," Erica told him. "And no, you've had enough sugar."

Melissa turned and asked, "Your son?"

"Yeah, that's him. And normally, he's better behaved than this, but I think the sugar is kicking in from that hot chocolate."

"I didn't know you come here," Melissa said.

"I do; more recently over the past few months. Is that a problem? Deacon and I—"

"It's not a problem, Erica," the woman interrupted her. "You can have coffee anywhere you want."

"I'll just go remind my son that we don't yell in public places, and you can order your coffee," Erica said.

"Sure," Melissa replied with a nod.

Erica turned to go but decided to take advantage of this moment.

"Listen, I promise I'm not trying to get some woman into bed. Well, that's not true; you caught me at a moment when I was interested in something specific. But I wasn't going to lie to you about my intentions. I was trying to be upfront about it, and I think I came off looking like an asshole. For that, I'm sorry."

Melissa nodded and said, "Your profile said you were looking for something real."

"I am. I was. I don't know," Erica sighed. "I look at him, and I remember when I had to watch and hear him cry when things didn't work out with my ex. Now I have to tell him his Little League coach had a heart attack and can't coach him this season when it's an important season for him, and I'm already picturing his disappointment. If I try again, and it doesn't work out, I'll just break his heart again. I don't think I can do that. I really thought I could try when I wrote that profile, I swear. But then… I don't know. Thinking about Deacon and thinking about what I knew I really needed – at least, in that moment – I just blew it with you, and I'm sorry about that."

"His coach can't coach?"

Erica looked at Melissa in confusion because she had given a pretty good speech that she thought explained her reasoning, and all Melissa had taken away was that the coach wouldn't be there this year.

"No, not this season, anyway. Deacon doesn't know yet." Erica looked over at her son. "I gave him sugar to, hopefully, lessen the blow. He's really close to his coach. He's the guy who taught him to pitch."

Melissa nodded and asked, "Is there a good assistant?"

"Why?"

"I used to coach at a Little League in the city. I have a nephew who played for years. He's playing in high school now and has a good chance of playing in college."

"So, *very* talented family," Erica said with a smile.

"Mom, can we go if I can't have a cupcake?" Deacon asked.

"One minute, Deacon. Finish your drink."

Melissa smiled over at him and said, "This might sound strange, given how you and I met, but I miss baseball. I've been thinking about volunteering my time teaching kids at the community center or coaching again. If the team needs someone to fill in, I could try to help out."

"Oh, really?" Erica asked. "Wait. Seriously? You'd want to coach my son's team?"

"Baseball's in my blood. Plus, there's something about knowing I'd be one of, if not the only, female coach." She smiled at Erica. "I know it might be awkward. I–"

"No, yeah," Erica interrupted. "I mean, I can get past it if you can."

"Of course," Melissa said like it was easy.

"I can get you the number of the other coach, and you could talk to him about it," Erica offered in response.

"I'll just reach out to the league," Melissa replied. "See if they even need my help."

"Mom, I finished my hot chocolate," Deacon said, walking over to them.

"Deacon, can you please be polite and say hello to my friend, Melissa?"

"Hi," he said.

Melissa knelt down in front of him and said, "I hear you're a good pitcher."

"Yeah."

"What are your pitches?" she asked.

He looked at her like he was surprised and replied, "Fastball and curveball. I'm working on my splitter."

"Splitter?" She looked up at Erica. "At your age?"

"Yeah. And I have two fastballs. My changeup is okay, but I need to work on my release. My coach tells me it's good, though."

"That's a lot of pitches," Melissa noted.

"You know baseball?" he asked.

"I do," she replied. "My whole family does. I played when I was your age. I was a second-basemen."

"You played? That's cool."

Melissa stood up and said, "Well, I just came in for coffee, but I'll call the league and see if they even need the help."

"Great," Erica replied. "We were just heading out, too."

"Mom, I have to pee," Deacon said.

Erica rolled her eyes and said, "Go to the bathroom." Deacon rushed off.

"I promise, he's usually more well-behaved, but I think he's just at that age, too. My little boy is gone; the rude pre-teen is upon me."

Melissa laughed and said, "He's right where he should be, then. It was good to see you."

"You too," Erica replied.

***

"Melissa, can we practice tomorrow?"

"Deac, you just practiced today," Erica said, removing Deacon's baseball hat from his head when they sat down at the table.

"Your arm needs to rest tomorrow," Melissa told him. "You want to be ready for the game, right?"

"Can we do batting practice? Mom said she'd take me to the cages tomorrow. Can you come with us?"

Erica recognized her son's excited tone. It made her incredibly happy to know that he had something he loved as much as baseball, but it also worried her that he seemed to really like having Melissa as his new coach. So much so, that when Erica offered to take him to *The Meet Cute* for a cupcake and hot chocolate after practice, Deacon had invited Melissa to join them, and she, to Erica's surprise, had accepted.

"I don't know, Deacon. I think that's up to your

mom," Melissa replied.

"Here you go," Shelby said, dropping their drinks off at the table, along with Deacon's cupcake.

"Thanks," Melissa said.

Shelby gave Erica an expression that told her she'd have some explaining to do later. Melissa had called the league, and they'd loved the idea of having a baseball blue blood as well as a female coach on one of their teams. That had been over a month ago. The season had started, and Deacon's team had won every single one of their games so far. He was happy. He was pitching and playing shortstop whenever he wasn't on the mound. Erica knew little about how coaches could tell if there was a superstar on the team, but Melissa had confirmed what everyone else had told Erica about her son. He had it. He had that thing that made great players. He was also only eleven years old now, so things could change. He could fall out of love with the sport; he could find something else he's just as passionate about; he could get injured.

Deacon had really responded to Melissa's coaching style, and Erica found that she liked the woman in both pencil skirts and silk tops, as well as in an old Mariner's baseball hat, T-shirt, and jeans. She knew her stuff on the field and had a way with the boys that made them all trust and respect her.

Erica had started to attend more of Deacon's practices, where in the past, she'd just dropped him off and picked him up after. The three new sex toys she'd bought all those weeks ago had helped quell her need, but not by much, and she hadn't had any luck with LezConnect, either. So far, she'd met up with two other women for coffee at *The Meet Cute* after messaging back and forth. One of them, she wasn't interested in. The second one had promise, but when they had shared a kiss in the parking lot of the café, Erica hadn't liked the other woman's very sloppy approach. Having been turned off, she'd gone home, and after putting Deacon to bed, she went to her room, pulled out the purple dildo she'd bought, and slipped it inside. In the end, it was the thought of Melissa in that old baseball hat that had taken her over the edge, which was why her son inviting Melissa everywhere with them now was becoming a problem.

***

"So, she's meeting you here?" Shelby asked.

"She just texted that she's on her way," Erica said.

"And you're meeting without Deacon? I've only seen you in here with Melissa with him here."

"He's with my mom tonight."

Shelby gave her that eyebrow that told Erica she needed to explain – she remembered it well from their relationship.

"I didn't plan it. Melissa asked *me* here tonight," she said. "And my mom and dad wanted Deacon to sleep over because his cousins are doing the same thing."

"Does Melissa know you're by yourself tonight?"

"No, but like I said, *she* called me."

"Any idea why?"

"She said she just wanted to hang out with an adult. She's been spending so much time coaching lately. She's really dedicated, Shelby. You can tell she cares, and I think she's made the team better."

"Hey," Melissa greeted, smiling when she walked into the café.

"Hey." Erica smiled back. "I was just about to order. What can I get you? Columbian blend or cappuccino?"

"Actually, can I just get a water?"

"Water?"

"To-go?" she asked.

"You want water to-go? I thought we were going to have coffee."

"Can you get yours to-go, too?" Melissa asked.

Erica glanced at Shelby, confused, and said, "Can I just get two bottles of water?"

Minutes later, she was following Melissa out to the café parking lot.

"Melissa, what's going on? I thought we were going to sit and have coffee like two adults that spend most of their time surrounded by children."

But Melissa just tugged Erica's free hand without saying anything until they were at the side of an SUV.

"This is mine," she said, unlocking and opening the back car door. "Get in?" she asked more than requested.

"Get in?"

"Erica…" The woman lifted both eyebrows at once.

"Okay. Are you kidnapping me? I'm not rich. You won't get any ransom money out of my family, either. My parents are retired and on a fixed income."

Erica climbed into the back seat of the SUV and was surprised when Melissa climbed in beside her and closed the door.

"Do you still…"

Erica put the water bottles into the dual holder between the two front seats and said, "What?"

"Do you still want what you wanted when we first met?"

"Sex?" Erica asked in a much higher tone than she'd planned on.

"Yes," Melissa smirked at her.

"With you?"

"Yes."

Erica looked around. The SUV had tinted windows. In fact, they might have even been tinted darker than was legal. The car faced the beach, but it was dark, and there was hardly anyone around.

"What? Here?"

"I've been watching you at practices, and you pace whenever Deacon is up to bat or pitching – it's adorable. And the other day, you came to practice after work wearing that sexy pantsuit, and I had to force myself to focus on the practice."

"Really?"

Melissa nodded.

"You weren't interested before."

"I am now," she said.

"Oh, wow," Erica said, getting wet just at the thought of touching Melissa.

"I'm wearing a skirt, and I took my underwear off before I went into the café."

"Fuck," Erica whispered.

Melissa cupped her cheek, brought her lips close to Erica's, and asked, "Is that a yes?"

"I didn't shave," Erica said, squeezing her eyes closed in embarrassment and opening them to see Melissa's eyes looking down her shirt, which Erica had unbuttoned at the top.

"I don't care," Melissa replied.

Then, she pulled on Erica's shirt and kissed her, and there was nothing slow about this kiss. It was hard and hot instantly, and it had Erica moaning into Melissa's mouth. She'd always wanted an assertive woman in the bedroom. And, apparently, she'd been right: Melissa was definitely assertive. This just *wasn't* a bedroom. She thought about saying that they could get caught, that they should stop or slow down, but Melissa had her hand inside Erica's shirt now, massaging her breast and trying to pull it out of the bra at the same time.

Erica reached for the buttons and undid them all. She watched as Melissa disconnected their lips and connected her mouth to Erica's nipple. She sucked so hard, Erica almost came.

"Yes," she said, pressing her palms to the roof of the SUV.

She watched Melissa suck and lick before she moved to the next nipple, popped it out of the cup of the bra, and did the same to it. Melissa's hands went to Erica's belt buckle next, and she undid the thing before Erica even realized it. Then, Erica was on her back, and Melissa had her knees on the floorboards. She was pulling and tugging at Erica's pants until they were at her ankles. Then, she climbed up and straddled Erica's stomach.

"You're wet," Erica said, moving Melissa's hips back and forth over her own abdomen, feeling the woman's wetness coat her skin.

"I've thought about this for weeks, but today, I was sitting at my desk, picturing you underneath it with your head between my legs, and I almost got off right there."

"Fuck. Really?" Erica asked, reaching up with a hand to get under Melissa's shirt and touch her breast.

Melissa was still fully clothed, but Erica's breasts were bare, and her pants and underwear were around her ankles. She had a shoe hanging off her foot and didn't know where the other one was, but when Melissa backed up and slid two fingers inside her, Erica couldn't think about anything else.

"You're so sexy," Melissa said, leaning down and kissing Erica. "I wanted you that first day."

"Why didn't you… Oh, fuck," she said, closing her eyes when Melissa's thumb met her clit.

"Because this is a bad idea. I want a relationship; you want sex."

"Fuck me," Erica requested. "If this is all it'll be, then fuck me." She stared up at Melissa, who licked her lips and obliged.

Minutes later, Erica was coming. Melissa was sucking on her neck as she brought her down from one of the most intense orgasms of Erica's life. When Erica finally came down, she slipped into a seated position, tore Melissa's shirt apart, shoved the bra down, and sucked as Melissa moved quickly to straddle her.

"I really, really like that," Melissa told her. "But I need you inside me. I want to ride your fingers."

Erica kept sucking and moved her hand between them under Melissa's skirt, letting Melissa ride her fingers until she came hard against them, and Erica felt wetness coat them. When Melissa came down, Erica brought those fingers to her mouth and sucked them in.

"Do you like that?" Melissa asked, moving her hair to one shoulder.

"Yes," Erica stated. "I want my mouth on you."

"We can try that, but it might be difficult in the back seat."

"My place," Erica said.

"Deacon?"

"Is with his grandparents tonight," Erica replied, kissing and sucking on Melissa's jawline.

"What? We could have done this at your place?" Melissa laughed.

"You're the one that brought me to your car."

"I thought Deacon would…"

"What about *your* place?" Erica asked.

"My brother lost his job last month, so he's been staying with me since. I didn't want to bring you there; he's nosy," Melissa replied.

"My place?" Erica offered again, lowering her lips to Melissa's breast. "I want all of you before the night is over."

"I'll follow you," Melissa replied.

***

"So, it's weird now?" Shelby asked.

"Shelby, we had sex all night long. I didn't sleep at all. And she left for work the next morning wearing one of my shirts because I tore the buttons off of hers. It was hot, and perfect, and I was hoping we could do it again, but I called her and texted, and she didn't respond. I've only seen her at practices and games, and whenever Deacon asks if she can come somewhere with us, I make up an excuse."

"Well, you *did* tell her you only wanted sex."

"Hot sex," Erica said. "It was… Can I even say this to you? *We* used to have sex."

"Hot sex," Shelby corrected with a smile.

"Yes, it was." Erica laughed. "But it's been a million

years, so we can talk about this, right?"

"Yes." Shelby laughed.

"No offense, okay?"

"Just say it's the best sex you've ever had, Erica."

"It really fucking was," Erica said.

"So, you want it again?"

"Yes."

"Have you told her that in your messages?"

"No, I just said we should talk."

"That's ominous."

"I know. I should just talk to her in person, but she's always around the kids."

"Ask her to talk at practice or something."

"Yeah, she can spare five minutes to tell me things are okay between us, right?"

"I'm sure she could," Shelby replied.

***

"Fuck," Erica gasped out.

Melissa's mouth was on her sex. Erica's leg was over her shoulder.

"God, I love your mouth," Erica told her.

"I love how you taste." Melissa looked up at her from between her legs. "We can't be long. I have to get back."

"This is really, really wrong," Erica said. "But that feels so good."

Melissa dipped her tongue inside.

"No one is here. We'll be fine."

Then, Melissa sucked on Erica's clit until Erica came in her mouth and nearly fell over the metal chip display behind her. She'd only asked the woman to talk, but Melissa had taken her into the locked concession stand that was closed during practices. As a coach, she had a key, and they had the place all to themselves. Melissa had pressed her up against the chip display that had crinkled and made a lot of other sounds as she'd taken Erica with her mouth.

"We have to go," Melissa told her a few minutes later, standing up and wiping her mouth. "I'll go first so I can go clean up in the bathroom."

"What about you?" Erica asked, tugging on Melissa's belt. "We can steal another couple of minutes."

"Confident you'll get me there that fast?" Melissa teased as she unbuckled her own belt.

Erica nodded and said, "Mouth or fingers?"

"Both," Melissa replied.

Erica wasted no time in pulling her pants and underwear down. She pressed Melissa to the counter behind her, spread her legs, and sucked hard as she thrust two fingers inside her.

"Make me come hard," Melissa said.

Erica grunted.

"Really fuck me, baby."

Erica thrust harder and deeper and sucked faster. Minutes later, Melissa came, pressing her own hand to her mouth to stop herself from screaming. Erica stood and smirked.

"Proud of yourself?"

Erica nodded.

"Can you get a babysitter tomorrow?" Melissa asked.

"I can try. What did you have in mind?"

"My place for a few hours."

"What about your brother?"

"He found a new apartment last week – he's moving out as we speak."

"I'll call my regular sitter when we get back out there."

Melissa kissed her and said, "We should talk."

"So, I'm coming to your place tomorrow to *talk*?"

"No, you're coming to my place to fuck me with that purple dildo of yours, but that doesn't mean we shouldn't talk," she replied.

Erica grunted again.

***

A month later, Erica was sitting at *The Meet Cute* with her son and Melissa, who was not her girlfriend but wasn't just her son's coach or a friend, either. They'd had sex at least ten nights of the past month, but they still had yet to talk about what they were to one another. Erica had slept over at Melissa's place on two occasions, and Melissa had only slept over at Erica's once, that night Deacon stayed with her parents. Usually, one of them would leave after their final round of sex, even if it was late. They hadn't put a label on what they had or put rules to it, and Erica had liked that until today.

"LezConnect?" she asked as Melissa's phone dinged with the notification sound Erica recognized.

"What's that?" Deacon asked.

"An app for grown-ups."

"Can I play games on your phone, Mom?" he asked.

"You have your tablet."

"Oh, right," he replied, pulling it from his backpack on the floor.

"So? Is it?" Erica asked Melissa.

They hadn't gone to the café together. Erica and Deacon had stopped by mainly for the view of the ocean and because Deacon loved the cupcakes Shelby made from scratch. Melissa had seen them from the parking lot and joined them when Deacon practically demanded it.

"Yes, it's a message."

Erica nodded.

"You're still on the app, too," Melissa added. "Your profile comes up a lot when I'm scrolling."

"Do you scroll *often*?" Erica asked.

"Not often," she said. "Why?"

"Just making conversation."

"Melissa, can we watch my video again?" Deacon asked.

Melissa had made Deacon a video compilation of his greatest strikeouts since she'd taken over as coach, and she shared it with him. Erica thought it was sweet, but now her son wanted to watch the thing a million times a day.

"Sure, buddy," Melissa replied, rubbing Deacon's head in the same way Erica did.

Erica bit her lower lip and tried not to worry.

"Don't," Shelby said a few minutes later when Erica went to the counter to order a refill. "I can see what you're thinking. I can still read you."

"What am I thinking?" Erica countered.

"You're freaking out because Deacon likes Melissa, and so do you."

"I'm not freaking out. Can I get a refill before she wonders what the hell is taking so long?"

Shelby took her cup and moved to refill it.

"Erica, you like her."

"So?"

"So, she wants a relationship. And it's clear she likes you, too."

"She's scrolling through messages on the dumb app you made me join," Erica replied.

"Because you aren't interested in being anything more than a *something else* friend with her."

"Right. So, what are we talking about?"

"I'm going to head home," Melissa said, sounding like she was right behind her.

That was because Melissa *was* right behind Erica.

"I thought I was getting us refills."

"I wasn't planning on staying this long. I have plans."

"Oh," Erica said. "Sure. I should be getting Deacon home, anyway."

"I'll see you tomorrow at practice?"

"I'll be there," Erica replied.

Melissa and Erica walked back over to the table so that Melissa could grab her purse and Erica could grab her son.

"I'll see you at practice tomorrow, Deacon."

"You're leaving?" he asked, sounding disappointed.

"So are we. Come on. Get your stuff," Erica told him, hoping that would ease his disappointment.

"Okay," Deacon replied, tucking his tablet into his backpack.

"It's not a date," Melissa said.

"What?" Erica asked.

"My plans; it's not a date, Erica."

"Oh, okay."

"I'm just meeting up with some friends."

"Sounds good."

"Mom, can Melissa come over for dinner after practice tomorrow?" Deacon asked as he stood and shouldered his backpack.

"Oh, I'm sure she has other plans," Erica replied.

Melissa shook her head at Erica and said, "I'll see you at practice, Deacon."

Then, Melissa left the café.

"Don't ruin this," Shelby told Erica from behind the counter.

***

Erica lifted her head from between Melissa's legs and asked, "Again?"

"No, I need a break," she replied, breathing hard. "God, you are determined tonight, aren't you?"

Erica slid up Melissa's body, kissing every bit of skin she could as she went.

"I like when you feel good."

Melissa looked at the bedside clock and said, "I should go."

"Deacon is with my parents tonight. There's no rush." Erica kissed her neck.

"Yeah, but I should still go."

"Why?" She looked down at Melissa.

"You know why, Erica."

"You've slept over before when he wasn't here."

"That first night when neither of us planned on this becoming a regular thing." Melissa slipped out from under her.

"Okay." Erica sat on the side of the bed. "I guess I'll see you at the tournament this weekend."

"We win this, we go to regionals, and then it's one more tournament before the–"

"I know. I know. Deacon won't shut up about the possibility of going to The Little League World Series. You know, he practices his follow-through in the living room and asks me all the time if *you* think they'll win the whole thing."

"He does?" Melissa asked as she slid into her panties.

"He cares what you think."

"And that's why you're so scared of this?"

"Scared of what?"

"Of me and you becoming more than just two people who have sex."

"Mel…"

"I love Deacon, Erica. I don't want to hurt him, either."

"I know that," she replied.

Melissa put on her skirt, and Erica stood, moved behind her, and helped her zip it up. She kissed Melissa's shoulder and stood still for a moment.

"You could stay," she said.

"I can't. It's already confusing enough."

Erica didn't know what to say to that.

"I think we should stop," Melissa said a moment later.

"Stop?"

"I want real, Erica. I want a relationship with someone who wants to be with me. I understand why you're worried about your son – I really do, and I'm trying to respect that – but I'm turning down women I meet on LezConnect for dates because…" Melissa sighed. "I'm waiting for you, which is very stupid of me – you aren't willing to take a chance on me, so I need to find someone who will."

"Mel…"

"Mom!"

Erica's eyes practically exploded. That was her son.

"Did you just hear…"

"Mom?"

"Shit. Deacon's home," Erica said, rushing to find anything to put on.

Melissa did the same. They were covered just in time for Deacon to arrive at the closed but not locked bedroom door and open it.

"Oh, there you are," he said.

"Baby, what are you doing here? Where's Grandma?"

"She's here. Oh," Erica's mother said when she noticed Erica's guest standing there, looking like they very much just had sex and dressed quickly. "Sorry, Deacon begged to come home. He said he was not feeling well. I tried to call you, but I couldn't get through."

"My phone is in the kitchen."

"Melissa is here," Deacon said, sounding happy and not at all confused. "Mom, can I have ice cream?"

"No. What's going on? You don't feel well?"

"My stomach hurts," he said. "And Patrick and Josh wouldn't stop fighting. I just wanted to come home."

She knelt in front of him, pressed her hand to his forehead, and said, "Well, you're definitely not having ice cream, then." Erica looked up at her mom then. "Did he eat something he shouldn't have?"

"No, he was fine at dinner. But he begged and begged, so I thought I better bring him here."

"Thanks, Mom," Erica said. Then, she turned her head to Melissa, who was standing with her arms crossed over her chest. "This is Melissa. Melissa, this is my mom."

"*The* Melissa?"

"Oh, I don't know," Melissa replied.

"Coach Melissa," Deacon explained, looking up at his grandmother. "She's the best coach ever, too. Plus, she's Mom's girlfriend, so I get to hang out with her all the time."

Erica looked at her son first. Then, she looked at her mother, who had an inquisitive eyebrow aimed at her. She turned to see Melissa standing there with her arms at her sides now.

"She's not–" Erica stopped herself. "Buddy, you can't just say stuff like that, okay?"

"Okay. Can I go lie down?"

"Sure. I'll take your temperature in a minute and bring some medicine, okay?"

"Can I have some water?"

"Of course." Erica kissed his forehead. "I'll be right there. Say goodnight to Grandma. Tell her thank you for taking care of you, okay?"

Her mother followed Deacon out of the bedroom, which just left the two of them standing there with nothing to say to one another.

"I should get going," Melissa said.

"I'm sorry. I don't know why he said that."

"Kids are smart." Melissa shrugged a shoulder. "They see things we *don't* sometimes."

"Yeah, I guess," Erica replied.

"Melissa is really cool, Grandma. She knows all about baseball."

"I know. You've told me that."

"And Mom really likes her. I think she likes her how she liked Rosa, but like, *more* than that," Deacon said as his voice faded.

Melissa stared down at the floor of Erica's bedroom, and Erica realized it then. She wanted Melissa, too. She'd been so worried about Deacon and his feelings that she hadn't taken stock of her own. Melissa was kind. She was brilliant, successful, and independent. She was beautiful in that skirt right now, but just, as if not more so, when she was staring at the lineup card, wearing the team hat and shirt that said 'Coach' on the back. Melissa also loved Deacon. Erica could tell the woman liked kids, and she cared about all of the ones she coached, but she seemed to care about Deacon differently. She spent more time with him, helping him grow and develop in the sport, but also as a leader on the field despite his young age.

The times they'd shared alone had been primarily about sex, but not only about sex. They'd talked about what they wanted for themselves, and Erica hadn't laughed this much since she'd been with Shelby during the good years. Melissa was still standing in her bedroom as if she were waiting for Erica to say something, and Erica knew that she was. This was it. She could let this woman go and make a huge mistake, or she could do something else.

"Stay," she said softly.

"Stay?"

"Yes, stay."

"Deacon's here," Melissa replied.

"I know. I need to make sure he's okay, but I want you to stay."

"I don't think I'm up for–"

"I don't mean for that, Mel. I mean, I want you to stay and just *be* here."

"What about Deacon?"

"He already thinks you're my girlfriend," Erica replied, smiling at Melissa.

"We're not there yet."

"I know. Let's talk," she suggested, walking over to her. "You can put on anything of mine to sleep in, and I'll come back as soon as I have him settled and say goodnight to my mom." She took Melissa's hands in her own.

"This is weird, Erica. Your mom is here. And Deacon. I should just go home. We can talk later."

"Mom," Deacon said, sounding like he was really close.

She turned to see him standing in the doorway.

"Deacon, you're supposed to be in bed."

"Can Melissa read me a story?"

"Oh, I don't–"

"This is part of it, babe," Melissa whispered from behind her. "This is part of it."

"Mom?"

"Sure, Deac. Can you ask *her*, though?"

"Melissa, can you read me a story?" Deacon asked. "Please," he added.

Erica smiled at her son as he wiped at his tired eyes.

"Give me just a minute, and I'll be right there, okay?" Melissa said.

"Okay. Mom, Grandma said she was leaving, but you can talk later. Bye!"

With that message, he ran off to his room, not looking like a boy who didn't feel well at all. Erica turned back around and smiled at Melissa.

"*Babe*, huh?"

Melissa wrapped her arms around Erica's neck and said, "I call you *baby* all the time."

"In bed," Erica said, laughing a little.

"So? It's *baby* in the bedroom and *babe* outside of it," Melissa said. "Are you okay with this? Really?"

Erica nodded and wrapped her arms around Melissa's waist.

"Can you deal with me worrying about him from time to time where you're concerned?"

"Yes," Melissa replied. "He's your son. I'd worry if you *weren't* worried."

Erica leaned in and pressed her lips to Melissa's for a quick kiss that Melissa turned into a long, slow one.

"Gross, Mom!"

"Deacon, go to your room," she said, laughing.

***

"I'll be right back. I just need to check in on that report." Melissa stood, kissed Erica quickly, and answered her ringing phone as she walked out onto the patio of *The Meet Cute*.

"Did I just witness a kiss?" Shelby teased.

"Yes," Erica replied, laughing a little. "We're on a date, actually. It's our fifth official one. We just left the theater down the street and decided to stop by for coffee before we go relieve the babysitter."

"*We?*"

"Yes, she's staying over tonight."

Shelby sat down at the table next to her and asked, "So, you have a girlfriend?"

"I have someone I'm dating," Erica replied. "We're taking it slow."

"Slow? You had sex with her in my parking lot before you went on one of those five dates."

Erica laughed and said, "I know. But we're taking *this* part slowly. I really like her, Shell. She's kind of just what I needed. She's happy on her own, you know? She's not looking for me to fulfill something within her. She and Deacon cooked dinner for all of us last night, and I just sat there watching them throw shredded cheese at each other."

"Cheese?"

"They were making pizza." Erica laughed again. "I still hope I don't screw this up because I think this would be worse than what happened with Rosa, but I just talked to him and told him that we're early in our relationship and that things aren't guaranteed."

"How did that go?"

"He seemed to understand, but he's also eleven years old, so I don't know what really stuck."

Erica looked over at the patio where Melissa hung up the phone and turned to see Erica staring. Then, she smiled at her, looked off to the side behind the café, and looked back at Erica, wiggling her eyebrows. She tilted her head to the side and walked out of sight.

"Oh, I've… I think I'm going to go. Mel just waved at me. Something with work. I'll talk to you later," she said all that quickly, standing and grabbing Melissa's purse along with her own.

"You okay?"

"Yup. Bye, Shell!"

Erica left out the backdoor and made her way down the patio stairs, finding Melissa's car, which they'd driven here, parked. She reached for the back door, somehow knowing it would be unlocked, and opened it to find Melissa spreading her legs for her as she lay in the back seat.

"Close the door and get in," she instructed.

Erica did as she was told and climbed on top of her.

"Get *in*, Erica," Melissa said firmly and looked down at her own spread legs.

Erica smirked, moved her hand to Melissa's center, and slipped inside.

"Now, fuck me, baby," Melissa told her, closing her eyes.

CHAPTER FOURTEEN

"Can I get a double shot?" Anna asked the teenager behind the counter with the nametag that said 'Chelsea' on it and had the logo of *The Meet Cute Café* next to it.

"Sure. Can I get you anything else?"

"No, thank you. I'm meeting someone here, and I don't want to have anything to keep me here just in case."

"Oh," the girl uttered, looking a little surprised as she rang up Anna's order. "Blind date?"

"How did you know?" Anna asked.

"We get a lot of those here," Chelsea replied.

"I've never been on one," Anna shared, looking around and seeing a busy café with a predominantly female crowd. "A lot of women here," she added.

"You could say that," Chelsea replied, laughing as she moved over to the espresso machine. "I'll have your drink at the bar in just a second."

"Thank you," she said, looking around still.

She'd been set up by her boss, and there were so many things wrong with that sentence. Anna worked as the office manager, and the owner of the small company only had ten employees, so they were all essentially an extended family. Anna had only worked there for a year, but she liked it so far and was just now being included in the things the long-term employees got included in regularly. It was as if she were finally being accepted as a member of that family, and that both made her happy and worried her. Anna wasn't much of a joiner; she never had been. And that work-family often socialized after-hours and had frequent summer barbeques. Anna was much more of a regular employee: she went to work, did a good job while there, and then went home to her one-bedroom apartment, her microwave dinner, and a good book.

She'd been that way for much of her life. When girls her age got excited about school dances, Anna preferred to skip them. When the kids in the neighborhood wanted to go on long bike rides and invited her to join, she declined and sat in the grass of the backyard, staring up at the sky. In high school, she hadn't played sports or joined clubs; she hadn't participated in academic competitions. She'd stayed at home and read books. Sometimes, she'd watch TV or put on a movie, but she liked being on her own.

Well, that wasn't entirely true. She didn't like it *all the time.* There were times when she wanted to go on those bike rides. She also thought about attending dances because of the idea of being included in that group of girls that always stood in a circle and talked about things like the dress someone was wearing or the boy whom they wanted to ask them to dance. She played the piano only because her parents had signed her up for lessons when she was seven, and she'd almost signed up for the talent show one year.

She hadn't because she was the outcast. In some ways, she didn't mind that moniker, but in others, she wanted to wash it away and pretend she was just like everyone else. That was a hard thing to do growing up. Anna was the name her American parents had given her when they'd adopted her from Korea. She didn't even know her Korean name. She'd been three months old when they'd gone to pick her up and brought her to her new home. She was five years old before she really noticed she was different than all the other kids. Her parents were very well-off. Anna grew up with a whole bunch of rich white kids with blonde hair and blue eyes. She'd gone to a Christian school through junior high and had been the only one of Asian descent there. When she finally left for boarding school in Vermont, she'd thought she'd meet a more diverse group of kids, but that hadn't happened. She'd been one of two Asian students, and there had only been one African-American student in the whole school.

No boy had ever asked her to the shared dances between the boys' campus and the girls' campus. No one suggested she play the piano in the annual talent show. Her roommate was polite but didn't invite Anna to join her and her friends as they smoked their illicit cigarettes in the old science building. Anna had been out of place and alone her whole life.

When her boss, Courtney, suggested she consider going on a date with the child of a family friend, Anna had declined politely more than once. On the fourth suggestion that Troy was great and also available, Anna had said yes. She'd rolled her eyes at her own acquiescence later, but her thought was that this yes was her playing the long game. If she said yes to this, they could have a cup of coffee and go their separate ways, but she'd then be able to use that yes to get her out of a few after-work happy hours in the future.

So, Anna grabbed her double shot in her to-go cup and sat at one of the few empty tables in the place filled with women, waiting for Troy to walk through the front door.

"How is everything?" a woman asked, walking up to Anna's table.

"I haven't tried it yet," Anna said.

"Well, let me know. And if it's okay, can I put this on your table?"

"Sure," Anna replied.

The woman looked to be in her mid-to-late-thirties and wore an apron indicating that she worked here. Her nametag said 'Shelby' on it, and she placed a small placard in the middle of Anna's table.

"We have an open mic night coming up," Shelby told her. "Friday at six."

"Great," Anna said.

"I'll leave you with your coffee. Let me know if you need anything else."

Shelby walked to the next table, where she put another sign and continued on as Anna took her first sip of what was very good coffee.

"Anna?"

Anna looked up toward the door but didn't see anyone looking her way.

"Are you Anna?"

She turned to her right to see a woman with short blonde hair and blue eyes giving her a soft smile.

"Yeah, I'm Anna."

"I'm Troy," the woman said, standing up. "Sorry, I didn't notice you come in. I had to take a work call and got distracted. Not the best way to start a blind date, huh?" The woman walked over to Anna's table, carrying her coffee in a mug, and held out her hand. "Nice to meet you."

"I'm sorry. What?" Anna said, setting her own to-go cup down on the table.

"Nice to meet you?" the woman asked this time.

"You're…"

"Troy. I got here a little early. I thought I'd catch you at the door and order something for you, but there was an issue at the site, and I had to take care of it."

"The site?"

"Construction," Troy explained. "I thought Courtney told you a little about me – I'm a contractor." She placed her cup on the table and ran a hand through her hair that had no product in it and looked a little tousled.

Anna shook her head and said, "*You're* Troy?"

"Yes, I'm Troy."

"But you're…"

"Holding out my hand for you to shake and kind of looking like an idiot now," Troy said.

Anna put out her own hand without really thinking about it and let Troy shake it.

"Are you okay?" Troy asked.

"You're a woman," Anna finally said.

"I am." Troy laughed a little. Then, she sobered. "Wait. Did you not know that?"

"Courtney said she wanted to set me up with a family friend's kid, and *his* name was Troy."

"Well, I'm a little on the butch side, but I'm *not* a him," she replied. "Courtney told you I was a guy?"

Anna thought about it, recalling every conversation they'd had about Troy, searching for pronouns.

"No, I don't think she did, actually. I just assumed."

"Can I sit?" Troy asked.

"Oh, sure," Anna replied.

Troy sat across from her at the small table and said, "So, you thought I was a guy, which is why you agreed to this blind date?"

"Yeah."

"And knowing I'm *not* a guy changes things for you?"

"I'm straight," Anna said.

"Got it." Troy nodded.

"Your name is really Troy? I've never met a woman named Troy before."

"My name is Danielle Troy. I go by Troy, though."

"Right. Courtney could've told me that."

"The better question is why Courtney set you up with a woman," Troy noted.

"You're right," Anna agreed as she realized her boss's mistake. "Why *did* she do that?"

"Does she know you're straight?"

"I don't advertise my sexuality at work," Anna stated.

"Well, you might want to let her know that if she's going to set you up again, you're interested in men, not women."

"I guess so," Anna said.

"Well, I'm here, and you're here… Do you at least want to finish your coffee with me?"

"Hey, Troy," the woman named Shelby said as she approached the table.

"Hey, Shelby. What's up?"

"Just thought I'd stop by and say hi. I'm taking the rest of the day off. Maria and I are going to get away from work for a bit."

"Sounds good," Troy replied.

"How's that coffee?"

"It's great. Thank you," Anna told her.

"Oh, Shelby, this is my new friend, Anna. Anna, this is Shelby. I come here a lot."

"Nice to meet you," Shelby said with a smile.

"You too," Anna said.

Shelby patted Troy on the shoulder and left them alone.

"You really *do* come here a lot," Anna commented.

"Small community," Troy shrugged. "It's one of the main queer hangouts and the only one I know of on the beach."

"Queer hangouts?" Anna asked.

Troy nodded and said, "You didn't notice? There's a rainbow flag in that corner and a few brochures for LGBTQ centers, support lines, and the like over on the counter."

"I guess I wasn't paying attention," Anna said.

"Does it bother you?" Troy asked, taking a drink.

"What? The LGBT thing?"

"Yeah."

"No," Anna replied, shaking her head. "I'm only confused as to why–" She stopped when she put it together.

"Penny for *that* thought," Troy said.

"I think I know why Courtney thought I was interested in women."

"Do tell."

"There was a holiday party last year, and I didn't want to go alone, so I asked my best friend from college to go with me. She's gay, and well, this is going to come out wrong, but I don't know how to say it."

"Let me guess. She looks the part?" Troy asked.

"You could say that."

"Courtney probably thought you brought a date."

"I guess so," Anna said.

"So, you can tell her you met up with me, we were very confused for a minute and finished our coffee, at least. It gives you a chance to clear things up."

"Yeah," Anna said.

"So, you and that best friend never…" Troy attempted to ask a minute later after a shared silence.

"What? No," Anna replied. "Honestly, we only became friends because the university roomed us together, and she was nice. She took time to get to know me, and when we both moved out of the dorm, we kept in touch, but I don't even see her that often anymore. That holiday party was the last time I've seen her, actually."

"*That's* your best friend?" Troy asked. "Someone you think was being nice to you back in school and someone you hardly see now?"

"I'm thirty years old; I have a job and responsibilities," Anna countered. "Do you see your friends all the time?"

"Well, yeah. I work with most of them, but I see my friends from college every few months, at least."

"How old are you, exactly?"

"I'm twenty-seven."

"Well, I don't know what happens as you get older, but it gets harder and harder to keep up with people," Anna said. "I suppose if you work with some of them, it makes it easier, though."

"Hey, are you going to this?" Troy asked, picking up the sign on the table advertising the open mic night.

"No," she said.

"Why not? Could be fun."

"I have plans," Anna replied.

"With that best friend you never see?" Troy teased.

"I think I'll take my coffee to-go," Anna said.

"No, I'm sorry. Come on. Stay." Troy leaned over the table. "I didn't mean it like that. It was my lame attempt at a joke."

"I really should be going, though," Anna told her.

"You thought this was a date. I highly doubt you had plans that started ten minutes after you got here," Troy said.

"You're presumptuous."

"I'm right," Troy replied, laughing.

Anna had to smile at that because Troy *was* right. She

had no plans. She rarely had plans. She should've thought of something to get her out of this date in case it was bad, but she'd only gotten as far as getting a small coffee in a paper cup.

"Come on," Troy encouraged. "Invite that best friend of yours if you want. She's gay, right? Maybe she'd like to come."

"She's out of town for two weeks; just left on vacation."

Anna hadn't talked to her about it, but she'd seen it on Facebook. That was her best friend, going on vacation, and Anna had no idea she was leaving because they rarely talked.

"Well, *I'll* be here," Troy replied.

"Do you sing or play something?"

"No, I just come to hang out and watch."

"It's not really my thing," Anna said.

"What is *your* thing?"

"Books," she blurted out.

"Books? Any book in particular?" Troy took another drink of her coffee, but her blue eyes remained on Anna.

"I read a lot."

"Genre?"

"Anything, really."

Troy laughed and replied, "Okay. I'll take the hint. If you change your mind about Friday, I'll be here. We can just hang out. You might meet some new people, or you might hate it." The woman laughed again. "But I can tell you're trying to be nice right now. You really want to flee, don't you?"

"What? No. Why would you–"

"You haven't stopped tapping your foot since before I sat down. And I've seen you look at the door like it's your way out of a bank robbery at least three times since I sat down."

"I'm not... I'm sorry. I–"

"No, it's fine," Troy interrupted. "I can pick up on the signals of a woman who isn't interested just fine. But you

80

should know, I'm not trying to pick you up. I heard you when you said you were straight. I just like meeting new people. I'll let you go, though. It was nice meeting you, Anna."

Troy stood and carried her cup to the bar, where she placed it down, waved at the barista that had served Anna her double shot, and walked out the door without turning back.

***

Anna walked into *The Meet Cute Café* Friday night just after six. She hadn't planned on coming tonight. Her plan had involved a good book, a glass of wine, and her very soft blanket, but there was just something about how Troy had left her there at the café. Anna hadn't handled the situation well, and she regretted it. She didn't socialize much, but she *did* hate when people didn't think well of her. Her plan was to find Troy, apologize for how she behaved, then grab a coffee on her way out, and go home to enjoy it in private.

"Hey, you."

Anna turned to her right to see Troy leaning against the coffee bar, giving her a smirk.

"Oh, hi," Anna said.

"Decided to come after all, huh?"

"What can I get for you?" Chelsea asked.

Anna realized that she'd remembered the girl's name without having to read her nametag.

"Oh, I–" She looked back and forth between Chelsea and Troy. "I just came to…"

"Can I make a suggestion?" Troy asked, moving a little closer.

"Okay."

"Try their cupcakes. The vanilla one is really good, and it goes great with just a regular cappuccino."

"I wasn't going to stay," Anna stated.

"Then, you can take it with you," Troy said, grabbing her own drink from the counter. "I'm over there with a couple of my friends if you decide to stick around."

With that, the woman walked off. How was Anna supposed to apologize to her if she just kept walking off like that? Why was it even so important to Anna to apologize to Troy, to begin with?

"Can I get a cappuccino?" she asked the barista.

"What size?"

"Large. And I guess I'll try that cupcake."

"For here or to-go?"

"Here," she said definitively.

"Good choice," Chelsea, the barista, replied with a small laugh.

A few minutes later, Anna stood there, holding a mug and a plate with a cupcake on it. She looked over at the table where Troy was sitting with two other women, and one of those women had her arm around the other one. Troy was laughing at something someone said, and Anna smiled, too. Troy looked really happy. She looked comfortable in her own skin. Then, she looked Anna up and down. Wait. What? Troy lifted an eyebrow at her. She'd definitely just looked Anna up and down. Anna hadn't dressed up to come here, exactly, but she had thrown on a nice pair of jeans, short heels, and a decent-looking sweater.

"Let's get things started," someone said into the microphone.

Anna was standing in the middle of the café, holding on to a cup and a plate, and she was staring at Troy, who was a woman, not a man. Troy ran her hand through her hair again, and Anna opened her mouth in response. What the fuck was that? She walked over to the table, and Troy stood up when she arrived, taking her cup and plate for her. After Troy set them down, she helped Anna move through the chairs to the one empty one at the table.

"Guys, this is Anna. Anna, this is Tara and Angie."

"Hi," Tara said.

"Nice to meet you," Angie added.

"You too," Anna said.

The first musician started with an original song and played the guitar. Anna took sips of her coffee but didn't touch her cupcake yet. She just stared at the woman on the stage for most of the song, but Troy was in her eyeline, which meant she was also staring at *her*. Not again. Not this again. She picked up her cappuccino and took another sip, trying to push the thoughts out of her head. She had been such a disappointment to her parents that she'd tried so hard to not think about the thing that would make her even more of a disappointment.

"Refill?" Troy asked when the musician finished.

"Oh, I should–"

"Be going, right?" Troy interrupted. "Why did you even come?"

"I came to apologize," Anna replied as the next performer took the stage.

"Apologize for what?"

"How I treated you last time."

"We're going to go grab a smoke," Angie said, leaning over the table toward Troy.

Troy nodded, and Angie and Tara stood up to go.

"Are they together?"

"Yeah, three years now," Troy replied. "Why do you need to apologize for last time?"

"I think I handled it wrong."

"How exactly are you supposed to handle when your boss sets you up with a woman named Troy, and you're straight?"

"*You* seemed to handle it fine," she replied.

Troy's laugh drew Anna's eyes to her full lips, and she seemed to notice that. She gave Anna an inquisitive look just as the second performer began.

"I'm getting you a refill. I'll be right back."

"I don't…"

Troy leaned over and whispered, "Just let me buy you a drink, Anna."

Anna didn't say anything else. Troy walked over to the

counter to order, and Anna just watched. She watched and remembered how she'd felt when she'd been at boarding school. Her roommate, Jen, had no problem changing in front of Anna. She'd walk into their room in a hurry, throw off her uniform, and put on either her sleep clothes or her going-out clothes. That had been the first time Anna had noticed the pull, and it wouldn't be the last.

She hadn't dated much in college and had used school as the reason why. She'd planned on becoming a doctor one day. Her parents would've loved that. Unfortunately, Anna couldn't stand needles or the sight of blood, so she would have had to stick to research, but she couldn't seem to find any real interest in medicine. When she'd graduated with an undergraduate business degree, her parents assumed she'd go for her MBA, but Anna had found a job as an office manager and liked it. It paid well enough to pay rent and support her book habit. It was enough for her.

That was when her parents started making suggestions. Anna would love the guy from church. There was a cute doctor who played tennis at the club. Her mother made a new recommendation nearly every time she saw Anna, and Anna had just obliged each time. She hadn't wanted to fight about it. She hadn't wanted to admit to the pull. She'd never even admitted to herself what that pull meant. She'd had sex with men, and it had been fine. It would be enough.

"Are you going to eat that cupcake or just stare at it all night?" Troy asked when the second performer exited the stage.

"Oh, I got it for you," Anna lied and pushed the plate over to Troy.

"You got me a cupcake?" Troy asked, smiling. "Split it with me?"

"Okay." Anna nodded.

***

"I got you a cappuccino," Anna said as Troy sat down

across from her.

"Thanks," Troy replied and looked out at the water. "God, it's beautiful out there, huh?"

"It is," Anna said.

This was their fourth time grabbing coffee together, but the first time they'd sat on the patio overlooking the water.

"How was work?" Troy asked.

"Fine. I got the new computers for sales approved. Courtney wanted me to get the vendor to go down at least another thousand dollars, but I got them to throw in some upgrades for the same price, so she's happy, and the sales team gets better laptops."

"That's awesome," Troy replied.

Anna noted how Troy's arm moved over the back of Anna's chair and stayed there as she continued to stare out at the water.

"How was work for *you*?"

"Things are coming along at the site. My dad's still annoying, but I'll forgive him, I guess."

Troy had explained on their previous coffee chat that she worked for her father's company and that he was in the process of teaching her everything he knew in order to retire early. The retirement was supposed to take place this year, but he seemed to be taking his time passing the torch.

"Is he having a hard time letting go?"

"It's his baby even more than *I* am," Troy replied, taking a drink of her coffee. "One day, my mom will press him to finally be done with it, though. She's going to talk to him about it this Sunday at dinner, and we're going to try to tag-team him."

"How often do you have dinner with your parents?" Anna asked.

"Every week. Sometimes, it could be twice a week. It just depends."

"Every week?"

"Yeah. Why?"

She looked at Anna with those blue eyes, and Anna looked away.

"I haven't had dinner with my parents in, God, over a year."

"Do they not live here?" Troy asked.

"No, they live about fifteen minutes in that direction," she said, pointing to the right. "They have a vacation house on the water here, a condo in the city, and their main residence is on the other side of the town."

"They have three houses here?"

"The condo is mainly for my dad. His office is in the city, and he sometimes just goes there after work instead of driving home. My mom wanted the place on the water, so they'd planned to sell their old place and move over here when they found one, but they ended up keeping the other house, too. They probably spend a weekend a month in the new one."

"Damn. My parents have a two-bedroom and an RV they take out every so often," Troy replied.

"I would *love* to see my parents in an RV." Anna laughed.

"Not the long road trip types?"

"Not in the slightest," she said.

"What about you?" Troy asked.

"Me and road trips?"

"Yeah. Do you like them?"

"I've never been on one," Anna replied.

"What?" Troy looked completely surprised. "You've never been on a road trip?"

"No, I never saw the point."

"Long, winding roads with beautiful landscapes on either side, your music blaring, windows rolled down, and wind in your hair."

"Where am I going, though?"

"That's not the point. It's the journey that counts."

"But there has to be a destination, doesn't there?" she asked.

"*Does* there?" Troy asked with that smile Anna always found herself staring at.

"Sorry to cut this short, but I have to run," Anna told her, reaching for her purse.

"I just got here," Troy said.

"I know. I thought I had more time, but–"

"Anna?"

"Yeah?"

"There's something you're not telling me."

"What? No, there's–"

"There is. But you don't trust me yet, and that's okay. Just know that you can. If there *is* something, you can tell me. I won't pressure you or anything. I just wanted you to know you could trust me."

"There's nothing I'm not telling you," Anna replied. "I mean, we just met a month ago. So, there are things you don't know because we're getting to know each other, but there's nothing I'm…"

Troy nodded and said, "Okay. I'll text you later. Maybe we can have a *whole* cup of coffee next time."

"Yeah, sounds good. Bye."

When she got to her car, Anna closed her eyes and leaned back against the headrest. She couldn't be like this. She couldn't want this. She had already made her parents' lives so difficult. They couldn't have children of their own – they had tried for years to no avail – so they'd traveled all the way to South Korea to get her. They'd given her a great life, and she'd repaid them by being a recluse who couldn't hack it at much. She couldn't also be the one thing she knew they'd never support.

***

"So, I got you this," Troy said, placing a gift bag on the table.

"What's this for?" Anna asked, smiling at the bag in front of her.

"Open it," Troy replied.

They'd been having coffee once a week for two months now. It wasn't always on the same day or at the same time. Troy's job meant that she couldn't just be there Wednesdays before work. Anna found herself not wanting to miss their weekly meetings, so she worked around Troy's schedule when needed. It didn't take much work on her part, though, since she didn't exactly have much else to do.

"It's a book," Anna stated, pulling a book from the bag that she'd never heard of.

"It is. You really *are* smart," Troy teased.

"Shut up," Anna said, laughing.

"Have you read it?"

"I've never even heard of it," Anna replied.

"It's one of my favorites," Troy shared. "I thought since you read, like, a million books a week, you might need a new one. I went with a paperback over an e-book because you seem like the type of woman who likes the smell of books. Am I right?"

"How did you—"

"I am," Troy said, laughing. "Well, I hope you like it."

"But what's it for?" Anna asked.

"What do you mean? It's *for* you to read."

"No, I mean, it's not my birthday. It's not Christmas."

"It's just because."

"Just because?"

"No one's ever gotten you a gift just because they can?"

"No," she said.

"Not even your ex-boyfriends?"

Anna shook her head.

"Who have you dated, Anna?" Troy asked, laughing a little.

"One vanilla cupcake with two forks," Chelsea announced as she set the plate down between them with two forks on top of it.

"Thanks, Chels."

"I'll be right back with your drinks."

"I haven't ordered yet," Anna said.

"I got you your usual," Troy replied as she picked up one of the forks.

Anna had a usual. She smiled at that thought, but really at the one that Troy had known her usual and had ordered it for her.

"Angie, Tara, and I are going to hit this art show this weekend. Do you want to come with us?"

"When is it?"

"Nope." Troy took a bite. "Answer *my* question, and *then* I'll answer yours."

"What?" Anna laughed.

"If I tell you when it is, you'll just make up some excuse for being busy that day."

"I will not."

"You do it all the time." Troy laughed. "I don't take offense to it because I know you like hanging out with me, since you come here with me every week, but you don't seem to want to get out of *The Meet Cute* comfort zone."

"It's not that."

"Then, what is it? You've met Ang and Tara. You told me you liked them."

"I do. They're nice."

"Do you have something against art?"

"No," Anna said, laughing and taking a bite of the cupcake they were sharing.

"Then, what is it?"

"I like it here. I like it here with you. I don't know about some art show with your friends."

"You like it here with me?" Troy said with a smile.

"You know I do." Anna rolled her eyes.

"Come to the art show; I can pick you up. You can drive separately, I guess, if you're worried you're going to need to make a run for it, though."

"I don't need to make a run for it."

"You've done that to me literally three times," Troy

replied.

"And two cappuccinos," Chelsea said, placing their drinks on the table in front of each of them.

"Thanks," Anna said, smiling up at Chelsea.

The girl walked off, leaving Anna staring at Troy, who was staring back at her.

"I'll think about it and text you, okay?"

Troy laughed a little and said, "Fine, but I get the rest of this cupcake."

"Hey!" Anna laughed.

***

This was one of Troy's favorite books? Anna had cracked the spine practically the moment she'd gotten home. She'd poured the wine, put on her fluffy socks, and pulled the blanket over her on the sofa. Then, she'd opened the book and realized what it was about by the end of chapter two. This book was about two women falling in love.

It wasn't *just* about two women falling in love. They were having sex by chapter nine. In chapter ten, they were at it again, and this time, they were in public. In chapter fourteen, they were using toys. By five in the morning, Anna was reading the epilogue where one woman proposed to the other, and they celebrated by christening their new bedroom by making long, slow, and passionate love. By seven in the morning, Anna was in her shower, stroking herself to her fourth orgasm of the night. By eight in the morning, she was lying in bed, re-reading chapter fourteen and using the small bullet vibrator she'd bought online years ago to bring herself to another one. She'd never had this many orgasms in one night. Hell, Anna hadn't had this many orgasms in one week before; maybe even in a month. She went to work that day, showing up late and a little sore, and received a text message from Troy around lunchtime.

Troy: Art show?

Anna licked her lips as she stared down at her phone

and the carrot sticks that awaited her just beyond. She'd been picturing Troy as one of the main characters in the book, and she had also been picturing herself as the other main character. She'd thought about Troy's head between her legs, Troy behind her, Troy on top of her, and Troy pressing her against that wall while Anna ran her hands through that always tousled short blonde hair. She grew wet at the thought and wished she were in the privacy of her own bedroom to take care of the pulse between her legs.

Anna: Sure. Dinner after?

Troy: Dinner?

Anna: We don't have to.

Anna stared down at her phone, waiting for the three bubbles to turn into Troy's response.

Troy: It's an evening show. We could do dinner before and meet Angie and Tara there.

That would mean they'd be having dinner alone. She and Troy would be moving out of *The Meet Cute Café* and into a restaurant where there would likely be appetizers, wine, and maybe even dessert.

Anna: Okay.

***

"Can I ask you something?"

"Sure," Troy said as they walked along the sidewalk.

"Why did you give me that book?"

"Because it's one of my favorites," Troy said, tucking her hands into the front pocket of her jeans.

"That's the only reason?"

"It's *one* of the reasons."

Anna looked over at her and asked, "What are the other reasons?"

"This is me," Troy said.

"What?"

"I live here," Troy replied.

"You live where?"

"Up there," she said, laughing.

Troy looked up then, and Anna followed her head tilt.

"You live here?"

"Yes, that's my apartment," Troy confirmed.

"You live across the street from the café," Anna stated.

"I know. Why do you think I'm there all the time? It's really more like across the street and down the block, but the restaurant we're going to is on the corner, so I thought I'd just tell you that I live here. So, we can go now, I guess."

"You live above a bookstore?"

"Yeah."

Anna smiled.

"Do you want to go in before they close?" Troy offered, smiling back at her.

"Can we? I can eat fast so we won't be late for the show."

Troy laughed and pulled open the door to the bookstore. Anna walked in and looked around, trying to get her bearings.

"Have you ever been in here?" Troy asked.

"No, I didn't even know this was here."

"Well, it's got a pretty specific audience, so that makes sense."

"Audience?" Anna checked.

"It's owned by two lesbians. It's got bestsellers and well-known authors, but it also has…" Troy motioned to the back wall. "Lesbian fiction, non-fiction, romance, and just about everything else."

"Did you get the book you gave me from here?"

"Yeah," Troy said.

Anna walked back to the wall Troy had just referenced and saw books mostly with two women on the covers or a cup of coffee with a catchy title or a beach with two umbrella drinks and lounge chairs.

"Troy?"

"Yeah?"

"Why did you really get me that book?"

"Did you read it?"

"Yes."

"Did you like it?"

"Yes," she whispered.

Troy moved to stand next to her and said, "If you want to tell me, you can, but you don't have to."

"How did you know?"

"There's a way you look at me sometimes," she said with a shrug.

"A way I look at you?" She turned to Troy.

"You stare at my mouth a lot," Troy said, chuckling a little. "And I've seen you watching girls kiss in *The Meet Cute*. You don't stare at them in disgust, more like curiosity. It's like you might want to know what that's like. I figured I could be wrong, but I didn't think I was, so I got you the book."

"I've never…"

"Do you think you might want to?"

"I can't, Troy," she replied.

"Why not?"

"Because I just can't. I can't do that to my parents."

"The parents you see, like, twice a year, even though they live close by?" Troy said.

"They're still my parents."

"And they'd have a problem with you being gay?"

"I never said I was," Anna argued.

"Fine. They'd have a problem with you being anything other than straight?"

"Yes."

"How do you know?"

"Because they're very religious and very conservative. I went to a Christian school and church every Sunday until I was in high school. Then, they sent me to a conservative boarding school. They wouldn't support it, but I don't even think they'd tolerate it."

"That's *their* loss, then. You have to be who you are, Anna. You should be happy."

"It's not that simple."

"I'm not saying it is. I'm just–"

"We should just go to the restaurant," she interrupted.

"Where we can continue this conversation, I hope," Troy said.

"Can we just drop it, please?"

"Anna, I–"

"You said you wouldn't pressure me, Troy."

Troy took a step back and said, "You're right. I *did* say that. I'm sorry."

"Actually, I think I'll just skip the dinner and a show thing."

"No, Anna… Please, don't. I'm sorry," Troy said, moving into her and taking her hand. "I didn't mean to make you upset. I didn't plan on us coming in here. Let's just start over."

"You didn't do anything wrong. I just don't think I'm in the mood to be with your friends tonight."

"Okay. I'll cancel."

"You made plans with them and *then* invited me," Anna reasoned, giving her a small smile.

"So? I'll tell them something came up. It's not a lie; something *did* come up."

"You don't have to sacrifice time with your friends for a thirty-year-old woman who's already having a mid-life crisis."

"I wouldn't call it a mid-life crisis."

"What would you call it, then?"

"A woman coming out," Troy replied, looking at her so softly, it nearly broke Anna.

***

Anna hadn't been ready to hear those two words together in a sentence about her. She wasn't coming out. She couldn't be coming out. Regardless of how she felt, she wasn't going to do anything about it. Her parents wouldn't exactly welcome Anna and her girlfriend into their home for a Sunday night dinner. They wouldn't want to hear about her engagement. They wouldn't celebrate with her at her wedding to a woman. They definitely wouldn't want her having kids and raising them with her wife. Anna had been raised to respect her parents, and she'd been raised to believe they'd given her an opportunity she wouldn't have had otherwise growing up in a South Korean orphanage.

Still, she couldn't shake the look on Troy's face that night when she'd pulled their hands apart and told the woman she was going to call it a night. Troy had looked disappointed, but she'd also looked scared, like she was worried that Anna was pulling away for more than just that night.

"Cappuccino and vanilla cupcake with two forks?" Chelsea asked.

"Actually, can I just get the cappuccino?"

"Anna?"

Anna turned to see Troy sitting at the table with that Shelby woman. If she were being honest with herself, Anna would admit that she'd come here in hopes of running into Troy after having not seen her for over two weeks. She'd skipped their last two coffee dates and hadn't responded to Troy's texts. She was being awful to someone who had been so kind to her, and she hated it. She'd left work that day, gone home and changed, and found herself staring in her mirror, surprised because she hadn't put on her sweats and fluffy socks like she normally would. She'd put on a pair of jeans and a nice shirt, along with a pair of her favorite heels. Then, she grabbed her purse and keys, and she'd ended up here, hoping and not hoping at the same time that Troy might be here, too.

"Hi," she said to Troy.

"I should get back to work," Shelby said as she stood. "Good catching up, though, Troy."

"Yeah, you too." Troy looked back up at Anna when she approached the table, and added, "I didn't expect to see *you* here."

"Because I can't come here on my own?"

"*Have* you?" Troy asked.

"You're infuriating sometimes. Do you know that?"

"I've heard that from my parents, my brother, and many an ex-girlfriend," Troy replied. "Are you staying?"

"I was just…"

"Right." Troy looked down at the table. "I'll see you around, then."

"No, I meant… I was just going to grab a coffee and go if I didn't see you here."

Troy looked back up and said, "So, you were hoping I was here?"

Anna nodded because she couldn't think of what to say.

"Do you want to sit?" Troy offered.

"I'll grab my drink and be right back," she replied.

Troy smiled at that, and Anna allowed herself to think that it was an adorable look on her. When she returned to the table, Troy had moved her napkin and now-empty plate to the side in order for Anna to be able to sit next to her.

"You haven't returned my messages. I assumed you were avoiding me."

"I was," Anna admitted after she sat down.

"Because I said something that upset you? Offended you?"

"No, Troy, you didn't do anything wrong. I told you that. It's just me."

"I'm not going to bring it up again if that's what you're worried about," Troy told her. "I shouldn't have even said anything that night. I just… we were talking about the book, and you said you liked it."

"I *did* like it. It was sweet."

"Sweet?" Troy lifted an eyebrow.

Anna laughed and added, "And sexy."

Troy smirked and said, "Yes, it's sexy first, though."

"Really? I think it's sweet first."

"How so?"

"They're just sweet together. I don't know. I could just see them walking down the street holding hands and staring longingly into each other's eyes."

"Yeah, that's common in romance novels," Troy told her with a smile.

"I'm surprised you liked it."

"Why?"

"Because you don't seem like the romance-novel type," Anna replied.

"Because I basically look like a dude with my short hair and lack of hips and boobs?"

"What? No. You don't look like a–" Anna stopped herself. "You don't look like a guy, Troy. You're… beautiful." Anna swallowed hard and picked up her coffee cup to cover it up.

Troy cleared her throat and said, "I like it when two women end up together. I like the happy ending part."

"Yeah, that was nice," Anna echoed.

"Did you like the other parts?"

"The sexy parts?" she asked, knowing perfectly well what other parts Troy was talking about.

"Yes, Anna. Did you like those parts?"

"I did," she said, sounding a little more confident in her tone now.

"*All* of them?" Troy asked, scooting her chair forward just a bit.

"Yes." Anna looked up and saw that Troy was much closer now than she had been only a moment ago.

"I like them, too," Troy said. "*All* of them."

"You do?" Anna asked, clearing her own throat now.

"Especially, chapter fourteen," Troy said. "Do you remember chapter fourteen?"

Anna nodded.

"What did you think about that?" Troy asked her.

"Have you… Have you done…"

Troy nodded and said, "It's one of my favorite things

to do."

"Oh," Anna said.

"But I also like working up to that."

"Working up?"

"Yeah," Troy replied, leaning forward and placing her hand on Anna's chair next to her thigh. "You don't start with that; you work your way up to it. When I'm with a woman, I don't want it to be one and done, if you know what I mean. I like to take my time. I like it when we enjoy each other, touch each other, make each other feel good. Nice and slow."

"Slow," Anna uttered, taking a deep breath right after.

"Yes, nice and slow." Troy drew out the words. "Sometimes, anyway."

"Sometimes?"

"After the nice and slow, after the work-up, I like to go faster. That's where chapter fourteen comes in."

"Right," Anna said.

"Anna?"

"Yeah?"

"I like you," Troy said, making their eyes meet despite Anna's attempt to look away. "I like you."

"I like you too, Troy. I—"

"No, not like that. I like you in the way that I think about you and me and chapter fourteen a lot."

"You do?" Anna asked, failing to mention that she'd had the same thoughts.

Troy nodded before adding, "But I don't need chapter fourteen. Well, not right now. Not anytime soon. I just need to know if I'm wrong here."

"Wrong about what?"

"I think you feel it, too," Troy stated.

Anna leaned back in her chair, needing to have some space between them.

"Troy, I can't."

"Because of your parents? They don't have to know anything about chapter fourteen. I'd prefer we never mention it to them, actually."

Anna laughed and said, "It's different for you. Your parents are supportive."

"I know. But I'm not asking you to come out to your parents, Anna. I'm just asking if you feel the same way I do. If I'm wrong and you don't – I'll back off, and we can go back to our weekly coffees. I just sat here before you arrived and poured my heart out to Shelby, over there. I told her I was totally into you and that I thought you felt the same, but that I didn't know if you'd be willing to give me a chance."

"You told someone about me?"

"Shelby is a friend."

"Troy, I don't need people knowing." Anna crossed her arms over her chest. "I don't need people thinking I'm– "

"Gay?" Troy asked, sitting back in her chair as well now. "It's not contagious, Anna. You're either gay, or you're not. Maybe you're some other color of the rainbow, but you can't get it from me or from Shelby knowing."

"I know that. I didn't…" Anna faded out and said, "I'm sorry. I keep messing up."

"Am I wrong, Anna?" Troy asked. "Am I imagining the whole thing? Am I making this up in my mind? Every time we're here, I put my arm over the back of your chair, and sometimes, you lean into it. We share cupcakes, and I open doors for you, pull out your chairs. You bought me that shirt you saw in the store one day because you said it made you think of me, Anna. I don't know… It just feels like there's something here."

Anna nodded and said, "There is. I just don't know what to do about it."

Troy smiled slightly and said, "What do you need?"

"I think some time, maybe."

"Time," Troy repeated.

"Yeah. I never thought I'd be interested in a woman beyond a passing crush, Troy. And we're friends. You're probably the closest person to me now, and I don't want to lose that, but I don't know if I can give you what you want, either."

"All I want is a date, Anna," Troy replied. "Just one date, and we see how it goes from there."

"It's the 'from there' part that I'm worried about."

"We can figure that out together if things go well."

Anna laughed and said, "Why do you even like me? I'm such a mess."

"No, you're not. You're just figuring yourself out. It's different for all of us," Troy reasoned. "Besides, you're beautiful, Anna. You're smart and funny. I love spending time with you." She paused for a second before adding, "And I'll give you what you need, okay? If you need time, I'll back off."

"I don't want you to back off," Anna replied. "I don't want us to not see each other. I shouldn't have been avoiding you."

"We can still do our weekly coffees if you want," Troy suggested.

Anna nodded.

***

Anna got home later and stared at the book on her coffee table. She smiled at the thought of Troy giving it to her because she'd known all along that Anna wasn't exactly straight. Then, Anna stared at the photo of her with her parents that she had hanging on the wall in the hallway. They were all wearing black and white. Her father had on a black tailored suit that made him look like he was going to a funeral. Her mother was in a white dress with a black belt and collar. Anna had worn a black dress with white heels and white pearls that had been a gift from her parents on her twenty-first birthday. They were all smiling their perfectly white smiles, but Anna recalled that day well and knew the smiles were all for the camera.

Her mother had been yelling at her father only an hour before the photographer had arrived. He'd been staying in his condo more nights than not, and she'd suspected him of having an affair. He'd denied it, of course, but Anna was fairly certain he was still sleeping with one of his business partners multiple times a week. Her mother wasn't exactly innocent, either. She'd had a few affairs herself, and the idea of the beach house had been hers. Anna always thought it was because her mother's best friend lived down the street, along with her husband. Anna's mother had spent a lot of time with the man as she pretended to learn how to play tennis, which Anna's father hated.

Anna had overheard the fighting that day they sat through the photos. She'd listened as her mother suggested she have a drink with the new intern at her father's office. She'd also admonished Anna for not wearing earrings and for not doing anything with her life beyond being an office manager. She had even called Anna out on not continuing with her piano lessons after she graduated high school. Anna had been good, sure, but she was never going to be a concert pianist. Her parents had always wanted more for her. No, that wasn't right. Anna glared at the picture now. Her parents had always *expected more from* her. Anna had let those expectations guide her entire life, and she shook her head at herself for it.

***

"Anna?" Troy said when she opened the door.

"Yes," Anna said.

"Yes, what? What's going on? It's late," Troy said, wiping her eyes.

"Is that what you sleep in?" Anna asked.

"Tank top and boxers? Yeah, usually. What are you doing here?"

"I woke you up," Anna stated the obvious.

"It's okay. Are you all right? Did something happen?"

"I want chapter fourteen," Anna said.

That seemed to wake Troy up.

"Sorry?" she said, clearing her throat.

"Not tonight. I mean, in the future."

"The future?"

"I want the slow part."

"Slow?" Troy asked, seemingly having a hard time keeping up. "Do you want to come in?"

"Is that okay? I just showed up."

"It's fine. Come in." Troy moved out of the way to allow Anna to walk inside.

"Oh, my God. This is your place?" she asked.

"Yeah. It's not much, but I don't need a lot of space, so a studio works for me."

"It has shelves everywhere," Anna gasped out, looking around the space.

The apartment was one main room with floor-to-ceiling shelves lining all four of the walls. There were two doors. Anna guessed one was a closet, and the other one, she assumed, was the bathroom. The bed was unmade, likely because Troy had been sleeping in it before Anna had arrived, and the kitchen was small but tidy. The living area had a sofa, a chair, and a TV that faced the wall with the window that overlooked the main street below.

"Oh, yeah," Troy replied. "It used to be the second floor of the bookstore. They had to downsize a few years ago, and they turned this into a studio to rent out. I was lucky enough to find it, and they don't raise my rent twenty percent a year like some of the other places around here."

Anna smiled at her. This woman looked so cute wearing a pair of red and yellow boxer shorts and a white tank top. Then, it clicked for Anna: Troy was wearing a *white* tank top. Anna stared, unable to do anything about it. She could see everything through it. She could see Troy's small but firm-looking breasts and nipples that were likely hard because it was cold in the apartment.

"You okay?" Troy asked, walking toward her.

"Yeah, I think I am." Anna smiled. "I'm saying yes to your question from earlier."

"Remind me because I just got woken abruptly by a beautiful woman standing at my door telling me she wants chapter fourteen."

"I'd like to go on a date with you," Anna replied. "If you're still interested in doing that with me."

"Yeah? I thought you said you needed some time."

"I thought I did. But I went home tonight and thought about it, and I don't need any more time. I've known I was interested in girls since I was fifteen years old. Well, women now – I'm interested in women now. *You*, actually. I'm interested in you."

"So, you'd like to go on a date with me?" Troy checked.

"Can you put on a robe or something? I can see…" Anna pointed. "Not that I don't like what I see… That's not the problem. It's that I *do* like what I see, and now that I've said all these things out loud, I can't seem to hold them in any longer."

"My boobs?" Troy said with a laugh. "I'll just change shirts."

She walked over to a dresser next to her bed, pulled the tank top off, and Anna saw her muscled back ripple as she put on a new shirt.

"You did that on purpose," Anna scolded playfully. "You could have just put another shirt on over it."

"I know," Troy said, turning around and smirking at her. "So, a date, huh? You and me?"

"You and me."

"Okay. When?"

"Friday."

"Friday," Troy repeated. "I'll pick you up."

"Okay," Anna said. "Okay," she repeated. "I should go now."

"Nope," Troy said, moving to her.

"Nope?"

"Stay," Troy replied.

"Stay? Stay the night?"

"It's already after midnight. Just stay. We can sleep." She took a few more steps toward Anna.

"Just sleep?"

"We haven't even been on a first date yet, Anna. What kind of woman do you think I am?"

"I don't have clothes," Anna replied, looking down at her jeans and the jacket she'd thrown on over an old sweatshirt.

"You can wear something of mine."

"Boxers?"

Troy laughed and said, "No. I don't take you for a boxers kind of woman."

"Bikinis," Anna shared before she could stop herself.

Troy stood there with an open mouth, and Anna had to laugh at that. Then, Troy shook her head as if shaking dirty thoughts out of her mind.

"So, sweatpants for you and a T-shirt."

"Okay."

Troy went to her dresser and pulled out clothes for Anna to change into. She motioned to the bathroom. Anna went inside to change, noting that it wasn't the tidiest of bathrooms, but it also wasn't disgusting, either.

"I don't have a toothbrush!" she yelled through the closed door.

"Second drawer!" Troy yelled back.

Anna opened the drawer and saw at least ten toothbrushes.

"Do you have company a lot that requires a toothbrush?"

"No, my brother is a dentist." Troy laughed. "He disappointed my dad by not taking over the business and became a dentist instead. Notice how they all say Dr. Marcus J. Troy on them?"

"Oh," Anna uttered.

She brushed her teeth, changed, and left the bathroom.

Troy was sitting on the side of the bed when she emerged.

"He gives me a new bunch of those every time he gets a new shipment in from a different vendor," she said. "I never have to buy toothbrushes."

"Right," Anna said, looking down at her bare feet.

"So, sleep?" Troy asked.

"Yeah," Anna replied.

Minutes later, Anna was lying in Troy's bed, staring up at the ceiling. Troy was at least a foot away, doing the same thing. It was awkward, but she knew Troy was trying to be patient and give her space. Anna, for her part, wanted to show Troy that this was the first of many, many steps, but that she was willing to take it. She reached for Troy's hand, entwined their fingers, and placed their now-joined ones between them on the bed.

***

Troy's kiss was still amazing. They'd kissed like this, sweetly and with no intention of taking things any further, more times than Anna could count now. They'd done a lot more than that in the two months they'd been dating, too, and Anna hadn't ever been so happy. Of course, she still had a lot of steps to take. Her parents had no idea she was dating a woman. They had no clue that she'd decided to stay at Courtney's company for the long haul since it was expanding, and she might have a team of office managers under her one day. They had no idea about a lot of things where Anna was concerned, but for the first time, she did not care. She didn't feel like she owed them anything anymore. She'd already decided she'd tell them eventually, and as much as she wanted them to like Troy and accept that their daughter was gay, she also wouldn't live her life by their rules, expectations, or standards anymore.

"So, two months, huh?" Shelby asked, sitting down at their table in the café.

"Two *great* months," Troy replied, smiling at Anna.

"And I understand you'll be playing for us at the next open mic night?" she said to Anna.

"Keyboard, yes," Anna said. "Angie, Troy's friend, is a singer-songwriter. She asked me to accompany her when she plays here for the first time."

"Can't wait to hear it," Shelby said. "And this one is on the house. Happy anniversary." She placed a vanilla cupcake down on their table with two forks.

"Thank you," Troy said.

"Thanks, Shelby," Anna replied.

Shelby winked at them and walked off.

"So, anniversary, huh?" Troy asked.

"I guess," Anna shrugged. "I've never celebrated a two-month anniversary."

"No?"

"No, I've never really made it to two months with someone I *wanted* to celebrate with."

"And you want to celebrate this one with me?" Troy asked, taking the fork from the plate.

"I do. I just don't know what that means, exactly."

"Well, first, I think it means that we make this official. We've been dating for two months, but we haven't used a certain word to describe each other yet."

"Ah," Anna said, picking up her own fork. "You want to be my girlfriend?"

"I do." Troy nodded.

"I've never had one of those."

"I know."

Anna smiled at her and said, "I think it's about time I do."

"Yeah?"

"Yes. And I was also thinking about something else."

"Something else?" Troy asked.

"Yes, you've been very patient with me." Anna took a bite of the cupcake. "You waited until our third date to even try for a goodnight kiss. You let me decide when we have public displays of affection. You never pressured me to sleep over or to sleep over at my place until I brought it up. You waited until I was ready for sex. Then, you took it very slow."

"I like slow. I told you that," Troy replied, sipping her coffee.

"So, do I." Anna leaned over and kissed the icing Troy had on her lip before licking it away.

"Oh, you're such a tease." Troy laughed.

"Not if we celebrate tonight."

"Anniversary sex?" Troy asked, lifting an eyebrow at her. "Your place or mine?"

"Yours. You have what we need there."

"What we need?"

"You said you bought a–"

"A new one. Yeah, I did. Wait…" Troy's eyes went wide. "You want *that* tonight?"

"Can I have it?"

Troy nodded rapidly and said, "You're sure?"

"Yes, I'm sure," Anna told her.

"We can take this cupcake and coffee to-go," Troy suggested. "I'll ask Shelby to wrap it up. We can leave now."

Anna laughed and said, "Okay."

"Shelby, can we move these things into to-go cups?"

"Sure. Everything okay?"

"Chapter fourteen," Troy whispered to Anna as Shelby approached with the cups and a plastic container for the cupcake.

Anna nodded.

"What's chapter fourteen?" Shelby asked.

THE SALES PITCH

"Come on. We've talked about this," Shelby said.

"I know, but this is a new number," Ryan replied.

"You're making me not want to serve you coffee, Ryan." Shelby gave Ryan a playful glare.

"Hey, I pay when I come in, and I tip well," she said.

"And you keep asking me to sell my place."

"For a very, very good price. It's way over what you could get if you actually put this place on the market."

"Ryan, my wife and I bought this place because we love it. We don't want to sell it. I plan on retiring here, not selling it so that I can retire early."

"Shelby, you have the prime location between a whole lot of other people who are actively considering selling or who have already sold. Condos will come whether you sell or not."

"Great. More people to buy coffee from me," Shelby said, smirking at Ryan.

"Are you holding out for a better offer? Waiting to be the last person to sell, knowing the number could go up."

"What? No." Shelby placed Ryan's caramel latte on the counter for her. "I don't care about the money. If I did, I wouldn't be slinging coffee. I'd still be an attorney."

"If I can go higher…" she said.

"I still wouldn't take it." Shelby laughed.

"God. Leave the woman alone already," someone else said.

Ryan turned to see a young African American woman standing at the counter, staring at her phone.

"Sorry?" Ryan asked.

"She said no, like, ten times; and I've only been here for a minute."

"Hey, Kelsey," Shelby greeted.

"Hi, Shelby."

"Bagel, toasted?"

"Yes, please. And Earl Grey."

"To-go?"

"Yes," she said.

"Shelby, what if you could just move this place to another location?"

"Oh, my God!" the girl Ryan now knew as Kelsey said, exasperated. "You do *not* take a hint, do you? Are you like this with women, too?"

"I'm sorry. I'm not talking to you, am I?"

"No, but you're in public and harassing a business owner, and I'm standing here, so I'm just doing my part to get you to back off. Besides, why would Shelby even want to sell this place? It's got the beach location, it's pretty much always busy, and it's a paradise for those of us who want a place to call our own instead of going to Starbucks or some other chain. Most LGBTQ places are disappearing, but this place is still here, and you're trying to turn it into a condo? God, why?"

"Not really any of your business, is it?" Ryan asked.

"It is when part of my livelihood depends on this place. I play here on Saturday nights, and Shelby takes care of the artists that perform here. Plus, like I said, I have a vested interest in keeping this place around when most of the others like it are disappearing," Kelsey said.

"Well, I *am* suggesting she take the money she makes from selling and turn it into another location," Ryan replied, walking over to the table closest to the counter.

"Why would she do that when she's already here?"

"Actually, she's right here." Shelby waved from behind the counter. "And she can hear everything you're saying about her. Ryan, we've been over this. Tell your bosses you tried. I can even call them myself and tell them you've given it a valiant effort. This place is home to me; I don't plan on giving it up anytime soon."

"Fine." Ryan sat down with her coffee cup.

"Here you go," Shelby said to Kelsey and placed the tea on the bar for her. "Bagel will be right out."

"Thanks," Kelsey said.

"You play?" Ryan asked.

"Sorry?"

"You play here?"

"Yeah, I have a regular slot every Saturday, and sometimes, I come in on open mic night to try out new stuff. Why?"

"I've never been here at night before. I guess I'm missing out on the action."

"You're trying to buy a place you've never seen at its busiest?" Kelsey asked, placing her phone in her purse.

"My company is; I'm in commercial real estate."

"So, you're trying to get your commission."

"I'm trying to make a sale. It's my job," Ryan replied.

"Well, leave this place alone. *The Meet Cute Café* is important for the community I *think* you're a part of. Am I right?"

"That's ballsy of you to just assume," Ryan told her.

"I have a good gaydar," Kelsey replied.

"So do I, normally, but you don't seem to be pinging it." Ryan squinted at her.

"Well, I'm bi, so maybe you need to recalibrate."

"I'll get right on that," Ryan said, smirking at her.

"Bagel, toasted, with cream cheese," Chelsea yelled from behind the counter. "Oh, hey."

"Hey. How have you been?" Kelsey asked her.

"Good. You?"

"Pretty good. School's kicking my ass, but I'm heading to campus to get some studying in."

"Taylor's there now," Chelsea said.

"Yeah, she texted me earlier. I'm going to meet her for

lunch."

"I'm working, unfortunately, or I'd join you. Will you be there later?"

"Yeah. Are you stopping by?" Kelsey asked.

"I'm staying over tonight," Chelsea replied.

"I'll get the earplugs out."

"Hey!" Chelsea said, laughing.

"No, it's good. I'm glad you two are happy. I'm so ready to move on from my ex, but I'm not even sure when I'd find the time. I'm glad at least you and Taylor are getting some action."

"Okay. Don't say it like that," Chelsea said, laughing. "I'll see you later."

Ryan watched Kelsey as she left the café without another word in Ryan's direction.

"You know her?" Ryan asked Chelsea, whom she'd met a few times here on her quest to buy the place for her employer.

"She's my girlfriend's roommate. Well, she's *one* of them."

"How old is she?" Ryan asked.

"I don't know that I should answer that," Chelsea told her. "She's a senior in college. How's that?"

"Oh," Ryan said.

Ryan had just turned thirty-two. She should *not* be looking at a twenty-two-year-old woman the way she'd just been looking at Kelsey, but fuck if she wasn't totally turned on right now.

***

Her voice was low and melodic. Ryan didn't know anything about music, but she knew that Kelsey was good. The woman's eyes closed when she got really into the song she was performing. Ryan had entered the café after Kelsey had taken the stage, so she wasn't sure what she'd missed so far. She'd gotten herself a cup of coffee and sat near the back.

The café itself was large, and with the back doors wide open, the patio could be seen, making it appear even larger.

Ryan had initially come into the café years ago as a customer. She'd been a grad student then, going for her MBA with the plan to get her real estate license and own her own company one day. She'd gotten that MBA *and* that license, and now she needed to make contacts and get her name out there while she saved money to start her own small firm.

She hadn't planned on commercial real estate at first, but she liked it enough. The place she worked for now had an entry-level office job opening when she'd graduated, so she'd snatched that and worked her way up to a full-on agent. Now, at thirty-two, she was starting to feel like the commercial grind wasn't her thing.

Still, if she could just get Shelby and Maria to sell this place, her commission would be massive. She'd begged her boss to let her work this account, and he was about to give up on Ryan's ability to close. That meant she'd either have to share her commission or give the account to someone else entirely. She had tried every angle she could think of with the co-owners, but she also knew her own heart just wasn't in it. Kelsey had been right: this place was sacred ground to the community. And Ryan might just go straight to lesbian hell if she actually got them to sell to the developer who wanted to turn this whole beach strip into condos.

"Thank you," Kelsey said in a deeper voice than Ryan remembered her having the other day.

It must be the voice the woman used when she performed. Ryan watched as she moved off of the small stage that had been placed there for these nighttime events. Kelsey was hugged by a few women and had others give her smiles, handshakes, and small talk.

Ryan finished her coffee and thought about leaving. She hadn't been certain she was going to come tonight until right before she left her apartment. She'd been in meetings all day on Friday and had to spend much of her Saturday doing her actual work, making calls to clients and potential clients, so she'd been wiped by six and ready to order dinner in and binge-watch something on Netflix.

There had just been something in the back of her mind that kept pulling her toward *The Meet Cute*, though. She'd dressed in her suede jacket, matching boots, and nicest pair of jeans. Under her jacket, she'd worn her old rock-'n'-roll T-shirt that had gotten her compliments from many ladies in the past. She wasn't even sure why she cared. She wasn't going to the café to pick someone up tonight. Though, if the opportunity arose, she likely wouldn't turn a woman down.

"Ryan, hey," Chelsea greeted. "I don't think I've ever seen you at one of these events before."

"First time," Ryan replied.

"So, you're a virgin, then?"

Ryan turned to see Kelsey standing next to her, giving her a smirk and a lifted eyebrow.

"I assure you, I'm no virgin," Ryan said.

"Hey," someone else said, walking up to Chelsea and kissing her on the cheek.

This must be Chelsea's girlfriend, who also happened to be roommates with Kelsey. God, this was all confusing and yet, all so very lesbian. Their names even rhymed. How did the roommate handle that?

"Hey," Chelsea said, smiling. "Oh, Ryan, this is Taylor. Taylor is my girlfriend."

"Nice to meet you," Taylor said, offering her free hand since the other was wrapped protectively around Chelsea's waist.

"You too."

"Ryan is here to try to steal the café from Shelby," Kelsey said.

"I am not." Ryan turned to her and laughed a little. "I'm actually just here to enjoy my night."

"Aunt Shelby won't sell this place," Chelsea stated. "And you won't convince her to move it, either. *I'm* trying to convince her to open another location, but she won't leave this one behind. It was her and Aunt Maria's dream to open it here."

"I know." Ryan held up a hand, palm facing forward. "I'm off-duty, I promise. I just came here for the coffee and the entertainment. Trust me, I've been working all day; I don't plan to work all night."

"Well, we're heading out now that Kelsey's set is over, so I guess we'll see you around." Taylor looked from Ryan to Kelsey. "Are you sticking around or coming with us?"

"I think I'll give you two a head start," Kelsey said with a laugh. "We share a wall."

Chelsea looked down at her shoes, and Ryan laughed.

"Thank you," Taylor replied.

"I can't wait until you get your own place," Chelsea said. "Or, for me to get out of my parents' house."

As they walked away, Ryan realized just how young these women were. Chelsea looked younger than her girlfriend, but Ryan didn't know her age. If Taylor was a senior, Chelsea was probably a freshman or sophomore, especially if she was still living at home. And if Kelsey was Taylor's age, that meant she was only twenty-one or twenty-two. So, she was at least ten years younger than Ryan and not at all someone Ryan should be staring at right now.

"I like your look," Kelsey said.

"Yeah, I like yours, too," Ryan replied, looking at Kelsey's tight jeans and bright-blue shirt.

"Did you dress up special for tonight, or is that your go-out and pick-up women look?"

"You *sure* do have an oddly specific opinion of me, don't you?" Ryan asked, laughing.

"Is it wrong?" Kelsey asked.

"I didn't come here to pick anyone up." Ryan rubbed the back of her neck. "I came to watch *you* perform."

"Oh, yeah?"

"Yeah, you're really good."

"Thanks," Kelsey replied. "But I'm not sleeping with

you tonight."

Ryan laughed harder just as the next performer took the stage.

"I'm not trying to get you to sleep with me," she said, shaking her head back and forth.

"Good," Kelsey stated.

"Good," Ryan echoed. "Glad we got that settled," she added sarcastically.

"I've got some work to do, so I guess I'll see you around, assuming you don't try to tear this place down and turn it—"

"Okay. I get it; I'm the worst person in the world for trying to do my job," Ryan said softly as the performer began to sing. "I told you, I'm not here to work tonight. I've left Shelby alone for days. My company wants this place, so even if I don't get the sale, they will just keep sending people until *they* do. I came here to watch you perform because I got curious. I wasn't trying to pick you or anyone else up. I'm not expecting you to sleep with me tonight. I'm just a boring, old lesbian, enjoying coffee at her favorite café, okay?" Ryan let out a deep sigh. "I'm just going to go home. This was a mistake."

"Wait." Kelsey placed a hand on Ryan's forearm. "I'm sorry. I just…" She looked around. "Can we go out there?" She nodded toward the front door. "I don't want to talk while someone else is performing."

"We're talking now?" Ryan asked.

"I come on a little strong at first. I'm sorry," Kelsey replied.

The performer grew louder. Ryan nodded toward the door, and they walked outside, stopping after a few steps to the right of the café entrance.

"I'm sorry," Kelsey said.

"It's cool. I like assertive just fine, but I think you have this impression of me that may or may not be accurate, and for whatever reason, it bugs me that you do."

Kelsey smiled and said, "My friend is watching my guitar for me right now. Let me grab it, and, I don't know, you can come with me down the street."

"With you where, exactly?"

"The bookstore down the street," Kelsey replied. "It's one of my favorite places to work."

"Work on what?"

"School. I go there to study sometimes."

"College, right?"

Kelsey laughed and said, "Yes. You're not hanging out with some sixteen-year-old kid, Ryan."

"So, we're hanging out now?

"Are you too cool to hang out? Does that change when you hit thirty? You don't hang out anymore? You just give up on new friends?"

"How do *you* know I'm over thirty? Should I take offense to that?"

"You don't look a day over twenty-eight. Better?" she asked. "I'll be right back. I hope you're still here. If not, though – no worries. I still have studying to do."

Ryan watched as Kelsey went back inside the café. What was Ryan still doing here? Was she just going to watch Kelsey study at some bookstore? That seemed creepy. On top of it, Kelsey was in college. Ryan had left undergrad behind ten years ago. In fact, she'd gotten an invitation to her ten-year sorority class reunion just a few weeks ago. God, she had really enjoyed sorority life. She'd known she was gay but hadn't been out at first. She'd had a lot of fun during those years and even more fun during their five-year reunion when the sorority social chair had asked Ryan to go outside with her. Ryan still had nights where she got herself off, remembering the hot sex they'd had in her car and then again later, at the hotel.

"Ready?" Kelsey asked.

"Oh, yeah. I guess."

"Have you ever been?"

"Where?"

"The bookstore."

"Well, I've been to several bookstores, but I'm not sure I've been to the one you're referring to."

"Lesbian-owned and operated. It has a great section for queer history, romance, and a bunch of other stuff."

"So, you go there because of that?"

"I went there at first because of that, but I keep going because I want to support their business. I buy something every time I'm there, and I'm there at least once a week. Sometimes, it's just a bookmark – I *am* a starving college student with three roommates. Other times, I pick up a book."

"It's cool that you support the community," Ryan said as they walked.

"I'm right here." Kelsey pointed to a car. "Just let me put this in the trunk and get my bag."

"Sure."

Ryan waited, but she wasn't certain what she was waiting for, exactly. Kelsey put her guitar in the trunk and pulled out a backpack.

"Can I ask you something?"

"Yeah," Kelsey replied.

"If you're planning on studying, why exactly am I going with you? I'm not sure you need a study buddy, and I've been out of school for a while, so I doubt I'd even be a good one."

"I get that you're just doing your job, but I thought it might be good for you to check out the other lesbian-owned business just down the street. There used to be a bar there." Kelsey pointed as they started walking again. "It went out of business about three years ago. I was too young to get in back then, but I had a fake ID and went a couple of times. It was owned by a bisexual, Black woman, like me. She had to sell it to that pet store when she couldn't make rent. Then, there was a trans-owned hair and nail salon over there. It went out of business last year. I have a friend who was a senior when I was a freshman. They wanted to start their own art gallery and even rented the building just over there to do it." Kelsey pointed again. "They had two shows and sold a few things, but not enough to make the rent on the lease, and someone else came in and swooped the place out from under them. This whole street – three blocks that way and four back where we came from – used to be predominantly LGBTQ businesses with some banks and grocery stores sprinkled in. Now, there's just the bookstore and the café."

"I didn't know that," Ryan replied.

"You didn't grow up here, did you?" Kelsey asked.

"No, I grew up a few hours from here."

"*I* grew up here," Kelsey told her. "I was thirteen when I first figured out that I liked girls in the same way I liked guys. At fifteen, I came out to my parents as bisexual. They tolerated it, but they still think that since it's possible I'll end up with a guy one day, they're just going to wait it out."

"Wait it out?" Ryan asked.

"Yeah, most of the rest of my family doesn't know. We're not super close, so I don't really care or need them to know about my life. If I end up with a guy, my parents think there's no point in telling people that I could have ended up with a woman, you know?"

"Yeah, I guess. I'm gay, so it doesn't work that way for me."

"Do you have problems with bisexuality?"

"What? No." Ryan laughed. "I don't care who people are attracted to, who they sleep with, or who they fall in love with. I just know that I like women."

"How did your family deal with it?"

"Well, I'm full-blooded Italian and not just Italian. My grandparents came over forty years ago, so my mom was born just outside of Rome. My dad's Italian, too, but his family's been here for a while. I grew up going to Mass every Sunday and confession every Wednesday, so I kept the whole gay thing to myself until I was in college. They're still processing; let's just put it that way."

"So, that olive skin of yours isn't just a tan?"

"No." Ryan laughed.

They arrived at the bookstore, and Ryan pulled the door open for Kelsey, who nodded, smiled, and then walked in before her.

"Kels!"

"Hey, Marianne. How are things?"

"Things are good. Slow, but it's late."

"This is my friend, Ryan. She's here to buy that whole romance series that just came out this week."

"The box set?" Marianne asked, looking at Ryan.

Ryan looked at Kelsey and said, "Yeah, I'm a big romance reader."

She wasn't.

"You're in luck, then. I have the whole eight book set in the back."

"Eight books?" Ryan whispered to Kelsey.

"It's a beloved series," Kelsey replied, obviously teasing her.

Marianne appeared behind the register with the book set in hand. She rang it up, and Ryan saw the total on the register – it was over a hundred dollars.

"You know what? Can you throw in a couple of bookmarks, too?" she said.

Kelsey laughed and said, "I'm going to set up shop in the back. Is that okay?"

"Of course," Marianne replied.

"Well, I have to study, so I'll see you around, Ryan."

"Maybe not. I have eight new books to read."

Kelsey laughed some more.

***

"Ryan, right?"

"Oh, hey," she said to Taylor, who stood next to Ryan's table.

"Kelsey said she got you to buy a whole bunch of books the other day," Taylor replied, laughing.

"That she did. Interested in romance by chance? I'll give them to you."

"Not a big romance fan?" Taylor asked.

"Not in books, at least."

"Well, I don't need any more books to read. I've got enough reading to do, being pre-law, but I do like a good romance book. I wouldn't have always said that about myself, but…" She turned to look at Chelsea, who was placing a scone on a plate at the coffee bar. "Then, I met her. That's my cinnamon scone, so I should go grab it."

"Sure," Ryan said, smiling.

She watched as Chelsea came around the counter and pulled Taylor into a hug, smiling the whole time. Ryan had had a lot of sex in her life, but she hadn't yet had a lasting relationship that made her hug a woman like that while beaming like they hung the moon just for her. Of course, Taylor and Chelsea were young; it was probably first love more than anything. And Ryan was too jaded to believe that would ever be for her.

"Well, long time no see."

Ryan looked up from her laptop again to see Kelsey standing there in front of her.

"Hey," Ryan said.

"How goes the reading of the great lesbian romance novel?" Kelsey asked.

"I haven't started," Ryan said.

Kelsey sat down across from her and asked, "Not interested in romance?"

"Not really, no."

"Of the book variety, or the real thing kind?"

"Haven't had much of the real thing, so I don't know about that, and I've never really cared much for the romance genre. I'm a classics fan."

"Like Austen or something?"

"Yes, I like Jane Austen."

"Then, you *are* a romance fan," Kelsey replied.

"I'm a fan of sassy women, I think." Ryan laughed.

"It's a workday. What are you doing here? I had hoped I'd gotten through to you the other night about not stealing away our businesses."

"I'm just here for the coffee and to work between my meetings, which are nearby. I don't even know if Shelby's here today, okay?" Ryan closed her laptop. "Can I ask you something? Why do you care so much?"

"Because we should be growing our businesses, not watching them disappear. That bookstore used to be two floors. They had to rent it out as an apartment because they needed the extra cash."

"Yeah, but bookstores, owned by lesbians or not, are failing in general. People buy e-books and read them on their phones and iPads. They don't all rush to pick up the newest hardback book at the store anymore."

"But the bookstore is just an example. Think of the gay bar I told you about. Lesbian bars are very specifically disappearing all over the country in a time when people are more out and proud than ever. I mean, I came out at fifteen because thousands, millions of people before me made that possible – made it so I could even understand what I was feeling; made it so I could express it and be myself. Those people are the people who own these businesses, and for whatever reason, those businesses are dying. I hate that. It seems it's already hard enough for people to support Black-owned businesses. I try to do my part there, too, but I want to have bars I can go to where I feel like I can be my true self. And I'd want my future kids to have the same thing regardless of who they love. I want bookstores that sell books *I* can relate to, that my friends can relate to." Kelsey nodded toward Taylor and Chelsea, who were still talking. "If they go away – yes, we can still buy books online, and we can still go to other bars, but our visibility diminishes, and the people who own these businesses had dreams just like Shelby and Maria did when they bought this place. I want them to be able to have those dreams because I want my own."

Ryan swallowed as she listened to Kelsey speak so eloquently about a topic she hadn't given much thought to.

"What *are* those dreams?"

"I have a few, actually," Kelsey said.

"Like?"

"Well, I want a record deal, with a Black-owned label, preferably. I'd like to go to graduate school and then maybe get my Ph. D in sociology. Those two things aren't mutually exclusive. I can record an album by day and go to school at night."

"Is sociology your major?"

"Yeah," Kelsey said. "What was yours?"

"In college? I was a marketing major in undergrad, but I got my MBA after that."

"And what is *your* dream, Ryan?"

"To own my own real estate company one day."

Kelsey nodded and said, "Which is why you really want this commission? Seed money?"

"Something like that. I wasn't planning on commercial real estate. I was thinking about residential, and I didn't want to be an agent forever. Eventually, I want to be a CEO of a nationwide real estate company, with thousands of agents doing the work I'm doing now."

"That's a big dream."

"So is getting a record deal *and* a Ph. D."

"Yeah, but you're all old. *I* still have time." Kelsey winked.

Ryan laughed and replied, "Hey, we're only ten years apart."

"Only, huh?"

Ryan realized what she'd said then. Before, she'd been thinking about how far apart they were in age. Now, she was trying to tell Kelsey how close they were instead.

"We're going home. Chels is off shift."

"Okay. Coming," Kelsey said to Taylor. "She drove."

"Ah," Ryan said.

Kelsey stood and added, "We're going to watch a

movie and order pizza. Want to join us?"

"I still have some work to do."

"Well, I'm sure they'll have sex for at least an hour before we even order dinner, so you have time to finish up here," Kelsey replied. "Come on. Hang out with us. We can buy beer ourselves, so you don't have to worry that I'm only inviting you because we need you to bring the booze."

Ryan laughed and joked, "Well, I'm so old that I can't even have more than one drink before I just pass out asleep."

"You'd be safe on the couch," Kelsey chuckled in response. "It doesn't fold out, but if you move the lumps around just right, you can get a decent night's sleep."

***

"So, Ryan, any advice for two seniors who are about to graduate?" Taylor asked.

"Not really, no," Ryan replied.

"Tay is going to law school," Chelsea said, sitting down next to Taylor on the sofa and offering Taylor a plate with two slices of pizza on it.

"Yeah, congrats," Ryan said.

"Thanks," Taylor replied. "We were thinking of an action movie tonight. Is that okay with you?"

"Sure. I'm not picky," Ryan said, sitting on the love seat that was perpendicular to the sofa.

"Good to know," Kelsey added, sitting down next to her and handing Ryan a beer. "It's light beer. Can you handle it?"

Ryan just rolled her eyes at her. She looked around the apartment, which was actually a townhome with two floors. There were four roommates in total. Taylor and Kelsey were friends outside of just being roommates. The other two just lived here, and on the lower floor. Kelsey and Taylor were on the top floor where the living room, kitchen, and one of the bathrooms were located. The space was large, and it reminded Ryan of her own apartment when she'd been in college. She'd moved out of the sorority house her senior year, wanting her own space. Ryan's apartment had been a lot smaller, and she'd only had *one* roommate, but there was just something about college apartments. As different as they could all be, they all had a similar vibe to them. There were the futons, the hand-me-down furniture from parents, the empty beer bottles in the trash, oftentimes, and the vague smell of cigarette or marijuana smoke, which wasn't the case in this particular apartment, thankfully. It was something Ryan had left behind ten years ago, and she'd been glad to be rid of it all then.

"Are you okay?"

"Huh?"

"You just seem a little lost," Kelsey said.

"Oh, I'm fine."

"This is weird for you, isn't it?" she asked, turning toward Ryan.

"A little, yeah."

"You can go if you want; you don't have to stay. I get that this isn't really your thing."

"It's a movie and pizza. Plus, there's beer."

"Cheap beer," Kelsey replied. "I'm sure *you* can afford the good stuff."

"I'm not usually much of a beer drinker."

"Wine?"

"If I drink, it's usually Grey Goose."

"The hard stuff." Kelsey nodded. "No wonder you can only handle one drink."

"Well, I *do* usually make it a double," Ryan teased.

"If you two are going to talk, can you do it in Kelsey's room?" Taylor said. "We're trying to watch the movie."

"Watch it in your room," Kelsey told her.

"The TV is out here," Taylor argued.

"You have a laptop," Kelsey replied.

"Babe, it's fine. We could snuggle up in bed and watch it," Chelsea said, moving into Taylor's side and wrapping an arm around her stomach.

"Maybe I should just go," Ryan said. "You guys had a whole thing worked out, and I'm crashing."

"We can just go to my room," Kelsey suggested. "If you want."

Ryan wasn't sure *what* she wanted.

"Here." She handed Kelsey her untouched beer. "Thank you for having me. I should go."

"Ryan, I didn't mean–" Taylor began. "I was just giving Kelsey a hard time."

"No, it's fine. I have work to do at home, anyway."

"I thought you finished before you came over here," Kelsey said.

Ryan stood and said, "There's always more to do. I'll see you around?"

"Yeah, okay." Kelsey stood up and followed Ryan to the staircase that led down to the door. "Hey, when?"

"When, what?" Ryan asked when she got to the bottom of it.

"When will you see me?"

"Oh, I don't know."

"Café? Tomorrow?" Kelsey asked.

"I have to work."

"Okay. Saturday night? I'll be performing."

Ryan nodded and said, "Yeah, maybe."

***

Ryan hadn't gone to *The Meet Cute* on Saturday night. She'd thought about it a lot but decided it was probably a bad idea. Kelsey was nice. She was beautiful, intelligent, and passionate. Ryan loved all of those things, but Kelsey was also a senior in college. She was just at a different point in her life than Ryan. And while they hadn't really said anything about romantic intentions toward one another, the look on Kelsey's face the night Ryan had basically run out of her apartment had been, in Ryan's opinion, disappointment.

Ryan had been disappointed, too. She hardly knew this woman, but what she did know intrigued her. She wanted to spend more time with Kelsey, but she also had an idea that if she *did* spend that time together, they wouldn't be doing so as just friends for very long, and Ryan wasn't sure that was what she wanted.

***

"I'm here to tell you that I've been taken off the account," Ryan said to Shelby two weeks after the movie and dinner disaster.

"Oh?"

"And to tell you that they're going to send someone else to talk to you, and it won't be coming from me. I told them you wouldn't sell. I told them your reasons. They just believe you're holding out for more money, no matter what I say."

"Well, thanks for trying anyway, but they're about to be disappointed. Can I get you something on the house?"

"Really? I've been trying to buy your beloved café, and you're offering me a coffee for free?"

"You're doing your job, and you've never been rude or unreasonable. Besides, you've become quite the regular customer lately. I like to reward my regulars."

"I'm okay. I really did just come by to tell you. Now, I need to get home and make a few more calls before I can finally end my work week."

"So, you *do* remember where this place is?"

Ryan turned to see Kelsey standing there with her guitar case.

"I thought you played on Saturdays."

"And on open mic nights sometimes, remember?"

Ryan nodded. She'd actually forgotten about that.

"So, I was right to think you've been avoiding me?" Kelsey asked.

"How about that free coffee now?" Shelby offered.

"I was just on my way out. Thank you, though," she said to Shelby. "It's good to see you, Kelsey."

Ryan turned to head out the back door toward the patio and then the parking lot. She hadn't heard footsteps, but then Kelsey was walking next to her without her guitar.

"You're freaking out because I'm twenty-two, aren't you?"

"What?"

"Ryan, I'm not an idiot. We've hung out a few times. We've flirted."

"We *have*?"

Kelsey pulled back on Ryan's arm gently to get her to stop walking.

"Come on," Kelsey said. "I'm being serious here. Tell me I'm crazy. There's something here."

"The first time we met, you practically ran me through the Spanish Inquisition. You then gave me a lesson in business the second time, while you also made me buy over a hundred dollars worth of books I won't read, and told me we *weren't* going to sleep together. Now, you're telling me *that* was flirting?"

"I said I wouldn't be sleeping with you *that night*," Kelsey corrected. "I thought you were flirting back. Was I wrong?"

"No, you weren't. But I also flirt a bunch. You pegged me as a woman who picks up women a lot, and I do. I have in the past, at least, so you were right about that."

"So, you flirted with me?"

"Yes."

"But you don't want to sleep with me?" Kelsey checked.

"Oh, I'd *love* to sleep with you. You're sexy as hell, especially when you're up on stage. I've had many thoughts about sleeping with you since we met, but…"

"But? You're too… sophisticated for me?"

Ryan laughed and said, "Is *sophisticated* your new way of saying the word *old*?"

"It doesn't bother me," Kelsey replied.

"My age?"

Kelsey shrugged and said, "Yes. Mine bothers you, though, doesn't it?"

"It's not the age; it's the phase."

"I know you're not actually saying I'm in a phase."

"What? No," Ryan replied. "I meant a *life* phase. You're in that end-of-college phase, where you're planning your next move, and I did all that once. I'm just in a different phase."

"Aren't you literally planning your next move with your career right now?"

"Not the same thing, really."

"It is, though. Look, I'm not going to try to convince you to go out with me. I don't convince people to date me. They either want to, or they don't. But, Ryan, I like you." She shrugged adorably. "I like sassy women, too; and you're obviously one. You seem nice and smart, and I know you're funny. I don't know much else about you yet, but I'd like to. You and I might be of different ages – I'm applying to grad school while I work on my music, and you're trying to figure out how to do a job you clearly don't like as much as you used to and move on to owning your own business – and they're not the same things, that's true, but we're both in transitional phases of our lives right now."

"So, we've gone from flirting to talking about sleeping together to dating?" Ryan said, smiling at her.

"Flirting usually leads to one or the other; sometimes, both. Right?"

Ryan laughed and said, "I guess so."

"Do you like me? And I don't mean 'do you want to sleep with me.' I'm asking if you like me."

"Yes," Ryan replied.

"Then, stay for open mic night. We can just hang out after I perform, get to know each other a little more, and see what happens."

Ryan stared out at the parking lot and her car. She

could just climb in and go home, pretend like she hadn't run into a beautiful woman who wanted to get to know her better, and then never come back to the café. She could also go back inside and listen to Kelsey's songs while she pictured what could be between them.

***

"I'm the President of the LGBTQ+ group at the university right now, and I was the VP last year. I joined as a freshman and never looked back."

"I wasn't a joiner in school," Ryan replied.

"You don't say," Kelsey said sarcastically as she ate a French fry from the basket they were sharing.

"Hey," Ryan said.

"You don't seem like much of a joiner."

"I guess I went to school to go to school. I mean, I was in a sorority, but that was about it."

"*You* were in a sorority? You?"

"Yes." Ryan laughed and took a fry for herself. "Is that really that hard to believe?"

"Yes," Kelsey said, laughing, too. "Were you out with them?"

"Not initially, but later, yeah."

"How many did you hook up with?"

"Why do you assume I hooked up with any?"

"Just a guess."

"Are we including after I graduated or just while I was in school?"

"After? You hooked up with someone after?"

"Freshman year, I was a pledge, and I hooked up with another pledge. That was it. Sophomore and junior year, I lived in the house and hooked up with four. One of them wasn't just a hookup, but she wasn't out as anything other than straight, and as far as I know, is married to a man now. Senior year, I moved out of the house; I wanted a change." Ryan shrugged. "But I was still a member of the sorority."

"And?" Kelsey asked.

"And there was one more. Another later, at the five-year reunion."

"So, seven? You hooked up with seven?"

"I was young, and I'd just discovered sex with girls. I really liked it, and they seemed pretty happy about it, too."

"If you do say so yourself."

"Well, they said so, too," Ryan replied, taking a drink of her water.

"I bet they did," Kelsey said, laughing.

"What about you?"

"What *about* me?" Kelsey asked.

"I'm not asking for your number or anything…"

"Good. You haven't really even told me yours. You've only told me about the sorority girls."

"Technically, I only told you about the girls in *my* sorority."

Kelsey laughed and sat back in her chair.

"Oh, my God. Really? Where are these girls? Why won't they sleep with *me*?"

"No idea," Ryan said, meaning it.

Kelsey stopped laughing and said, "This isn't a date."

"I know."

"I don't even sleep with women on first dates," Kelsey added.

"Okay."

"This is a hangout to see if we want to have a first date."

"I get it," Ryan said.

"So, if you want a first date, you'd still have to wait for that if–"

"Kels?"

"Yeah?"

"I like spending time with you. I'm *definitely* attracted to you. I still don't know if it's a good idea for us to date, though."

"I see," Kelsey said. "I told you, I'm not going to try

to convince someone to go out with me."

"I know."

Kelsey nodded.

"Kelsey?"

"Hey, Troy," Kelsey said to a woman with short blonde hair who approached their outdoor table at the diner.

"How have you been?"

"Good. You?" Kelsey asked.

"Good. Hi," the woman said, looking at Ryan.

"Oh, hi," Ryan replied. "Ryan. Nice to meet you." She held out her hand for the woman named Troy to shake.

"Troy. You too." She shook it and turned to Kelsey. "I was just heading home, and I saw you. Thought I'd say hi, but I'll leave you two to your dinner."

"Oh, it's not dinner. It's French fries, and we're wrapping up. I think I'm going to go get some studying in at the store, actually."

Was this Troy an ex-girlfriend of Kelsey's? If so, they sounded like they'd been able to remain friends, which was not something Ryan had ever been able to do with her exes.

"Cool. I won't see you there. Anna is parking the car; we're going upstairs to watch a movie."

"Tell her I said hi," Kelsey replied.

"Tell her yourself. She's here." Troy smiled. "Hey, babe. I ran into Kelsey here."

A woman walked up and instantly pressed herself to Troy's side. Troy kissed her on the temple and wrapped an arm around her waist.

"Hi, Kels," Anna said.

"And this is her friend, Ryan. I've seen you around, I think. *The Meet Cute*?"

"Yeah, I go there sometimes," Ryan said.

"Well, I'll see you there, then. We've got food being delivered to the apartment in a few minutes, so we should get going." Troy looked down at the bag Anna was holding and added, "You know, if you just moved in with me, you wouldn't have to pack a bag every time you stayed over." She took the bag from Anna.

"Yeah, yeah," Anna said, leaning in and giving Troy a quick kiss. "It was nice to meet you, Ryan."

Ryan nodded. Then, she watched the two women turn and head down the sidewalk. They held hands, and Troy hefted Anna's bag over her shoulder. Anna rested her head on Troy's other one, and Ryan recalled Taylor and Chelsea's public display in the café. Her first thought would normally be that it was all temporary bullshit, but tonight, her mind took her elsewhere instead.

"How do you know them?" Ryan asked.

"Café, mainly, but I've also run into Troy at the bookstore. She lives in the studio above it. Anna is her girl-friend."

"So, you and Troy never…"

"No." Kelsey laughed. "Why? You don't want me, but you don't like the idea that someone else might?"

"I never said I–" Ryan paused and pushed the half-eaten fries away, leaning over the table. "It's not all about the age difference thing. I've never been a big believer in love, Kels. And I don't date a lot because when I've tried it in the past, it's always blown up in my face. I don't have some grand plan to never fall in love or anything; I just don't often pursue it."

Kelsey leaned over the table and said, "Instead of pushing me away because of all of that, you could try talking to me about it."

"What would that look like? A first date where I tell you my sob story?"

"Maybe not the whole thing on the first date," Kelsey replied. "We could work up to the *whole* story."

"One date," Ryan said. "And when I inevitably say or do something to ruin it, we can still try to be friends. Is that possible?"

"I don't know," Kelsey replied with a shrug. "You're one-hundred-percent my type." She smiled. "I've been attracted to you since I saw you that first time in the café. Then, you spoke, and I was like, 'Damn, I like this woman. Who the hell is she?'"

"Really? You *argued* with me." Ryan laughed.

"I know. It was hot."

"It was," Ryan said and stopped laughing.

"I can't guarantee I can just be your friend, Ryan. I'm not, like, madly in love with you or anything, so don't get a big head, but I don't know that I really want to be a friend you talk to about your future hookups, either."

Ryan nodded and replied, "I get it."

"But I can try," Kelsey told her. "Can we go on a real date and just see?"

Ryan smiled and said, "I can pick you up. I already know where you live."

***

"And they went for the full annulment."

"Not just a divorce?" Kelsey asked.

"They're very Catholic, remember?" Ryan said. "My parents were married for three good years. After that, things got bad. My dad moved out for a year or so but moved back in when he got pressure from my grandparents to make things work. They tried separate bedrooms in the house for a while. Then, he met someone and had an affair. My mom did the same later."

"So, they'll have affairs, but won't get divorced?"

"Have you ever noticed how some very religious people are selectively religious?" Ryan asked rhetorically. "That would be my parents in a nutshell. They could justify the affairs because they both knew about them and they weren't having sex with each other. It wasn't exactly an easy house to grow up in. Then, I came out, and that just made things worse. I think me being gay was the thing that finally pushed them toward an annulment. The interesting thing about an annulment is that it means the marriage itself never happened, so in the eyes of the Catholic church, I'm a child out of wedlock, which is also not really allowed."

"So, you've got that parental damage to work through?" Kelsey said.

"I've chosen to just push it aside. It works for me."

"Does it?" Kelsey asked as they arrived at her front door. "I mean, from what you've told me, you're not all that happy in your career, and you avoid relationships because your parents had a messed up one. I'm sure having casual sex is fun and all, but is that all you really want out of your life?"

"You're sure casual sex is fun? You've never had it."

"I've had sex after dates and relationship sex. I don't do one-night stands."

Ryan nodded.

"And nice attempt at a deflection, by the way," Kelsey added. Then, she pulled out her keys. "I had fun tonight."

"Me too," Ryan said.

"So, this was the one date," Kelsey replied.

"It was, yeah."

"Do you want another?"

Ryan had had a great time. They'd gone to a nice dinner and walked along the beach after just talking and getting to know one another some more. Kelsey had this confident way about her that Ryan was drawn to, and despite every part of her brain telling her that this wouldn't work and that she'd end up hurting Kelsey how her parents had hurt each other, she still nodded. She wanted to give this a try.

"I don't know if–"

"You nodded. That's a yes. You can't take it back now," Kelsey interjected with a smile. "I get that your parents kind of screwed up your view of relationships, Ryan. And I'm not saying I'm the one for you or anything, but I really, really had a good time tonight. I do every time we hang out. I know you think I'm young, and I might be, but I've tried dating women my own age, and it never works out. Maybe it's at least in part because I want to be with someone older, in a different transitional phase of their life than graduating." She took a step toward Ryan and placed a soft hand on her neck. "Do you want to come up? We can keep talking."

"What about your roommates?"

"We can go to my room," Kelsey offered. "If any of them are home, they'll leave us alone."

Ryan nodded again, and they made their way up the stairs until they were on the top floor. No one was in the living room, so Ryan stood in the kitchen as Kelsey grabbed them both a bottle of water, and then she followed Kelsey into her bedroom, which was much nicer than the rest of the apartment.

"I got the master," she said. "Bathroom is through there. I pay a little more in rent than the rest of them, but it's worth it: I have my own bathroom and a small balcony. Plus, the bedroom itself is bigger. I have a desk for school stuff, and room for my guitar set up. Closet is smaller than I'd like, but it works for me."

"It's nice," Ryan commented. "Nicer than my room. You have an actual bed set with sheets, pillowcases, and a comforter that all matches; I have a blanket."

"What?" Kelsey laughed.

"I have sheets, too. I mean, I have pillowcases and stuff, but they don't all match. I mostly just buy something when something else tears or there's a stain."

Kelsey shook her head and said, "Want to sit?"

"Sure," Ryan said, sitting awkwardly on the edge of the bed.

Kelsey pulled her desk chair around and sat down. Sounds from the living room started up, but Ryan wasn't sure what they were.

"Video games; they play all the time," Kelsey explained. "It's one of the reasons I go to the café or the bookstore to study whenever I'm not on campus."

"I never got into video games," Ryan replied, placing the bottle of water on the floor next to her foot.

"Neither did I," Kelsey said. "One day, I will have a place of my own where no one is yelling into a headset about killing a Nazi or a zombie."

Ryan laughed and said, "A girl can dream."

***

Ryan had met Kelsey at the café for their second date. Kelsey had been performing that night, and they'd gone out after. They'd held hands this time as they'd walked along the beach and then sat down on the sand to look out at the water under a full moon. Kelsey's head had ended up on Ryan's shoulder, and Ryan had liked that. Then, they'd climbed into her car and gone to an ice cream shop. Kelsey had insisted on buying, and they'd sat there talking for over an hour, long after the ice cream had melted. Ryan had driven Kelsey home, and now they sat in her car laughing about how Ryan had gotten caught going down on a woman in the campus library when she'd been in school.

"We were in a study room I'd reserved. No one should have gone in," Ryan defended.

"There aren't locks on those doors, Ryan," Kelsey replied.

"It was still *my* room."

"Did you get kicked out?"

"Obviously," Ryan replied, laughing still. "It wasn't something I'd planned. We went there to study, but she'd been giving me the look that told me she was interested. Then, we were making out, and things happened."

"Do you want to come up?" Kelsey asked when she finally stopped laughing.

"To listen to boys kill zombies?" Ryan asked.

"We can turn up the music," Kelsey said.

Ryan smiled and replied, "I have to get up early tomorrow. I should go."

"Tomorrow is Sunday."

"I know. I have a new possible listing I need to check

out, and before you say anything, it's not a LGBT business. The owner reached out to me; I'm not trying to convince them to sell."

"Come up, Ryan," Kelsey said seriously. "You don't have to stay long. We've had fun tonight. I just…" She took Ryan's hand over the center console. "I don't know that I want it to end yet."

They walked up the stairs again, past the roommates playing video games, and then into Kelsey's room. The last time Ryan had been here, she'd kissed Kelsey on the cheek when she'd left after about another hour or so of talking. Kelsey had remained in her desk chair then, and Ryan had sat on the edge of the bed. Tonight, though, Kelsey kicked off her shoes and lay down on her bed. Ryan stood there, not knowing what to do. This thing between them was still so fragile, so new. She knew she liked it. She knew she was scared. She knew she didn't want to ruin it.

"Ryan, lie down with me," Kelsey said softly.

"I can just sit," Ryan replied, motioning to the desk chair.

"What are you so worried about?"

"I'm not worried about anything," she said, sitting in the chair.

"*I* invited you up, Ryan. I asked you to lie down with me."

"I like this," Ryan stated. "I don't want you to think that I want something and *only* that something."

"If you only wanted sex, you wouldn't be here right now," Kelsey replied. "I've seen the women staring at you at the café and other places we've been. Obviously, if you wanted just sex, you would've gone home with one of them, not me."

"I don't go on a lot of second or third dates," Ryan admitted.

"I know," Kelsey replied softly. "You're probably LezConnect's primary audience, aren't you?" she laughed.

Ryan laughed and said, "I've made a few *connections*

on there, yes. I'm always upfront about what I want, though."

"Be upfront with me, then. What do you want right now?" Kelsey asked.

"Sex." Ryan laughed and leaned back in the chair. "You're lying there, wearing that cute dress with your ankles crossed, and I just want to slowly pull them apart and climb up your body."

She watched as Kelsey swallowed.

"You asked," Ryan noted.

"I did." Kelsey nodded. "What do you want after the sex, though?"

"After?"

"You climb up my body, we do all kinds of exciting things to each other, and then what? Do you leave, or do you stay?"

"Stay," Ryan replied.

"The whole night? Even though you have to get up early tomorrow?"

Ryan nodded.

"And then? Do you kiss me goodbye in the morning?"

She nodded again.

"Do you call me later?"

A third nod.

"Three days from now because that's what the cool kids do, or tomorrow when you get done with work so that we can arrange a third date?"

Ryan gave her a soft smile and said, "We can just arrange it now, but I'll call you tomorrow, too."

"Your place? Tomorrow night?" Kelsey asked.

"I can cook for you," Ryan replied, standing up. "I have a baked ziti recipe from my grandma that's amazing."

"And you have wine?"

Ryan nodded, bit her lip, and knelt down in front of the bed. When Kelsey didn't move or ask what she was doing, she placed her hands on Kelsey's ankles and slowly parted them.

"I do," she said. "Red *and* white."

"And will you freak out if you stay here tonight and I stay at your place tomorrow night?"

"Two nights in a row, huh?" Ryan asked, running her hands up and down the inside of Kelsey's legs slowly, taking in her soft, warm skin. "You like me a little bit."

"I like you a lot," Kelsey said, inhaling deeply. "That's good."

"Yeah?" Ryan asked, moving her hands a little higher until she was under the hem of Kelsey's dress.

"Yes," Kelsey said.

"Are you sure?" Ryan asked, watching Kelsey's face for any sign that she should stop.

Kelsey nodded and closed her eyes. Then, her legs spread farther apart, and Ryan leaned forward to kiss the skin of Kelsey's left calf. She repeated the action on the right and moved slowly up to Kelsey's knees. Kelsey's head went back against the pillow, and her eyes remained closed as Ryan moved to kneel on the bed between her legs now.

"Take off your shirt," Kelsey told her.

Ryan met her eyes and found that Kelsey was looking at her now.

"Are you sure you're sure?" Ryan checked again.

"Fuck, Ryan. I want you. Take off your damn shirt. I've been hot for you since I first saw you, remember?"

"Kels, are you home?"

The question came from the other side of the door and was likely from either Taylor or Chelsea, but Ryan couldn't tell. She froze and stared at Kelsey.

"Yes, and I'm busy. Good night!" Kelsey yelled.

"Oh," the person on the other side of the door said, drawing out the word.

Ryan laughed a little and said, "I don't have any roommates."

"Yeah… Like I said, your place tomorrow," Kelsey replied, sitting up and yanking Ryan's shirt off. "Now, where were we?"

***

"Ryan," Taylor said the following morning when Ryan was making her exit.

"Morning," Ryan said.

"Tay, can–" Chelsea stopped when she saw Ryan standing in the living room, putting on her shoes. "Ryan?"

"Good morning," Ryan replied, blushing completely now.

"So, that was *you* last night?" Taylor poured a cup of coffee and handed it to her girlfriend, who joined her in the kitchen.

"It was probably *me*, actually," Kelsey replied instead, coming out of her room. "Ryan's surprisingly quiet in bed." She walked over to Ryan and kissed her quickly. "Walk you out?"

"Yeah, sure," Ryan said.

"Nice to see you again, Ryan." Chelsea winked at her.

"Will we be seeing you again soon?" Taylor asked.

"Um… I don't–"

"Just let them make fun of me," Kelsey said as she pulled Ryan up by the hands and smiled at her. "Hi," she added softly.

"Hi," Ryan said, smiling back at her.

"Let's get out of here."

They made their way down the stairs and into the parking lot to Ryan's car.

"So, one to ten… How much are you freaking out at the thought of me coming over tonight?"

"About a four," Ryan said honestly, pulling Kelsey against her body.

"I expected at least a seven," Kelsey replied, smiling.

Ryan leaned in and pressed their lips together, placing one hand on the back of Kelsey's head and keeping the other one on the small of her back while Kelsey moved both around Ryan's neck.

"Do you *really* have to leave right now?" Kelsey asked.

"Yes," Ryan told her.

"I was hoping for morning sex," Kelsey said, moving her lips to Ryan's neck.

"Oh, that's not fair." Ryan laughed.

"I offered. You insisted you had to go."

"I'll call you when I'm done. It should be around lunchtime."

"You're calling me for a nooner?" Kelsey asked, quirking an eyebrow at her as she pulled back to meet Ryan's eyes.

"No." Ryan laughed and held on to Kelsey. "Can I take you to a late lunch? We can go to my place after. We can watch a movie or something, and then you can watch me cook."

"Do you or do you not wear an apron that says, 'Kiss the cook?'"

"I do not," Ryan said, pressing her lips to Kelsey's neck. "I don't have to wear anything at all."

"I knew I was smart going for an older woman," Kelsey replied. "You know what you're doing."

"Yeah?" Ryan sucked on her earlobe. "So do you. That thing with your tongue…" Ryan grew wet just at the thought of it. "Okay. I've got to go."

Kelsey laughed and said, "I'll see you later."

"Meet me at the café around one? We can eat there, and you can follow me to my place after. Pack an overnight bag, Kels."

"My, you got clingy all of a sudden," Kelsey teased.

***

"So, how freaked out are you *now*?" Kelsey checked.

"Are you going to ask me this forever?" Ryan asked back as she lay on top of Kelsey in Kelsey's bed.

"Maybe," she replied. "Take your shirt off."

Ryan laughed and said, "I came over here to take you to dinner. I made a reservation, babe."

"We can be late."

"I got all dressed up."

"I know. You look sexy. You turned me on." Kelsey sat up and put her arms around Ryan's neck. "Do you really want to go?"

"I did a whole thing."

Kelsey looked up at her with those big brown eyes.

"I've never celebrated an anniversary before. I know it's only three months and not a big deal, but–"

"It's a very big deal," Kelsey interrupted, pressing her lips to Ryan's. "And you're right, you did a whole thing. Let's go. Sex can wait."

Ryan turned her head when she heard something coming from the room next door.

"They're at it again," she said.

"They're at it all the time," Kelsey replied. "It would be cute if I didn't have to share a wall with them."

Ryan hadn't heard Taylor and Chelsea like *this* before.

"They think we're at dinner already," Kelsey said, laughing silently. "They're really going at it."

"I can hear the bed hitting the wall," Ryan whispered.

"Do you want to make *my* bed hit the wall?" Kelsey asked.

"Yes," Ryan said, kissing her quickly. "After dinner."

***

Ryan hadn't planned on falling in love. And she really hadn't planned on meeting an argumentative college student in a café and falling in love with *her*, but she had. Their relationship had been an easy one once Ryan had given in to it. Kelsey would graduate soon and move into an apartment with only one roommate, a little farther from campus but a little closer to Ryan. She'd still play at the café and a few other spots in town, and she'd be in grad school in the fall. Ryan still didn't have enough saved up to start her own firm, but she'd been thinking a lot more about taking out a loan with what she had saved up instead of waiting.

This feeling was so new and so foreign to Ryan that she almost didn't trust it. Then, Kelsey would show up at her place, or she'd see her perform at the café, and she'd know that it was right. It had only been three months, and Ryan knew she still had things to work out from her past dealing with relationships, but she just knew that Kelsey was the one for her. She could see them moving in together one day – maybe in a year or two. She could see them buying a house together and getting engaged and married, and she found herself laughing at just the idea of her settling down, but she had to admit it – it was happening.

"You plan a nice anniversary dinner, babe. Are you going to plan one of these for every anniversary?" Kelsey asked as she tipped her glass of white wine to her lips.

"Maybe not for every single month, but there are big ones, right? Six months, one year, and then every year after that."

Kelsey nearly choked on her wine. She put the glass down and cleared her throat.

"I like when you talk like that, but you know you don't have to, right?" she asked.

"I know." Ryan shrugged. "But I don't just talk – I mean what I say."

Kelsey nodded.

"Kels?"

"Yeah?"

"I love you," Ryan said.

It took a second, but Kelsey smiled. It was small at first, but then it went wide, and the brick pressing on Ryan's chest lifted. She had finally said it, and it felt good. Even if Kelsey wasn't ready to say it back, Ryan had said those words, and they'd been right.

"I love you, too, babe," Kelsey replied.

MOVING ON

Courtney sat at the small table on the patio, with her chair aimed at the water so that she could take in the view. She hadn't been to the café in a while. She recommended it to people all the time, including Anna and Troy, and now those two were a couple. Courtney, however, hadn't been there since before her wife died. They'd gone a few times right after it had been bought by Shelby and Maria and transformed into a lesbian hotspot in town, and they'd planned to make a regular thing of it. In fact, they'd decided they'd make time for one another every Sunday morning. They'd wake up together, watch the news for a bit to keep up with the current events, get dressed, and walk the four blocks from their beachfront house to the café to grab a coffee and a decadent pastry to eat as they looked out at the water. There wasn't supposed to be any talk of work; it was their time to catch up as a couple after a busy workweek with limited time together.

They'd had exactly two of those easy Sundays before Grace had been taken away from her so unexpectedly and so unfairly. They'd been talking about how they could retire early, how they could take a vacation later that year, and how they wanted to sell their beach house within the next five years. They'd been making plans for their future. Then, it had been taken away. Grace's job was supposed to be safer now that she'd been moved to a desk. She'd been on patrol for six years before she'd become a detective. Later, she'd been made a Sergeant and moved off the streets. After more than twenty years on the force, she had been eligible for retirement, but Grace hadn't been ready to let it go. She'd been hoping for a promotion to Lieutenant. She'd put in the work, passed the exam, and just wanted to retire in a few years as a Lieutenant. It had been her dream, and Courtney had supported her wife.

She regretted that support to this day and likely always would. Perhaps, if she had told Grace that she didn't want her to remain on the force... Maybe if she'd convinced her that retiring now would mean more time for them to be together... Courtney would've slowed down at work herself if Grace had retired. Grace could have still gotten a job somewhere, but they didn't need the money. Courtney's business and her family inheritance provided more than they'd ever needed, and they hadn't had any children to support. It was supposed to be their time.

Then, Grace had been in the car heading to work for her third day as a newly minted Lieutenant in one of the safest cities in the state, when she'd gotten a call for a domestic disturbance nearby. Normally, a patrol car would have been the first to respond, but she'd been just a block away, and there were reports of shots fired. She had been first on the scene, with two patrol cars right behind her. Unfortunately, the man with the gun hadn't wanted to give her time to put on her vest, which she was doing at her car when he walked out on his porch and shot her. Grace had died at the scene.

Courtney hadn't been back to *The Meet Cute Café* since their last time here, and that had been five years ago. As she sat there, staring out at the water and sipping her coffee, she thought back to their walks along this very beach. There hadn't been many of them, even though they'd been together for nearly two decades at the time of Grace's death. Grace's job meant she had odd hours, and Courtney's business was a demanding one that left them little time together week after week. That had been why they'd settled on Sunday mornings and made the commitment to reinvest in their relationship. Courtney hated that they'd had all those years together, but they only took a handful of walks on the beach, despite owning property on the water. That property had been sold since; Courtney couldn't live in the house they'd decorated and improved together. Now, she was in a lonely condo in the city, which made this trip to *The Meet Cute* completely out of her way, but one she felt she might finally be ready to take.

"Hey, I brought you a refill," Shelby said as she poured coffee into Courtney's cup.

Shelby had been someone Courtney had met years ago, when the woman had first bought the café, but they'd never been close. Grace had gone to the café on her own a lot, as she always needed coffee in her system to function, so Shelby had been more familiar with Grace than Courtney, but they'd been introduced one Sunday, and Shelby had made it a point to be at Grace's funeral with Maria. It was a kind gesture back then, and now Shelby was giving her a refill in another kind gesture that Courtney appreciated.

"Thank you," she replied.

"Can I get you anything else?"

"No, I'm meeting Troy and Anna here in a bit. I just needed some time to myself here first," she said.

"How are they doing? I haven't seen them here in a while."

"They decided to take a few weeks off work and road-trip. They rented an RV and just went wherever the day took them."

"That sounds very bohemian of them," Shelby noted.

"They've been on this kick lately to try to get me back out on the dating scene. I get it from Anna at work more now since she's been promoted and in leadership meetings, and Troy is basically like a daughter to me, so she hits me when her parents and I have dinner and she tags along. I think they both feel they can pick on me because I'm the reason they met."

"Ah. Yes, the confusing blind date."

"You know about that?" Courtney asked.

"Troy told me later, once they were a couple, how it all went down, but it happened here, and I see a lot that people don't know about." She winked at Courtney.

Courtney smiled up at her and said, "I don't know how to do this. I haven't dated in over twenty-five years. I turn forty-nine in a few weeks. When I dated the first time, gay marriage wasn't even a thought for our government, and now there are apps where you can meet women for sex or dates. The whole world changed while I was with Grace, and in the last five years, it seems to be changing even faster."

"Don't put any pressure on yourself. If you're not ready, just tell Anna and Troy to leave you alone. They will. They probably just want to see you happy."

"I know. They mean well. And it's not that I don't want to meet someone. It's just… I already did that. I wasn't supposed to have to do it again. Grace and I were supposed to grow old together and die at the same time in our warm bed." Courtney chuckled a little. "And if that didn't happen, if I went first or if she did, we'd be so old that we wouldn't even want to find anyone else. We'd just be waiting for the grim reaper to take us so that we could be together wherever we go when it ends here."

"Hey," Troy greeted, walking out to the patio hand in hand with Anna.

"Hey there, world travelers," Courtney said, happy to see Troy, who'd she'd known for Troy's entire life.

Troy's father owned a contracting company that Troy would take over one day, and he and Courtney had met years ago at a holiday party for people they both knew, and they'd maintained their friendship. Courtney had watched Troy and her brother both grow up, and she'd been there when Troy had come out and had supported her. When Anna had started working at Courtney's company, she'd been a private person, not really interested in coming out of her shell. When Courtney had seen her with a female friend at their company holiday party and drew a conclusion that had turned out to be correct, Anna hadn't been ready to believe it at the time. Courtney had suggested a setup with Troy, and while the two women had been friends at first, they'd been together in one way or another ever since.

"We're really more like *US* travelers since we didn't leave the continent," Troy replied.

"I'll go grab us coffee. Do you need anything?" Anna asked Courtney.

"No, Shelby just refilled my cup, so I'm good."

"I've got to get back to the counter. I'll walk with you, Anna," Shelby said.

Troy sat down in the chair to Courtney's right and asked, "How have you been?"

"Good. You?"

Troy smiled and looked to make sure Anna was out of earshot.

"I'm so great. I'm going to marry that woman."

"You *are*?" Courtney said with a smile. "Did you ask her if that's what *she* wants?"

"Not yet, but I will," Troy replied. "I did ask her to move in with me. She doesn't like her place, and she spends most of her time at mine, anyway. She said yes while we were on our trip."

"That's great, Troy," Courtney said.

"I want to have a ring ready, though, in case the moment strikes. I want to be prepared. It's why I asked if you could meet me."

"I don't sell engagement rings," Courtney joked.

"No, but you bought one once," she said, looking down at Courtney's hand.

After she lost Grace, Courtney had taken to wearing her own wedding band and engagement ring as normal but wore Grace's set on her other hand. Gay marriage hadn't been legal when they'd met all those years ago. They hadn't bothered with a civil ceremony or anything; they'd just started saying *wife* instead of *girlfriend* or *partner*, but once it had been legalized across the country, they'd planned a small wedding. Courtney had gotten down on one knee and presented the woman she'd loved forever with a ring.

"She's seen Grace's ring on your hand, and she's made

comments that she really loves it," Troy continued. "I was hoping you could tell me where you got it so I can see if they have something similar. I would have just texted you, but I knew you'd want to see me when we got back." She winked at Courtney. "You worry more about me than my actual parents."

"You're the daughter I never had," Courtney replied. "And I got this at a place downtown. It was expensive, Troy."

"I know. I've been saving up," she replied.

"For how long?"

"Since I met her," Troy stated, smiling over in Anna's direction. "She's the one. I knew it when you first set us up."

"Then, don't wait, sweetie. If you're ready to propose, don't spend time saving up for some expensive ring that'll take years for you to pay off. Tell her now what you want; don't waste time. You don't know what might happen, and you two deserve to be happy. If you're ready and you think she's ready, ask her with no ring at all. Anna isn't the kind of woman who cares about that anyway."

"Her parents are. They barely tolerate it when I'm in the same room with them. If I propose to their daughter with no ring, they're going to think I haven't thought this through or that I can't afford to take care of her."

"She doesn't need you to take care of her. She's perfectly capable of taking care of herself."

"I know. It's just that…"

Troy kept talking, but Courtney wasn't listening to her anymore. She'd turned to follow Troy's gaze in Anna's direction, which meant she was now turned facing the rest of the café and the front door. A woman with gray hair, cut just below her ears, and bright blue eyes that Courtney could see from all the way out on the patio, had just walked in. She was accompanied by two much younger women who were holding hands, and Courtney recognized one of them as Chelsea, Shelby's niece, who worked at the café. That must make the other young woman her girlfriend that

Courtney hadn't met. She had no idea who the older woman was, though, and there was just something drawing Courtney's attention to her.

"Anyway, I can't *not* get her a ring. I want to be down on one knee and do the whole thing right. Her parents won't ever give me their blessing for real, I know that, but they've been trying to listen to Anna when she talks about me and being gay, at least. I mean, it's the first step, right?"

"What, dear?" Courtney asked.

"Are you okay?" Troy asked back.

"I…" Courtney didn't know what to say to that.

The woman with Chelsea and her girlfriend now stood at the counter, placing an order, and Courtney watched as an elegant hand swiped a credit card and smiled at Shelby, who was behind the register. Courtney had to look away.

***

She'd made the trip back to *The Meet Cute* because Shelby had asked her to stop by and talk about her retirement fund. Financial planning wasn't a glamorous profession for most people, but Courtney liked it. She'd grown her business from the ground up and now had over twenty employees in her local office and two more remote people who were likely going to be the first in the new offices she had planned in her expansion. She'd been fine with the five or so employees she'd had before she'd lost Grace. They'd had the money, and she'd already worked hard enough – she'd wanted time with her wife over more work to do. But when she'd lost Grace, Courtney had poured everything she had into her business, which was how she'd met Anna – she needed an office manager to help run things.

Now, Shelby and Maria wanted to review their savings and retirement accounts, and they sounded interested in hiring Courtney's firm to manage things for them.

"She just stepped out," Chelsea said when Courtney asked for Shelby. "We ran out of whole milk, so she just went to the store to grab a few gallons until our delivery gets here later. She told me to get you whatever you wanted, and she'd be back in twenty minutes."

"No problem," Courtney replied. "I can wait. Can I just get a regular coffee?"

Chelsea's smile appeared as she turned her head to the front door.

"Hey," she said.

"Hi, babe," the young woman Courtney had seen with her before replied with an equally bright smile. "Mom and I were hoping you could take a break."

"I can when Shelby gets back," Chelsea said and turned back to Courtney. "Sorry. Let me get you that coffee, Courtney. How about a cinnamon scone? Taylor loves them."

"Who's Taylor?"

"That would be me," the young woman replied. "The lucky one who gets to call Chels, here, her girlfriend."

"She's sweet," Chelsea said.

"She better be; I raised her."

Courtney turned her head a little farther, and there she was. It was the woman who had been there with the two of them before.

"Taylor gets a cinnamon scone. Andrea, the usual?"

"Yes, please." The woman smiled at Chelsea.

"And, Courtney?"

"Sorry?" Courtney said, turning back to Chelsea.

"On the house, because Shelby's making you wait," she said with a smile.

"Oh, just the coffee is fine. Thank you."

"I'll bring it out to you," Chelsea replied.

"Thanks," Courtney said and turned around to find an empty table.

The café wasn't crazy busy, but there were only two empty tables. No, scratch that: there was now only one empty table. Taylor and the woman Courtney now knew to be Taylor's mother were now sitting at the table right next to the one Courtney would now have to take.

"How do you know Shelby?" Taylor asked her, sitting down next to her mother.

"Oh, just a customer," she replied. "You?"

"Dating her niece," Taylor said.

"Right. Obvious," Courtney replied, sitting down as well and feeling like a nervous idiot.

"Oh, this is my mom." Taylor motioned to the other woman.

"Hi," the woman said. "Andrea."

"Courtney," she replied with a half-hearted wave.

"Nice to meet you," Andrea said with a kind smile.

"You too," Courtney replied.

"So, what do you do?" Taylor asked.

"Sorry?" Courtney asked back.

"For work."

"Taylor, leave the woman alone," Andrea told her daughter. "Sorry, she's nosy."

"No, it's fine." Courtney chuckled a little and added, "I'm a financial planner. Well, I run a company of them now; I don't do much of the work myself anymore."

"That's cool. My mom needs one of those."

"Taylor!" Andrea laughed and said, "No, I don't."

"Yes, you do. You have to–"

"Taylor, stop," Andrea scolded, appearing annoyed now.

"Cinnamon scone and a panini, extra crispy," Chelsea said, placing plates in front of the two women. "I'll be right back with your drinks and your coffee, Courtney."

"Sure," Courtney said. "Enjoy your lunch," she added to Taylor and Andrea before pulling out her phone to check her email while she waited for Shelby.

A phone rang, and it wasn't Courtney's.

"It's Dad," Taylor said.

Courtney tried not to listen in, but they were only a few feet away.

"Answer it if you want, Tay."

"I haven't talked to him since…"

"I know, baby. But he's your dad."

"He treated you like shit."

"You might be about to graduate college, but you're still my kid, so watch your mouth." Andrea chuckled.

"Sorry, but it's true," Taylor replied.

The phone stopped ringing just in time for Chelsea to drop Courtney's coffee off and then give Taylor and Andrea their drinks.

"What's wrong?" she asked.

"How do you know something's wrong?" Taylor asked her girlfriend.

"I think I know all your faces by now, Tay," Chelsea said, running her hand through Taylor's hair.

"My dad called."

"You didn't answer?"

"No, I'm not talking to him."

"What's between your father and me isn't about you, Taylor."

"Oh, I'd say it is," Taylor replied to her mother. "He never treated *me* like this. Why is he treating *you* like this?"

"Courtney, I am so sorry." Shelby rushed in, holding on to four gallons of milk.

"Oh, I've got it," Chelsea said, moving to her aunt to help.

"I didn't think it would take as long as it did. There was a line, and I'm just really sorry. Did Chelsea give you anything you wanted?"

"I just got the coffee," Courtney replied. "And it's fine; I don't mind waiting." She stood up and placed her cell phone back into her bag. "Should we go somewhere more private, though?"

"Yes. I just need a second to put this away. You can come into the back."

Courtney looked over at Taylor, who was staring down at her phone, and then at Andrea, who looked up at her and gave Courtney a small smile.

***

"I think I've got what I need. Let me work it up, and I'll send you an email later for you to confirm," Courtney said before she exited the back room of the café with Shelby on her heels.

"That would be great. Sorry, Maria couldn't be here. But I'll review everything with her tonight."

"Sounds good," Courtney replied, hefting her bag over her shoulder.

"Can I grab you a coffee for the road?"

"No, thanks. Traffic's bad this time of day, and I'm going back into the city – don't want to have to pee halfway home." She laughed.

"Why not stay here for a bit?" Shelby suggested. "It's Friday; our open mic night is starting soon. You could stay through rush hour and let me make you a sandwich or something, at least, for being late today."

"You *should* stay," someone said from behind her.

Courtney turned to see Andrea standing there.

"Oh. Hi, again."

"Hi," Andrea said, smiling at her, and she looked a bit nervous. "I'm sorry about earlier. I'm sure you overheard my daughter and I talking, and she also tried to get in the way of you and your coffee. I just wanted to apologize again."

"No need," Courtney said. "She seems nice."

"She's twenty-two and thinks she knows everything. Thank God for Chelsea," Andrea said, looking at Shelby. "She's been a Godsend."

"I think they're good for each other," Shelby said.

"They're being nice to me, inviting me to spend time with them more these days, despite me being an old lady getting in their way." Andrea laughed. "My oldest daughter doesn't live nearby, so I think Taylor feels like she has to do twice the work."

"Work?" Courtney asked.

"Fresh off a divorce," Andrea explained. "Well, it's not *that* fresh, actually – we split about two years ago, but the ink just dried off on the paperwork about six months ago. Taylor's trying to keep me occupied when I'm not at work."

"Sounds like a good daughter. And sorry to hear about that," Courtney replied.

"It needed to happen." Andrea nodded. "Anyway, I just wanted to say I'm sorry. And if you're considering sticking around, open mic night here is pretty good. I've been coming for a few weeks now. It gets my daughter off my back and gives her time to study, which is what I'm choosing to believe she's doing now instead of thinking about her in her apartment with her girlfriend."

Courtney laughed at that and said, "Let's just agree that they've never even kissed each other. How about that?"

Andrea laughed as well and asked, "Do *you* have kids?"

"No," Courtney replied. "We never really had the desire to."

"We?" Andrea looked down at Courtney's left hand. "Husband? Wife?"

Courtney swallowed and said, "Wife. Grace."

"Beautiful name."

"Yes," Courtney replied, smiling softly. "She was beautiful in more than just her name."

Andrea's eyebrows pinched together.

"How long?"

"About five years," Courtney said.

"I'm sorry," Andrea replied.

"Me too," she said. "And I really *should* be going."

"Of course," Andrea said.

"But maybe I'll see you here next time," Courtney offered in response.

"I'm usually here without the kids in tow on Thursday mornings, around eight, before I head off to work."

Getting to *The Meet Cute* would be completely out of Courtney's way that early on a weekday, but something told her it might just be worth it.

"I'll see if I can make that work," she replied.

***

Courtney wasn't sure why she had dressed up more than she usually would for work, but she'd put on lipstick and eyeliner, where normally, she reserved those two things for meetings with important clients. She also had to leave around six-forty-five just to get over there, find a parking space, and make it into the café, and she'd have about twenty minutes in the café if she was going to make it into the office by her usual time. She wasn't even sure it was worth it. What was she hoping would happen? Andrea had said she was *usually* here around *eight*, and that hadn't guaranteed she'd be here. The coffee at *The Meet Cute* was good, but driving this far out of her way for it would be ridiculous.

"You made it?"

"Oh, hi. Yeah," Courtney replied.

Andrea was stirring something into her cup at the condiments station. It was a *to-go* cup. Of course, it was. Andrea had stopped in before work to get her coffee to-go. Courtney had driven all the way over here to have a thirty-second conversation with a woman she didn't know before said woman got in her car and ran off to work.

"So, you made it?" Andrea repeated.

"I did," Courtney replied as she stood in line now that she knew Andrea had a drink and was about to leave.

Andrea walked over and said, "I would have waited to order, but I–"

"Have to get to work; it's okay."

Andrea smiled and said, "I was going to say that I wasn't sure you'd be here. I waited until ten after."

"You waited?" Courtney asked.

Andrea nodded.

"I'm sorry. I tried to make it by eight... I live downtown."

"Is your office nearby here?"

Courtney laughed and said, "Not even close."

"No?"

"No. This time of day, it's going to take me about forty minutes."

Andrea smiled and asked, "So, you need to go?"

Courtney stepped up in line and said, "I have about twenty minutes."

"I can get a table."

"I thought *you* had to go."

"Why?"

"To-go cup."

"Oh, they were out of mugs when I ordered. I usually sit here for a bit and read the news on my phone."

"I don't want to interrupt your usual plans," Courtney said.

"No, please do. I could use some adult time," Andrea replied. "Work is work, and the rest of my time has been spent with my daughter and her girlfriend or with my other daughter on the phone with her asking how I'm doing."

"They love you. That's a good thing," Courtney said, moving up in line again.

"I know. I just… I wasn't expecting this."

"Your children caring enough about you to check on you?"

"No, being divorced at fifty," Andrea replied.

"Do you mind if I ask—"

"Hi," a barista Courtney didn't recognize said. "What can I get for you?"

"Oh, just a large coffee."

"Room for cream?"

"No, thanks," she said.

"Let me get it," Andrea offered when Courtney pulled out her credit card. "You came all the way here, and you're only ordering a plain coffee." Andrea handed the barista her own card.

"You didn't have to do that," Courtney replied.

"I wanted to," she said.

Courtney grabbed her coffee off the bar a moment later, and they walked toward the patio where they found the one tiny table in the corner. They headed in that direction, and Courtney turned her chair out to the ocean how she'd done the last time she'd sat out here.

"So, financial planning? How did you get into that?"

"It's not a great story. I was in college and needed a job after graduation. My father had a financial planning firm, so I worked there for a while. Then, I went out on my own. That's about it."

"I doubt that," Andrea said. "If it were that easy, everyone would do it, right?"

Courtney took a sip of her very hot coffee, regretting it instantly.

"What do you do?"

"I'm a teacher. I teach second grade. On Thursdays, we have a late start, so that's why I can come in here and grab a coffee and have a few minutes with the news before I have to go be surrounded by seven-year-olds."

"You're a better person than I am; I couldn't do that job."

"It doesn't pay well, but it's rewarding. Well, sometimes, it's rewarding. Other times, you just want the school day to end so that you can go home, open a bottle of wine, and get into a nice, hot bath."

"Hell, I want that every night," Courtney replied.

Andrea smiled at her, took a drink of her coffee, and said, "Inside, you were going to ask me about my divorce, weren't you?"

"I shouldn't have. It's way too personal."

"No, it's fine," Andrea replied. "It's part of me processing what happened."

"Did he… do something?"

"No, it wasn't him. It was me," she said, looking out over the water. "I realized I wanted something else."

"Something or someone?" Courtney asked.

"Not someone, specifically," Andrea replied. "I didn't cheat on my husband. I'm not sure *he* believes that, but it's the truth. It took me a while to realize it; much longer than most. I mean, my daughter figured out who she was as a teenager. And here I was, in my mid-forties, thinking I might not be as interested in my husband as I'd pretended to be." Andrea paused. "It's wrong to say that; *pretended* to be. I thought I was in love, and I thought we had a good…" She stopped again. "Anyway, I watched my daughter come out. Then, I saw her meet Chelsea and fall in love for the first time, and I knew that I could keep pretending, or I could try to be happy. I talked to my now ex-husband about my confusion, and he didn't take it well."

"Confusion?" Courtney checked.

"I'm not confused anymore, and I don't think I have been for a long time. But I didn't want to admit it. I didn't want to believe it. I was married. I had two grown daughters. I've lived most of my life already, right? What was the point in coming out now?"

Courtney turned to Andrea then and watched her as she took another drink of her coffee.

"He didn't react well," the woman continued, "and it wasn't worth fighting with him when he tried to claim I'd cheated on him, so I let him have the house and moved into a small apartment. He's always been the breadwinner, so that's why Taylor made those comments the other day: she wants to make sure I can support myself. Which, I can. She doesn't know all the details of the divorce, and I don't plan on telling her."

"I wasn't trying to listen, but I overheard the comment she made about him supporting her."

"He always has. He's a great father. He's never cared about Taylor being gay, and he loves Chelsea for her. It's young love, but there's just something about the two of them that we both believe in." Andrea smiled. "He loves his children; he's just angry with me."

"I'm sorry," Courtney replied.

"Well, it's my own fault for not coming clean sooner."

"You can't really help that. It's a process for everyone. For me, it wasn't something I'd planned on doing, but then I met Grace, and I couldn't see a life without her, so I came out, and we were together."

"Do you mind me asking what happened?"

"She was a police officer; shot in the line of duty."

"Oh, God. I'm sorry, Courtney," Andrea said, taking Courtney's hand in her own.

Courtney stared down at their now-joined hands and didn't know what to do. It felt so nice to be touching another woman like this after all this time, but it also felt strange. Andrea's hands were smaller than Grace's had been. They were a little softer, too. There also wasn't a wedding ring on the left ring finger. Courtney swallowed another gulp of hot coffee.

"I've only just started putting myself out there. I have sort of a daughter that's not really my daughter – she's the daughter of a friend of mine, and I've known her since she was born. Anyway, she's been trying to get me to put myself out there again."

"How's that going?" Andrea asked, still holding Courtney's hand.

"I don't know; I haven't tried yet."

"No?"

Courtney shook her head.

"Neither have I."

"What do you mean?"

"I haven't tried dating."

"Since your divorce?"

"Technically, since I dated my ex-husband, but not since the separation, no."

"So, you haven't–"

"No is the answer to any possible questions." Andrea laughed.

Then, she seemed to realize she was still holding Courtney's hand.

"I suppose, that might be why I mentioned to you I'd be here."

Courtney looked down at her now lonely hand before she moved her eyes back to Andrea's blue ones.

"What do you say?" Andrea asked.

"Oh. To what?"

"I'm doing a really bad job at this, aren't I?" Andrea laughed.

"Oh, you're asking…"

"You out, yes. That sounds so weird… I've never actually asked anyone out before."

"You want to go out with *me*?"

"I know we don't know each other, but people do that all the time – meet someone, have a shared interest, and get to know them as they date."

"Yes, they do." Courtney looked down at the rings on her fingers. "I just haven't done this in a long time."

"Would you be interested in letting me take you to dinner sometime?"

"I haven't been with anyone since Grace died; you should know that before you ask me out. I haven't even been remotely interested in…"

"It's okay. You can say no, or you could give it a chance, or you can say we could just try to be friends. I'll understand."

"I want to," Courtney said.

"Which one?" Andrea asked with a light laugh.

"Dinner. I just want you to be prepared for what you might get."

"I'm new to this, too. You'd be going on a date with a woman that's never even kissed another woman before."

Courtney smiled at her and asked, "What about tomorrow night?"

"I'm free tomorrow night," the woman replied. "I'm supposed to come here for open mic night because Taylor wants to make sure I stand a chance of meeting eligible lesbians." She laughed.

"Well, *I'm* an eligible lesbian," Courtney remarked, wondering how true that actually was the moment she said it.

***

"Is this okay?" Andrea asked.

"Of course," Courtney replied.

Andrea had taken her to an Indian restaurant on the other side of town. She'd even picked Courtney up at her condo and had insisted on planning the whole evening. Courtney hadn't even been to this restaurant, and she usually stuck to her regular take-out places for dinner, so being out in a nice restaurant with a beautiful woman was a welcomed change of pace.

"I wasn't sure what you ate… I should've asked before I made the reservation."

"I like Indian food," Courtney said, smiling as she sat down.

"Me too. I've only been here once, but it was really good."

Courtney could tell the woman was nervous, and she assumed Andrea could tell the same thing about her. Andrea had brought her flowers, and Courtney had had her hands shaking as she'd attempted to put them in the vase she kept under the kitchen sink. Then, she had motioned for Andrea to head out of the condo first at the exact same time Andrea had said, "After you." They'd laughed about it, but it was nice to laugh. Courtney needed that laugh to help ease the nervous tension that sat in a knot in her stomach.

"So, Taylor seems great," Courtney said when their entrées were placed in front of them.

"She is," Andrea replied, smiling with pride. "She's about to graduate with honors, and she's going to law school."

"Really?"

"She's following in her sister's footsteps. Tanner chose

environmental law. Taylor's thinking criminal, but we'll see. Their father is also a lawyer, but Taylor told me she's not doing it because of him."

"Things are tense between them?"

"She doesn't understand how he can be fine with her being gay but not be okay with *me* being gay."

"You were his wife; I think it's a little different."

"I know. I think she knows it, too, but she's still angry with him. And she has her own mind, so I just have to let her get through it." Andrea took a drink of her water. "But I don't want to talk about him tonight. And while I'm happy to talk about my kids anytime, I don't want to monopolize our evening, either."

"You're not," Courtney said. "Tell me about teaching second grade."

"Oh, there are a lot of stories I could tell you about that." The woman chuckled. "I've been doing it for twenty-five years."

"Wow. That's a lot of second graders."

"Our principal is retiring next year, and I thought about tossing my name into the ring. I love teaching my kids, but I think I'm ready for something else."

"You should go for it," Courtney encouraged.

"It's more administrative work, and I wouldn't have any teaching responsibilities, so I don't know… It's a big change."

"You should at least go for it if you think you might like it," Courtney told her. "I assume there's an interview process and everything."

"Yes, I'd have to be approved by the school board."

"Maybe talk to the current principal and get their thoughts on the job. Tell them to give you the good, the bad, and the ugly, so you know what you'd be getting yourself into."

"Yeah," Andrea said with a smile. "That's a good idea."

Later, Andrea drove Courtney home and then walked

her to the door of her condo. They stood there awkwardly for a moment, with neither of them saying anything.

"Well, I had a nice time," Andrea said eventually.

"Me too."

Courtney smiled because it was true. They'd stayed at the restaurant for over two hours, sharing a dessert and having refills for their coffees because they'd been enjoying their conversation. Courtney hadn't wanted the night to end, but the waiter had clearly grown tired of checking on their coffees and asking them if they needed anything else. Courtney felt bad and wanted to take care of the check to tip him extra, but Andrea took the check from her, insisting she wanted to pay.

"Do you want to come in?" Courtney offered. "I'd ask if you want a coffee, but I think we've both had enough of that tonight."

Andrea laughed and said, "I'd love to come in, but I think it's best that I don't."

"Why? I have more than just coffee. There's wine, and I have a full bar I hardly ever use. I've got iced tea in the fridge, I think."

Andrea smiled and took Courtney's hand, her right hand.

"Were these hers?" she asked softly, staring at Grace's rings.

"Yeah," Courtney said.

Andrea nodded and asked, "Can we do this again sometime?" She dropped Courtney's hand.

"I'd like that," Courtney replied.

"I'll call you?"

"Okay." Courtney nodded.

Andrea leaned in, and just something about the way she did it, told Courtney that she was going for her cheek. Andrea *did* kiss her cheek, but she also hovered there. She was so close, and it felt so good having her there. Courtney knew that it wasn't just because she hadn't been with another woman like this for a long time; it was Andrea. Courtney smiled and wrapped her arms around Andrea's waist, silently asking her to stay there just for another moment.

"Are you free tomorrow?" Andrea asked as she lay her head on Courtney's shoulder, embracing Courtney back.

"Yes," Courtney replied with a smile.

***

"You had a date?" Shelby said the following morning.

"I did," Courtney replied. "It was nice."

"Just nice?" Shelby asked, placing a cup of coffee in front of Courtney and then sitting down.

"It was nice and, I don't know, felt strangely right," she said.

"That's a good thing." Shelby nodded.

"We don't have to talk about my date. Is Maria joining us to discuss what I came up with for you guys?"

"She's still sleeping. Of the two of us, I'm the early riser. It's why I run this place, and she has a day job outside of it still." Shelby laughed. "I usually wake up around five when I open. She doesn't wake up until well after nine most days. It's cute, though. She'll do this thing where I'll tell her I love her before I go, and she just kind of grunts at me and pulls the pillow over her head."

Courtney thought about Grace at that moment. Grace had always been an early riser. She had worked irregular shifts as a patrol officer first and then as a detective, so she forced herself to be on some kind of schedule as much as she could. Then, Courtney furrowed her brow as she thought about something else – she wondered if Andrea slept in or woke early.

"So, I have a plan here that I'd like to go over with you if you're okay with it," Courtney spoke, trying to focus on the present. "If not, we can reschedule and have Maria join us."

"No, it's okay," Shelby told her. "I love my wife, but finances aren't her thing. I handle them for us because if I let her, we'd have forty credit cards with forty different interest rates, no retirement plan at all, and probably a boat we docked but never used."

"Impulsive?"

"Not necessarily," Shelby replied. "She just grew up with money and then made her own on top of it, so the concept of planning for the future with our finances isn't one she really understands or cares much about. She believes the money will always be there, and we have more than enough to support ourselves and the life we've made, so she doesn't see the point in bothering with all of this. I grew up with hand-me-downs and then put myself through college and law school, so I see things differently."

"That makes sense." Courtney nodded.

As she walked Shelby through what she'd put together for her approval, Courtney thought about how she'd been the one to handle the finances for her and Grace. It had just made sense; she did it for a living, so she should do it for the two of them as well. And Courtney loved it. She loved taking care of something for the two of them. Grace liked to be involved, but more as a consultant than as a decision-maker. Courtney loved their talks about their future. She missed having someone to bounce her ideas off of, someone to talk to about those future purchases and vacations, and well, just someone to talk to.

After her meeting with Shelby, Courtney got home a few hours later, having had a few errands to run, including picking up a new dress to wear for her date that night. She had more than enough dresses, but when she'd looked through her closet for their Friday night date, she'd felt like she needed something new, something fresh, something that Grace hadn't seen her in, hadn't helped Courtney zip up, or hadn't taken off of her at the end of their date night. As Courtney hung her new purchase up on the hanger and stared at it, she was both excited by the possibilities of her second date with Andrea and also terrified by what this meant for her life with Grace.

***

"Are you not feeling well?" Andrea asked.

Courtney didn't want to lie to Andrea; the woman didn't deserve that. She'd called Andrea two hours prior to the time she was supposed to leave to pick Andrea up for their second date to cancel the whole thing, and she had planned to make an excuse. She was going to suggest they postpone, or she'd tell Andrea she had more work to do than she'd planned on or something else. Having heard Andrea's concerned tone just now, though, she knew she couldn't lie to her.

"I'm feeling fine," Courtney replied. "I just…"

"Oh," Andrea said knowingly. "I see."

"I think it might be too soon," Courtney said.

"I understand," the woman replied softly. "I probably shouldn't have asked you out, to begin with. You're… You still wear your rings."

Courtney looked down at her right hand; her left one with her own rings was holding the phone.

"Yeah," she said, sighing. "I'm sorry. I thought–"

"No, it's fine. I really do understand," Andrea said. "Maybe we could just grab coffee sometime."

"I'd like that."

***

Their third Thursday morning coffee had been the best yet. Andrea had scrolled through the news app on her phone. Courtney had stared out at the water, and when Andrea had shared some of what she was reading with her, Courtney had commented. They'd spend twenty minutes together before they both had to leave for work, and they'd hardly spoken about anything of substance, but the silence between them had been a comfortable one.

"Are you going to be here tomorrow night?" Andrea asked.

"For open mic night? I don't know."

"Come on. If you're not there, I'll be by myself with my daughter and her girlfriend, who is sweet but can't keep her hands – and often, her lips – off of Taylor. A mother can only take so much…"

Courtney laughed and said, "Okay. I'll be here."

***

The performance was surprisingly good. The woman had introduced herself as Kelsey and sang along to the guitar she played. It was either an original song, or Courtney hadn't heard it. It could go either way because she didn't exactly keep up with music these days. She looked over at Taylor, who was sitting next to Andrea. Chelsea was working the event, so she only came over when she could. Andrea had been right, though: whenever Chelsea was near Taylor, she found an excuse to touch her. Courtney thought it was cute. Andrea kept rolling her eyes at it in Courtney's direction, making Courtney laugh. Kelsey finished her song, earning well-deserved applause, and Courtney watched her hop off the stage and walk straight into the arms of another woman who held on to her tightly before pulling back to kiss her sweetly. Was everyone here coupled off? No, *she* wasn't. She'd turned down a chance to be with Andrea, which she'd been regretting ever since.

They weren't just going to coffee together once a week; they were texting regularly and talking on the phone at least a few times a week. Courtney found herself looking forward to the texts and especially the calls. She looked over at Andrea, who she expected to see sitting next to her, but she wasn't in her chair. Andrea was standing now. She was hugging another woman over by the counter.

"That's Stephanie," Taylor said, looking at Courtney now. "She lives in Mom's building."

Courtney gave Taylor a nod.

"Mom invited her tonight but didn't think she'd show."

I guess they bonded over their divorces or something. Stephanie divorced her wife last year."

Courtney nodded again.

"You like my Mom, don't you?" Taylor asked.

"Sorry?"

"She talks about you a lot. I know you guys are talking on the phone and having coffee and stuff. She told me about your first date and what happened. I don't know what, if anything, will happen with her and Stephanie – they haven't gone out yet – but my mom likes you."

"I like her, too," Courtney said.

"I'm not trying to pressure you or anything, but she's pretty awesome," Taylor added. "And now that she's putting herself out there, I don't think she'll be single long."

"Hey, Courtney, this is my friend Stephanie. Stephanie, this is my friend Courtney."

And just like that, Andrea had introduced her as a friend to another friend. And that friend was now sitting between Courtney and Andrea at the small table as the next performer took the stage.

"I'm going to head home," Courtney said when the performer finished her spoken word poetry.

"It's early," Andrea remarked, leaning back behind Stephanie to talk to Courtney.

"I know. I'm a little tired. Long week."

"Okay. Let me walk you out," Andrea offered. "I'll be right back," she added to Stephanie.

"You don't have to. I'll be fine," Courtney replied, standing up and making her way quickly through the crowd and out the door toward the small parking lot.

"Hey, is everything okay?" Andrea asked, having followed Courtney out to her car.

"What? Yes, everything's fine."

"But you're leaving."

"You invited someone else, Andrea." Courtney hadn't meant to say that as loud as she had. "I'm sorry." She turned around to face her.

"You're leaving because of Stephanie?"

"It's just a little crowded at the table, and it's already a small table."

"She's just a friend, Courtney. She hadn't been out in a while, so I mentioned that I come here sometimes when I saw her taking out her trash today. She told me she didn't think she could make it."

"It's fine," Courtney replied, hitting the button on her key fob to unlock her car.

"No, it's not," Andrea replied. "You're upset." She took a few steps toward her. "Courtney, she's just a friend."

"It doesn't matter; I'm being unfair. She can be a friend or something more."

"I like *you*," Andrea replied. "You canceled on me, and I understand why, but it doesn't change the fact that I like you. That part doesn't just go away. And it's been getting stronger the more time we spend together. I didn't say anything because you said you weren't ready. But Stephanie is really just a friend; she's still in love with her ex-wife."

"So am I," Courtney replied. "Only she wasn't an ex."

"I know." Andrea moved closer. "You always will be in love with her. I wouldn't expect anything else, and no one should."

"That's not fair to anyone, is it? Me, always being in love with Grace?"

"She was your wife. She was taken from you."

"I miss having someone to wake up to every morning," Courtney said.

"So do I." Andrea chuckled a little.

"I like you, too. It's more than just having someone to wake up to for me – I like spending time with you. And yes, I definitely got jealous tonight when I saw you with Stephanie, but I'm the one who said I wasn't ready. You deserve more than me."

"Do you want to try again? We could go on that second date we missed and see how it goes."

"I don't know."

Andrea nodded and said, "Okay. Well, I should get back inside, then. I *did* invite Stephanie here. I'm being rude leaving her in there with my daughter and her girlfriend."

"Wait," Courtney said, swallowing.

She stared into Andrea's beautiful blue eyes, and for the first time in a long time, she wasn't thinking about Grace; Courtney was only thinking about the patient and understanding woman standing in front of her.

"I'd be an idiot if I let you walk in there without telling you that I really, really want to go out with you again."

"Telling me that doesn't mean you will; it just means you want to." Andrea looked over her shoulder back toward the café. "Have a good night, Courtney."

***

She knew she'd messed up. Courtney had gone home after that night and had stared at the photos of her with Grace hanging on the living room wall. Then, she looked down at her hands and stared at the rings they'd given each other years ago now.

"Baby, I don't know what I'm supposed to do here," she said to herself. "I know we talked about it all the time; you were a cop – it could always happen. But I never thought it would. I never thought I'd lose you on the job." Courtney wiped her tears from her cheeks. "I know you told me to move on – I know you want me to be happy – but it's harder than it looks." She let out a small chuckle. "You were the one I was supposed to grow old with, and you're not here, babe. I never wanted anyone but you." Courtney swallowed. "Until now. I don't know what to do. I feel like being with Andrea is betraying what you and I had, what we were supposed to have, but I like her. You'd like her, too." Courtney smiled at their wedding photo on the wall. "And I have this chance to try to make things work with her. I don't know if she'll even give me another chance now, but I know she won't be single long; she's a catch. And when I hugged her, babe, I just felt like I not only wanted that; I wanted more. I wanted to kiss her goodnight and hold her hand on our next date. I wanted to go to her apartment and– " Courtney looked away from the photo then and added, "I don't know what to do with all of these feelings. I haven't wanted anyone how I wanted you. And I know Andrea's not you – she can't ever be you – but she *is* special, and I am attracted to her. I want to be with her, babe. And if I'm going to do that, I think I need to make some changes. I hope you understand. I hope you're wherever you are telling me that you love me and that you get it. I love you, Grace; I will always love you. But I think I need to make room in my heart for someone else now."

***

"You didn't have to get me flowers," Andrea told her.

"These or the other ones?" Courtney asked.

"Both." Andrea laughed.

Courtney had sent Andrea a bouquet of flowers to the school the previous day, with a card asking for a second chance. Andrea had called her after, agreeing to a date, and now Courtney was standing at her apartment door, holding another bouquet out to her.

"Come in. I'll put these in water, and then we can go," she said, smiling at Courtney.

Courtney followed her into the apartment, which opened straight into a lightly furnished living room. She followed the woman farther into the kitchen and watched as she put the flowers into a large glass.

"I don't have a vase here," she said.

"Where's the one from the other bouquet?"

"Still holding the *other* flowers you got me." Andrea laughed. "On the kitchen table." She nodded.

Courtney took a few steps out of the kitchen and saw the flowers in the center of the table. She looked around the space a little more and then felt Andrea standing behind her.

"It's not much, but it's enough space for me."

"It's nice," Courtney replied.

"It's not," Andrea said, laughing. "I still have stuff at the house from after the divorce that I haven't picked up, but I wanted a fresh start here, so I bought all this stuff when I moved out."

Courtney felt the arms wrap around her waist from behind, so she looked down at them, smiled, and covered them with her own.

"I like this dress," Andrea said softly as she rested her head on Courtney's shoulder.

"I bought it for tonight. Well, I bought it for our second date that was supposed to happen, but I wore it tonight."

"Did you know this was my favorite color when you bought it?"

"No," Courtney replied.

"You look gorgeous."

"So do you," Courtney replied, meaning every word.

Andrea rubbed her nose along Courtney's neck and said, "Is this okay?"

"Definitely," she breathed out.

"I've never held a woman like this before."

"Well, you're really good at it."

"I almost wish you weren't wearing a dress, so I could feel your skin."

"You like this dress."

"I said *almost*," Andrea whispered into her ear.

Courtney wasn't sure what had come over her, but she reached down to the hem of her dress and lifted it up slowly. She knew Andrea couldn't see anything, but she wanted Andrea to feel her skin.

"Oh," Andrea said, lowering her hand until it was under the dress and on Courtney's stomach. "Wow."

"God, you feel good," Courtney gasped out.

Andrea kissed her neck and said, "I wanted to do that when we hugged that first time." Then, her other hand slipped under the dress and moved along Courtney's skin. "I don't know what I'm doing," she admitted.

"Trust me, you do." Courtney leaned back against her and closed her eyes.

"Should we stop?" Andrea asked.

"Only if you want to," Courtney told her.

"I don't," Andrea replied. "I want… more of you."

Courtney turned her head a bit and met Andrea's eyes. Then, she turned around completely, missing the contact of Andrea's hands on her stomach but wanting more, too. Andrea's hands found their way to Courtney's waist, and Courtney pulled Andrea to her, hovering her lips above Andrea's. She waited a second. Then, she pressed them together. Andrea's mouth was soft and hot. It was also moving against Courtney's in a way that told her she'd wanted this, too. When Andrea moaned, Courtney gasped into her mouth. Andrea's hands slipped under the dress again and landed on her lower back. Courtney placed her own hands on Andrea's neck, wanting the woman to shift so she could kiss her there.

"Wait," Andrea said.

Courtney pulled back, worried she was moving too quickly.

"What? Did I–"

"You're not…" Andrea pulled Courtney's hands down and looked at them. "You're not wearing your rings."

"I left them at home in my jewelry box."

Andrea looked up, meeting her eyes, and said, "You didn't have to do that for me."

"I know. I needed to do it for *me*," Courtney replied.

***

"One second," Andrea told her.

"No, don't get it," Courtney replied, pulling Andrea back into bed. "It's probably just a package or something; it can wait."

"Wait. What day is it?"

"Sunday, I think. Why?"

"Shit," Andrea said, standing up quickly.

The knock at the door had come a few seconds into Courtney's first exploration of Andrea's body of the day. It would *not* be her last. They hadn't left Andrea's house since she had arrived for their date Friday night. Courtney had been wearing Andrea's clothes for a few days now, using the extra toothbrush and borrowing the woman's hairbrush and body wash in the shower. This morning, Andrea stood there naked, though, because they'd slept naked. While sex with Andrea was amazing, waking up next to her had been even better. Now, someone was disturbing their little love nest, and Courtney wasn't all that happy about it.

"Taylor and Chelsea," Andrea explained as she slipped into her robe. "They were coming over for breakfast this morning; I totally forgot."

Courtney hopped out of bed and tossed on a pair of Andrea's sleep shorts and T-shirt.

"It's okay. Just tell them you'll be right there again."

"Taylor has a key," Andrea replied.

"Shit."

An instant later, the front door opened.

"Mom, we're here. Where are you?"

"Coming, honey!" Andrea yelled. "Just give me a second! Late start to the morning!"

"We brought scones and coffee from the café. I have an inside woman," Taylor replied.

"What do you want me to do?" Courtney asked, moving toward Andrea. "I can hide out in here until they go."

"What? No way." She took Courtney's hand. "It took me forever to get this, to find you; I'm not hiding you, Courtney."

Then, Courtney was pulled out into the living room by the hand.

"I hope you brought enough for four," Andrea told her daughter.

"What? Why–" Taylor noticed them then. "Oh."

"Hi, Courtney," Chelsea greeted, leaning into Taylor and smirking.

"Don't say a word," Andrea replied. "I'm going to go put on real clothes. I'll be right back." She leaned over and kissed Courtney on the cheek. "I'll be right back," she repeated in Courtney's ear.

"I can just come with you," Courtney suggested as Taylor crossed her arms over her chest.

"She's harmless," Andrea replied.

Then, she rushed back into her bedroom, leaving Courtney to deal with Taylor's glare.

"You had sex with my mother last night?"

"What? No, I mean, we just… I just…"

"Yes, she did!" Andrea shouted from her bedroom. "And, Taylor, knock it off!"

"Babe, come on; let's set everything up for breakfast," Chelsea said, still smiling at Courtney. "I'll share my coffee with Courtney."

"Seems like my *mother* is sharing a whole lot with Courtney!" Taylor yelled back to Andrea.

"No, we…"

Andrea emerged from the bedroom wearing a pair of sweatpants and a T-shirt.

"I watch you make out with your girlfriend nearly every time you two are around each other. You can at least be nice to mine when–" Andrea stopped and turned to Courtney with such wide, concerned eyes, that Courtney just wanted to kiss the worry away.

"No, it's okay. Keep going."

Courtney didn't mind being called Andrea's girlfriend in the slightest.

THE PROPOSITION

She loved watching the red hair between her legs. Madelyn had been growing it out since before they met, and Ashley was obsessed with giving it little tugs as her girlfriend worked her tongue into her folds.

"Fuck, that's good," she said, giving the hair one of those tugs.

Maddie groaned as she continued to lick while Ashley closed her eyes and let the orgasm begin to build. Maddie was so good at this. While they'd only been together for six months, this woman had known just how to touch Ashley from the very beginning.

"I love eating you out," Madelyn said as she climbed back up Ashley's body. "It's one of my very favorite things." She kissed Ashley, and Ashley tasted herself.

"*You* love it? That's *my* line," she said.

Ashley ran her hands through Madelyn's hair and stared up at her with those eyes that likely clearly told Madelyn that she was in love.

"We should probably get up now," Madelyn said, kissing Ashley's neck.

"You're not really giving me any reason to move right now," Ashley replied, pressing down on Madelyn's ass, silently asking her to rock her hips down and into her.

"Again?" Madelyn muttered against Ashley's neck.

"The first one turned me on even more," Ashley replied.

An hour later, they were showered and dressed. Ashley kissed Madelyn goodbye as the woman climbed onto her bicycle and took off to work. Ashley wasn't lucky enough to live within biking or walking distance, so she got into her car and drove to *The Meet Cute* to spend some time with her friend, Anna.

They hadn't hung out a lot in the past few years; really only when she'd called Anna to check in on her – the woman had been a bit of a hermit during their friendship. Recently, though, Anna had made a lot of life changes and was happy with her girlfriend, Troy. They'd also moved in together not so long ago, and Ashley knew that a proposal wasn't likely far off – Troy had that look in her eye. Ashley recognized it because she'd had it in her own eye recently. Madelyn made her happy. She made her so happy, and it had been totally unexpected.

Madelyn was only twenty-three and hadn't been looking for a relationship, and Ashley was twenty-eight, closer to twenty-nine, and not thinking about finding a younger woman to fall in love with. They'd run into each other at a frozen yogurt shop of all places. There hadn't been an empty table, and Ashley had noticed Madelyn looking around for a place to sit. That red hair and blue eyes combo had done Ashley in, and now they were celebrating their six-month anniversary by having an all-night sexathon at Ashley's place, leaving her sore and tired but still wanting.

"Hey," Anna said, motioning for Ashley to come over to her table. "I got you an iced vanilla latte."

"Cool. Thanks," Ashley said, sitting down. "Where's Troy?"

"Working," Anna replied with a smile.

"And?"

"And I told you, I don't think she's going to ask me."

"Of course, she is," Ashley replied. "She's planning a whole thing. She has to be. You guys did that long road trip not that long ago, and she's asking you to go away with her for the weekend."

"She just wants to get away. Her dad is about to give her the business. She knows it's long hours and more work after that."

"All the more reason for her to ask you to marry her before that happens, right?" Ashley argued. "I'm just saying; Troy is obviously crazy about you, and you're madly in love with her."

"Can we talk about something else?" Anna requested.

"Katelyn, I told you it's a no-go," a voice said from the counter. "They're not going to sell."

"They gave me this account, Ryan. I have to at least try," the other woman said. "Can I speak to the owner?"

"Sure," the barista replied.

But Ashley was too busy staring to follow the barista as she walked into the back room. She was staring at the woman who was dressed in that sexy pencil skirt and matching suit jacket with a button-down shirt under it. Ashley had a thing for unbuttoning a shirt on a woman. It was her weakness. Unfortunately for her, Madelyn had no reason to wear a button-down shirt. She wore a T-shirt to work most days, and when they dressed up for dates, Madelyn was usually in a dress. Ashley wasn't complaining; she loved her girlfriend in a dress. Sometimes, Madelyn wore tight dresses, and Ashley could picture everything underneath. Other times, they were loose, and Ashley could slip her hand under the hem and stroke her girlfriend to a quick orgasm. Now, she was looking this stranger up and down, and this stranger was definitely *not* her girlfriend.

"Are you okay?" Anna asked.

"I'm fine. Do you know them by any chance? You're here a lot, yeah?"

Anna turned and saw the women talking at the counter.

"Yeah, that's Ryan. I don't know who the other woman is, though."

"Her girlfriend?"

"No, Ryan is with Kelsey. She performs here a lot on

Fridays and Saturdays. They've been together for a while now. Oh, and that's Shelby." Anna pointed. "She owns the place with her wife. And the barista is new, so I don't know her."

"Hi, my name is Katelyn. I think you know my colleague, Ryan," the woman said, holding her hand out for Shelby to shake.

"Oh, no," Shelby replied, shaking it. "You're here to try to buy the place, aren't you?"

"I've just been handed the account, and–"

"You're the third person they've sent. The guy they sent after Ryan didn't convince me, either."

"I know. I was hoping we could sit down and–"

"Ryan, you could've saved her the trip," Shelby said.

"I tried," Ryan replied.

Ashley watched as Shelby shot down Katelyn's offer for a meeting about selling the café. That must mean Katelyn was an agent, worked for a bank, or something like that, at least. She looked too young to be as successful as she looked. Her dark brown hair was pulled up in a clip, and her heels looked designer, as did her bag. When she turned around toward the tables, Ashley noticed her eyes were gray. She wasn't sure she'd ever seen gray eyes on a woman in person before, and on Katelyn, they were beautiful. Katelyn was looking at her now. No, Katelyn was *smirking* at her. Ashley closed her mouth then, realizing she'd been gawking at the woman.

"Let's just grab a coffee," Ryan suggested. "Shelby, can we get…"

Ashley didn't hear the rest of Ryan's order because Katelyn was walking over to their table.

"Hi," she said with just the hint of a southern accent.

"Hi," Ashley replied.

"Katelyn," she introduced herself, holding out her hand for Ashley to shake.

"Ashley," she said, shaking it.

"I'm Anna."

"Oh," Katelyn looked over then, seemingly just now realizing someone was at Ashley's table. "Hi."

"Anna is my friend," Ashley said way too quickly.

"Right," Katelyn replied, turning back to Ashley and smiling wide.

"Hey, Anna. How are you?" Ryan asked.

"I'm good. Working today?"

"Yeah. I'll be here on Saturday night with Kels if you and Troy want to hang out with me while she performs."

"I'll ask her," Anna replied. "This is my friend, Ashley."

"Oh, hey. Nice to meet you," Ryan said with a smile.

"You too," Ashley replied, still looking at Katelyn.

"Can we join you?" Katelyn asked.

"Sure," Anna replied before Ashley could say she was just about to leave, which would have been a lie, but sitting next to Katelyn was *not* a good idea.

Ashley's heart was pounding in her chest, and it hadn't done *that* since Madelyn.

"Thanks," Katelyn said, pulling up a chair next to Ashley. "So, do you come here a lot?"

"Sometimes," Ashley replied. "With my girlfriend," she added, finally mentioning Madelyn. "She's at work."

"Got it," Katelyn replied, lowering her head for a second. "How long have you been together?"

"Six months as of yesterday," Ashley replied.

"That's nice. I've never been able to make it work with a woman that long."

"No?" Ashley asked for no reason.

"No. I work a lot, so they usually get upset when I have to cancel on them."

"Here you go," Shelby said, dropping drinks off at the table. "And, Katelyn, you can come into the café any time you want, but we won't be selling. So, if you could just kindly let your employer know that we're really not interested, no matter what they offer or try, my wife and I would appreciate it."

"Yeah, sure," Katelyn said, looking from Shelby to Ashley. "So, I clearly buy and sell commercial real estate. What do *you* do?" she asked Ashley.

***

"She's here again," Madelyn said, moving the hand that had been wandering up Ashley's thigh away.

"Hey, I was enjoying that," Ashley told her, putting Madelyn's hand back in place. "And who are you–" She looked toward the counter and saw only one person in line. "Katelyn."

"You know her?" Madelyn asked.

"I met her when I came here with Anna last week. She works with Ryan."

"Who's Ryan?"

"A friend of Anna's, I think. How do *you* know Katelyn?"

"I came in for coffee on a break from work, and I left my bike chained up outside. So, when I saw her looking at it, I went outside to make sure she wasn't thinking about stealing it or something."

"You think a woman dressed like that would steal your bike?"

"She wasn't dressed like *that*, babe. She had jeans on with holes in them, sandals, and a tank top. You never know, right? Anyway, she was just looking across the street at her car. I guess there was a meter maid there or something, and she was making sure she wasn't getting a ticket. We talked. She's cool."

"Yeah, she is." Ashley watched as Katelyn turned to look out at the patio and likely, the ocean beyond while she waited for her drink.

"You talked to her, too?"

"Just for a little while. She and Ryan had to get back to work."

"She's hot, right?" Madelyn checked.

"Excuse me?" Ashley joked. "Hi. Girlfriend. I'm sitting right here."

Madelyn laughed and said, "I know. I can still tell you when I think someone's hot, can't I?"

Ashley leaned forward and kissed her quickly.

"You can. And yes, I agree."

"Yeah? Her eyes are crazy intense. And I know she's dressed up now, but she looked good in those jeans."

"I don't know… I kind of like her all dressed up like she is now."

"Really? Should *I* dress up more?" Madelyn asked her. "You're dating a lowly dog groomer who can't afford her own car. Should I be worried?"

"No." Ashley laughed and moved Madelyn's hand higher on her thigh. "I like you in those T-shirts – they're easy to take off."

And they were. Ashley had taken them off hundreds of times by now. And while she had a thing for button-downs, she also loved her girlfriend's pale breasts revealing themselves to her as she pulled off Madelyn's shirt and the sports bra she usually wore to work.

"Hello," Katelyn said.

They both looked up, surprised to see her standing there.

"Oh, hey," Madelyn replied. "We were just talking about you."

Ashley stared wide-eyed at her girlfriend.

"You were, were you?" Katelyn said.

"Yeah, just that we'd both run into you," Ashley replied.

"Want to sit?" Madelyn offered.

"I just came in to grab a quick coffee and apologize to Shelby for coming on strong before. I've been schooled by Ryan's girlfriend that this place is pretty important to the community."

"Yeah, it's a great place," Madelyn agreed.

"We'll see you around, maybe," Ashley said.

Katelyn looked down and spotted Madelyn's hand, with Ashley's on top of it, and the location of them both.

"This is your girlfriend," Katelyn stated more than asked.

"Yes," Ashley replied.

"And this is *your* girlfriend," she said to Madelyn.

"Yeah," Maddie replied. "This is Ash."

"You two make a good couple."

"Thanks," Ashley said.

"And I asked both of you out." Katelyn laughed a little.

Ashley looked away from Madelyn.

"She asked–" Madelyn started.

"I was going to tell you, but she walked over. She asked *you* out, too?"

"Yeah, but–"

"You both said no," Katelyn interrupted. "I probably should've taken offense, but…" She sat down in the empty chair next to Ashley. "I don't know. It was… I liked talking to you both."

"So, you asked us both out?"

"Well, I asked *you* out." She turned to Ashley. "You said no. Then I met Madelyn, and I asked *her* out. So, technically, I asked you out separately, but…" She looked back and forth between them. "God, you're both really hot."

"Oh," Madelyn said, leaning back in her chair.

"I swear, I'm not like this," Katelyn added quickly. "I come on strong sometimes when I'm interested, but there was just something about meeting you both. I came back here the other day because I was hoping to run into you, Ashley. Then, I met Madelyn, and I came back *today* because I wanted to run into her."

"I thought you came here to talk to Shelby," Ashley remarked.

"Added benefit," Katelyn replied.

"So, you like both of us?" Madelyn replied.

"I don't really *know* either of you, but there's something here, isn't there?" The woman laughed a little. "I've never done this before."

"Done what?" Ashley asked.

"Asked what I'm about to ask."

"Which is?" Madelyn asked, squeezing Ashley's thigh.

"To have both of you."

"Have? Both?" Ashley squeezed Madelyn's hand on her thigh.

"Yeah, both."

***

"It's crazy, huh?" Madelyn said later while they sat on Ashley's couch.

"Yeah, nuts," Ashley replied half-heartedly.

They'd turned Katelyn down at the café, for obvious reasons; they were a couple. They were happy and in love, and not at all interested in having a threesome with someone.

"I mean, talk about forward," Madelyn added, rubbing Ashley's bare thigh.

"Yeah, we spent, like, five minutes with her, and she's telling us she wants to sleep with us." Ashley moved her own hand to Maddie's neck, rubbing the soft skin there.

"And we're just sitting there, having coffee."

"Right," Ashley echoed.

Madelyn's hand slipped into her shorts and stroked her clit over her panties.

"Fuck. You're hard, Ash." Madelyn turned her head to Ashley.

"I know," Ashley said, pressing her free hand on top of Madelyn's, encouraging her to press harder. "I need you."

Madelyn moved until she was on her knees in front of her girlfriend and pulled Ashley's shorts and panties off. Ashley spread wide for her, watching as Madelyn licked her lips.

"Ash…"

"I know," Ashley said.

"Do you want to?" She ran her index finger through Ashley's wetness. "Baby, you're soaked."

"I *have* been all day," Ashley stated, wanting to be honest.

"Me too," Madelyn replied, kissing the inside of Ashley's thigh. "Are we crazy?"

"I love you. You know that, right?"

"Yes. I love you, too," she replied, kissing up Ashley's thigh.

Ashley pulled at Madelyn's shirt until it was over her shoulders and on the floor.

"But I can't stop thinking about it. You, me, and her; how it would…"

"Feel?" Madelyn asked, kissing the top of Ashley's clit.

"Yes," Ashley gasped out.

"I can't believe I'm saying this, but I've been thinking about how much I want to watch her do this to you all day today." Madelyn's lips met her clit again.

"Wait. You have?"

"Yes," Madelyn admitted. "I know you're mine, and I'm yours, and I shouldn't want to–"

"Babe, do you want that? Forget what we should or shouldn't do."

"Yes," Madelyn repeated, looking up at her. "I've thought about it before today, too."

"Really?"

"Yeah," Madelyn replied. "I'd like you to watch me, too."

"What are you doing when I'm watching?" Ashley asked, running her hand through Madelyn's hair.

"Fucking her."

"Oh, Jesus," Ashley said. "Make me come."

"Yeah?" Madelyn checked.

"I need you. Now."

***

186

"So, it's just sex, right?"

"Yes, it would just be sex," Maddie told Katelyn. "And one time."

"Yeah," Ashley agreed. "Just once."

Katelyn nodded and said, "And you're both sure about this? I'm not trying to get in the way of your relationship."

"We're sure," Ashley replied, looking at Madelyn, who was nodding.

Katelyn nodded, too, and said, "Okay. Well, I can't say I ever saw myself doing this, but I'm in, too."

"Really?"

"Yeah."

"Okay. Um… when?" Ashley asked.

"Now?" Katelyn said.

"Now, as in *now*?" Ashley asked, clearing her throat.

"Are you free?" Katelyn asked.

"We're watching the performers," Ashley replied, motioning to the singer on the stage of *The Meet Cute.*

"You can keep watching them, or…" Katelyn leaned in, and Ashley thought she might kiss her. "We could get out of here." She didn't kiss her, but she leaned in closer, pressing their bodies together, and sucked Ashley's earlobe into her mouth.

Ashley looked at her girlfriend, whose blue eyes had darkened about three shades.

"Yeah, let's go," Maddie said, nodding rapidly.

Minutes later, they were back at Ashley's one-bedroom apartment that was the closest to the café.

"Rules?" Ashley asked once the door was closed behind them. "We should have rules, right?"

"What, like a safe word? Do you two get into that because I'm not really–"

"No," Maddie interrupted quickly. "Just, like… If anyone wants to stop, we do. Right, Ash?"

"Right," Ashley said. "And it's just that Maddie told me she wanted something specific, and I wanted to ask if you'd be okay with it."

Katelyn looked at Madelyn, running her hand down her chest, between her breasts, and asked, "What is it you want?"

"I want to watch you with Ash and to…"

Ashley walked over, stood next to her girlfriend, and took the hand that was at Madelyn's side. She moved it to the button on her own jeans and undid them. Katelyn looked down, watching the movement. Her gray eyes darkened, and she smirked then. Once the button and zipper had been undone, Ashley slipped Madelyn's hand inside her jeans and her panties.

"Oh," Madelyn uttered.

"Tell her what else you want, babe," she encouraged when Madelyn began to stroke her.

"I want to fuck you," Maddie told Katelyn, looking into Katelyn's eyes while she stroked Ashley, who was already so wet.

"With what?" Katelyn asked, leaning closer to Madelyn, her lips centimeters from Maddie's.

"My strap-on."

"And you're both… you know?"

"We're safe, and we've been…" Ashley stopped when Maddie hit a spot that had her practically ruining her panties.

"Tested. We're good," Madelyn finished. "You?"

"Yes," Katelyn replied, pressing her lips to Madelyn's, and Ashley just watched as they kissed.

She *should* have been jealous. And she'd be lying if she said she wasn't in part, but there was a much larger part of her that was so turned on, she wanted to come right now. Maddie's touches had nearly stopped, and Ashley rolled her hips into her girlfriend's palm to help her orgasm keep building. Katelyn placed her hand on the small of Ashley's back and pulled her in. Then, her lips moved from Maddie's and connected with Ashley's, and Ashley nearly exploded. Maddie's hand started moving again, her fingers finding their purpose.

"Okay?" Katelyn asked, pulling out of the kiss and

looking between them.

They both looked at each other and nodded.

Katelyn moved behind Ashley, lifted Ashley's shirt up and off, and unclasped her bra. Maddie moved into Ashley, still stroking, and then kissed her hard. Ashley now had Katelyn's hands on her breasts, massaging them while she kissed Ashley's neck. It was all too much. Well, almost. Ashley closed her eyes and let the sensations take her over.

"Can I take your pants off?" Katelyn whispered in her ear. "I've been dying to see all of you."

"Yes," Ashley replied.

Then, Katelyn's hands moved down her body, and she pushed at Ashley's jeans and panties all at once.

"You wanted to watch?" she asked.

"Yes," Maddie said.

Ashley kicked everything off, along with her shoes, and spread her legs, knowing what was about to happen. Madelyn took a step back until the back of her knees hit the sofa, and she practically flopped down. Katelyn stood up again behind Ashley, and her hand moved to Ashley's sex while the other one continued on her breast, massaging, twisting, and otherwise playing with Ashley's sensitive nipple.

"Oh, yes," Ashley moaned when Katelyn's fingers met her swollen clit.

"Babe, tell me…"

"So good," Ashley managed to get out. "Take off your shirt, baby. Let me see you play with…"

The whole time, Madelyn's eyes remained on Ashley's sex and Katelyn's hand as she pulled her shirt over her head and took off her sports bra. Then, she leaned back and began playing with her breasts.

"That's sexy," Katelyn said, nibbling on Ashley's neck. "Will you put your hand somewhere else for me?"

Ashley had to close her eyes. She was already so close.

"Fuck, that's hot," Katelyn added.

Ashley had to open her eyes then. Her girlfriend was

watching them and had one hand inside her jeans, likely inside her underwear, and the other playing with her nipple.

"Babe, I want…" Madelyn told her.

"I know," Ashley replied, knowing exactly what Madelyn wanted. "Katelyn, do you…"

"Kate."

"What?"

"My fingers are on your clit; you can call me Kate," she said. "God, you feel so good. Are you always this wet?"

Ashley didn't know what to say to that. If she said yes, she'd be lying. She got pretty wet, usually, but this was to the extreme. If she said no, Maddie might get offended or think that she'd never gotten Ashley this turned on, but Maddie had been the best sex of Ashley's life.

"Do you want to go down–" Ashley started and stopped.

"Can I?" Katelyn checked.

"Yes," Ashley replied.

"Will you keep standing up so that Maddie can see everything?"

"Yes," Ashley replied.

Normally, Ashley liked to be the only one to use her girlfriend's nickname, but it sounded so good falling from Katelyn's lips, that she let it go and instead, focused on the fact that someone other than Maddie was kneeling between her legs and sucking on her clit.

"Oh, my God," Ashley moaned, holding on to the back of Katelyn's head, keeping her in place while she connected her eyes to Maddie's. "Like this, baby?"

"Yes," Madelyn said with hooded eyes and that look that Ashley had come to love on her girlfriend. "Fuck. I'm going to come."

"No, wait for her," Katelyn told her, holding on to Ashley's legs and turning her a bit so that Madelyn had a better angle. Then, she licked Ashley once and added, "Let me make her come."

"God," Madelyn uttered.

Ashley looked down and met Katelyn's sexy as hell eyes as the woman licked her again. Then, she used just the tip of her tongue against Ashley's clit, meaning Maddie could see that tongue slip between Ashley's folds. And that was it; Maddie came hard. Katelyn moved back into Ashley and sucked on her clit. Ashley came a second later, holding Katelyn against her until she could hardly stand up anymore. Katelyn moved up her body and pulled Ashley's mouth to her own for a searing kiss. Thankfully, her arm had also wrapped around Ashley, and she was keeping Ashley on her feet. Madelyn was on the move then. Ashley opened her eyes to see Maddie heading toward the bedroom without saying a word to either of them.

"Bed," Ashley said, kissing Katelyn and moving the woman backward while she undid the buttons of Katelyn's shirt, just like in her fantasy but better because this was real.

By the time they'd gotten to Ashley's room, Katelyn was only in her light-blue panties; the rest of her clothes were strewn about Ashley's apartment. Ashley noticed Maddie standing with only her special shorts on and a dildo between her legs. A second later, Katelyn was pulling off those bikinis.

"Fuck, you're hot like that," Katelyn said, flopping back on the bed.

Ashley watched as Madelyn climbed on top of the other woman. She lay next to them as her girlfriend kissed Katelyn, sucked on her neck, and then her nipples. Every now and then, Maddie's hand would move to Ashley's breast or between her legs for a few strokes, but Ashley was more than content to just watch them like this.

"Inside," Katelyn breathed out as Maddie started stroking her clit. "Fuck me."

Maddie reached between her legs and coated the toy with Katelyn's wetness. Then, she slipped inside her.

"Oh, God," Ashley said, leaning down over Katelyn and kissing her while Maddie rocked into her.

Ashley squeezed Katelyn's breast, causing Maddie to

moan. She looked up at her then and kissed her as Maddie rocked. Then, she moved behind Maddie and waited. As Maddie rocked harder, Ashley reached into the shorts from behind and stroked Maddie's hard clit.

"God, baby. You're so ready."

"Yes," Maddie said.

"Fuck, so am I!" Katelyn yelled.

"Come for me," Maddie said to Katelyn. "God, Ash. Don't stop!"

They stayed like that, with Ashley staring down into Katelyn's eyes and stroking Maddie from behind as Maddie fucked Katelyn harder and harder by the woman's request. When Katelyn closed her eyes, Maddie came hard into Ashley's hand. Then, Katelyn yelled Maddie's name, and quickly after, she yelled Ashley's, too.

***

"She's here," Ashley said to Katelyn.

"Finally. I have to go to work, Ash," Katelyn told her. "Hey, Mads."

"Hey," Maddie replied, smiling at them both before sitting down at the table Katelyn had scored for them when she'd arrived first.

"So, you called. I came," Katelyn said. Then, she closed her eyes. "Poor choice of words." She laughed. "Is this where you tell me it was one time and that we should be friends? You already told me the one-time thing before we had the one time."

Katelyn hadn't slept over that night. They'd enjoyed one another one more time before she had left around midnight after kissing them both goodbye. Maddie and Ashley had taken a shower together and enjoyed each other again before they had talked for several hours. They'd been on the same, surprising page again, and they'd called Katelyn the next day asking to meet.

"No, that's not why we called," Madelyn said, looking

over at Ashley as if making sure this was still okay.

"You *don't* think we should be friends?" Katelyn asked. "Was the sex *that* bad?"

"Um…" Shelby set a plate between Katelyn and Ashley. "One chocolate cupcake. Sorry for interrupting." Then, she walked off.

"I got us three forks," Ashley said, holding one up to Madelyn and to Katelyn.

"I'm good," Maddie replied.

"These are your favorite."

"They're mine, too," Katelyn said, peeling the paper wrapper away.

"We want to be with you again," Madelyn blurted out.

"And here are your drinks," Shelby said, holding a tray with three coffees on it. She placed them all down and added, "Next time, I'll leave them on the bar for you." Then, she disappeared.

"You want to have sex again?" Katelyn asked.

"Yes," Ashley replied, taking a bite of the cupcake. "We talked about it, and if you're interested, we'd like to do that again another time."

Katelyn took a bite of the cupcake. Then, she put another piece on the fork and held it out for Madelyn.

"Just a bite," she said. "For me."

Maddie cleared her throat, leaned forward, and took it off the fork.

"Do you want to?" Ashley asked.

"My place this time," Katelyn said. "I have a vibrator I want to try on *you.*" She winked at Ashley. "And I didn't get to taste you last time." She met Maddie's eyes. "Friday night?"

"Yes," Maddie said quietly.

"I'll text you my address." She leaned over and kissed Ashley on the cheek. "I cannot wait to watch you come again." Then, she stood and kissed Maddie on the cheek. "And I want you behind me next time."

Maddie nodded.

***

It went on like that for the next several weeks. Every Friday night, they met at Ashley's or at Katelyn's place since Maddie still had roommates, and they didn't want them to know what they were doing. And it started differently every time. Sometimes, Katelyn would spread her legs once they were all inside, revealing that she hadn't been wearing any underwear. Other times, Maddie would wear her strap-on, coming prepared, and Ashley would rub her through her pants while Katelyn kissed her. It was thrilling, and despite their Friday night activities, Ashley and Maddie were having more sex than ever, which was saying something. It was as if Katelyn got them hotter for each other, which Ashley hadn't thought possible.

"Can I sit on your face while you're inside her?" Katelyn asked that fifth Friday.

Maddie just nodded. Ashley had the dildo inside her, and Maddie was on her back. Ashley was rolling her hips, letting the fullness slowly bring her to orgasm. Katelyn turned to face Ashley and lowered herself onto Maddie's face. She leaned forward and kissed Ashley. Then, Ashley felt Katelyn's palm against her clit.

"Fuck, Kate," she let out, holding on to Katelyn's hips for balance as the woman stroked her clit and Maddie filled her up.

"There, Mads," Katelyn said as Maddie sucked on her clit. "Fuck, I'm already…"

"Yes," Ashley echoed. "Me too. Baby, I'm coming."

At this point, she wasn't sure which woman she was calling *baby*, though.

Katelyn had stayed that night, and she'd fallen asleep between Ashley and Madelyn around four in the morning. The queen-sized bed was small for three people, but oddly, they seemed to fit together. Maddie had always slept hot, so she was on the outside, facing away from them. Ashley slept cold and liked to cuddle at night. Katelyn had wrapped her arms around her in the early morning. When Ashley had woken up like that, and it was nice. She didn't know where to put that feeling, so she'd gotten up before the other two and went to brush her teeth.

***

"Did you not get my message?" Ashley asked the following Friday.

"No, but my phone's in my bag." Katelyn pulled her phone out and checked the readout. "Oh, you canceled."

"Maddie is still at work."

"She's grooming dogs after nine at night?"

"Her other job," Ashley replied. "Come in." She motioned for Katelyn to enter the apartment. "She got a second job a few weeks ago. Dog grooming barely pays the bills, and her student loans are killing her. She's working as a barback a few nights a week. She's new, so normally she gets the non-busy nights, like Tuesday and Wednesday, but the regular Friday-night person called in sick, so they asked her to work instead."

"Oh, bummer," Katelyn replied. "I was really looking forward to tonight."

"Sorry. I texted as soon as I found out. She went straight to the bar from the groomers."

"Sure. Do you want to hang out?"

"Hang out?"

Katelyn laughed and said, "Yes. I know we have sex whenever I'm here, but we *can* just hang out."

"Oh, I know. I didn't mean it to sound like that," Ashley told her.

"Come on. Tell me about your day; I'll tell you about mine. I brought wine with me. It's been a long week for me."

They talked and finished that wine by the time Madelyn got to Ashley's around one in the morning.

"I'll call a car," Katelyn announced around two, after

they'd all sat talking about Maddie's night at the bar. "I'm too drunk to drive."

"Just stay," Madelyn said.

"Yeah, just stay," Ashley agreed.

***

That was the first time Katelyn stayed over when nothing happened. She had borrowed a pair of Ashley's shorts and a T-shirt of Madelyn's, and she slept between them again, leaving before the two of them woke up.

"Did you two do anything?" Madelyn asked.

"What? No."

"You didn't… Without me?"

"Maddie, no. Why would you think that?"

"I don't know. We never really talked about what might happen if one of us was busy and Katelyn was free."

"Is that something you *want* to talk about?"

"We've been honest with each other since this whole thing started, right?"

"Yes," Ashley said.

"So, we should continue being honest; totally open communication all the way."

"Agreed," Ashley replied.

Maddie sighed and said, "I love you."

"I know, Maddie. I love you, too. Just spit it out."

"I think about it sometimes," Maddie admitted.

"Being with Katelyn? Without me?"

"Yeah, but they're just thoughts."

"You want to just have sex with her without me there?"

"It's not just that… I wouldn't unless you were okay with it. And I'd want to know if you wanted to be with her that way, too."

"So, I have sex with her, you have sex with her, you and I have sex with each other, and then we all have sex together?" Ashley let out a small laugh. "That sounds complicated."

"It is, I think," Maddie agreed. "But… I don't know. It's been going on with all three of us for weeks now, and it seems like it's going well. It *is* going well, right?"

"I'm sore half the time," Ashley replied, smiling at her girlfriend.

"But the best kind of sore, right?" Madelyn checked.

"Yes." Ashley smiled at her and then cupped Maddie's cheek. "You know we can't just decide something like this; we need to talk to Katelyn."

"I know. I wasn't going to talk to her without talking to you first, though."

"How would this even work?" Ashley asked. "*You're* my girlfriend, Maddie."

"I know," Maddie replied, kissing Ashley sweetly. "That wouldn't change."

"But we're sleeping with someone else; the same person."

"Not yet. We have to talk to her about it."

"And if she says yes?"

"We figure it out from there, but the moment any of us changes our mind, we stop."

"Which part?"

"Whatever needs to stop."

***

Maddie's night with Katelyn had been last night, and Ashley and Katelyn had tomorrow night planned. That meant that tonight, Ashley was staring at her girlfriend from one end of the sofa, trying to figure out how to bring up the topic they'd both been avoiding since Maddie had come over an hour ago.

"Do you want to know?" Maddie checked.

She'd always been able to read Ashley so well. From moment one, Maddie had had her figured out.

"Yes."

Maddie turned to her on the sofa and said, "I went to her place. We fooled around."

"What does that mean, *fooled around?*"

"We did everything, but not at first."

"At first?" Ashley asked.

"We stopped to watch a movie." Maddie shrugged. "And then, we kind of started up again and…"

Ashley nodded rapidly, trying to take it all in.

"You watched a movie?"

"I know." Maddie laughed. "It was weird, but it just kind of happened. We were on her sofa; I had my mouth… Do you want the details, babe?"

"No." Ashley closed her eyes. "Yes."

Madelyn moved a little closer, putting Ashley's feet in her lap, and said, "I was sucking on her nipple, she was running her hands through my hair, and we just started talking." She laughed a little again. "She asked me about work, and I asked about her sister. They fought about their grandma moving–"

"Into the nursing home, yeah," Ashley recalled.

"At some point, I got up to get us some water, and we sat there, talking, until she turned the TV on, and then we were watching a movie. When it ended, she… Well, she started touching me again, and then we went to her room."

Ashley nodded rapidly again and asked, "And?"

"And, it was–" Madelyn rubbed Ashley's feet. "What am I allowed to say here, Ash?"

"Allowed? You can say whatever you want, Maddie. There's no *allowed* about it."

"I liked it," Maddie replied honestly. "I felt guilty right after, and then again this morning, but I liked it."

"Did you stay over there?"

"No, we didn't talk about that part, so I went home."

"Are you going to do it again?" Ashley checked.

"We didn't set anything up," Maddie said. "It depends on what we *all* want, though, right?"

"Right," Ashley said.

***

"Did you wear that just for me?" Ashley asked when Katelyn walked into her apartment.

"I might have," Katelyn replied. "I remember you telling me how much you like unbuttoning shirts." She moved into Ashley instantly and slammed the door behind her. "Hi." She smiled at her and pulled Ashley flush against her.

"Hi," Ashley said with a smile.

Katelyn squinted at her and said, "Do we need to talk about it?"

"Which part?" Ashley asked, laughing.

"Any of it. All of it." Katelyn brushed Ashley's long blonde hair away from her neck. "You know about Mads and me. I assume she told you everything."

"Yeah."

Katelyn kissed Ashley's neck and asked, "Did it bother you?"

"Yes," Ashley admitted.

"But not enough to cancel tonight?"

"No," Ashley replied.

"Did it bother you because you were jealous that I was touching her?"

"Yes."

"Do you think it's bothering her that I'm with you right now?"

"Yes," Ashley repeated as Katelyn's hands slipped up under her skirt, and she pulled Ashley's thong down her legs.

Ashley stepped out of it and stared at the finger it now dangled off of.

"For me?" Katelyn asked.

Ashley nodded.

"Will you sit down for me and spread those sexy as fuck legs?"

"Can I ask you something?"

"Anything," Katelyn said as she backed Ashley up

against her own sofa.

"You and Maddie didn't just have sex; you had a date."

"We watched a movie." Katelyn shoved Ashley down onto the sofa, smirking at her when Ashley immediately spread her legs for her.

"And then had sex – that's basically a date."

"Okay. I guess, yeah," Katelyn said, kneeling in front of her and holding on to Ashley's knees lightly. "Is that a problem? It wasn't intentional; it just kind of happened."

"But you don't want to watch a movie with me?"

"I will happily watch a movie with you tonight if you want," Katelyn replied. "But I'm already on my knees, babe. Can we get each other off before we take two hours to watch some lame rom-com?"

Ashley hadn't missed the term of endearment they hadn't used before, but she nodded. Katelyn moved her head between Ashley's legs and began licking at the wetness that had already pooled there.

"Do you need me, Ash? You seem like you need me right now."

"Yes," Ashley said, knowing it was true and feeling awful about it.

She didn't just need *someone.* She didn't even need Maddie right now. She needed Katelyn.

"I love when you're wet like this," Katelyn told her.

Ashley just closed her eyes in response and let Katelyn take her with her mouth.

An hour later, her own head had just emerged from between Katelyn's legs. They'd moved to her bedroom and had spent that whole hour exploring one another really for the first time, and Ashley had loved every minute of it.

"Movie?" Katelyn asked as Ashley pulled out of a kiss.

Ashley chuckled, "I think I need a shower first."

"Good call," Katelyn replied, kissing her again before she slipped out from underneath Ashley. "I'm joining you, by the way. I'm not going to be the only one smelling like sex while we watch a movie."

***

"So, it was a date?" Maddie asked the next day at the café. "You were on a date?"

"You guys were on a date, too," Ashley reminded.

"But you had sex and *then* watched a movie."

"So?"

"So, we fooled around, but we didn't have sex until after, and then I left. She slept over, Ash."

"It was five in the morning; I wasn't going to kick her out," Ashley replied.

"Did you kiss her when you woke up?" Maddie asked.

"No, she was gone before I woke up, Maddie."

"Would you *have*?" Maddie asked.

"Maddie, I don't–" Ashley stopped. "Maybe we should all talk. I think we might have taken this too far. We can go back to it just being the three of us, and you and I can go back to being just us, or we could tell Katelyn it's over."

"All of it?" Madelyn asked.

"I won't lose you, Maddie."

"I know," Maddie replied.

"Hey," Anna said, stopping by their table.

"Hey, I didn't see you come in," Ashley replied.

"Yeah, Troy is ordering. Are you guys sticking around? We can join you."

"Sure," Maddie said, smiling up at Anna.

***

"This is one of those serious talks, isn't it?" Katelyn asked the following Friday night.

They were at Ashley's place, and Maddie and Ashley were on the sofa. Katelyn moved to sit between them, which seemed about right given the circumstances.

"It's done?" she asked. "I assume that's why you both look so serious. Mads, your fists are clenched so tightly, you're going to have bruises. And, Ash, you look like you might throw up."

"I'm okay," Ashley replied.

"We took things too far, didn't we?" Katelyn asked.

"I don't know," Maddie replied. "It's weird."

"Okay." Katelyn took a breath. "Tell me. What's weird about it?"

"You went on a date with my girlfriend."

"No, I had *sex* with your girlfriend. I had sex with you, too, Mads."

"It wasn't just that, though. There were movies, and you stayed over with Ash."

"I fell asleep. It was crazy early. Are you mad I stayed at Ash's, but you didn't stay at my place? You left on your own. I told you that you could stay."

"I'm not mad," Maddie replied.

"What *are* you, then?" Ashley asked, realizing she didn't know, either.

"I don't know. Confused. Scared."

"I'm confused, too," Katelyn shared.

"You are?" Ashley asked.

"Yeah. You guys know I have feelings, too, right? I'm not just someone who has threesomes every week and then has sex with a couple separately. I've never done this before, either. I'm twenty-five; I've had sex with two women other than you guys – my first girlfriend in college and the woman I dumped about a year ago. That's it."

"Well, what are *you* thinking about all of this?" Ashley asked.

"That I like it. I'm confused and scared, too, but I'd like it to continue. I don't know what that means."

"You want to continue *all* of it?" Maddie asked.

"Yes. Look, it's weird for me. You two are a couple; you basically live together without living together. And I'm an outsider – I stop by every Friday night, we have sex, and I leave. Sometimes, I stay, but it's because it's late and you don't want me driving home, or it's really early, and it's easier for me to leave from here. But neither of you has actually told me you want me to stay because you *want* me here."

Ashley looked from Katelyn to Madelyn. Maddie gave Ashley a small smile.

"I love Ashley."

"I know that," Katelyn said.

"I just don't know what to do with what I…"

"It's okay, Maddie," Ashley told her.

Madelyn nodded and said, "With what I feel for you."

Ashley closed her eyes.

"Ash, I love you. Nothing will change that," Maddie said quickly.

Ashley opened her eyes and nodded at her.

"Ash, what are *you* feeling?" Katelyn asked her.

"I love Maddie. I saw her for the first time, and I knew something then. I wasn't looking for it, but there it was."

It was Katelyn's turn to nod.

"But when I saw you in *The Meet Cute* for the first time, it was like…"

Katelyn turned to her and said, "Yeah?"

"Yeah," Ashley replied.

"For me, too," Katelyn said, smiling. "It was why I came over and introduced myself." Then, she turned to Madelyn, adding, "And I felt it with you, too, when you accused me of being a potential bike thief."

"I couldn't tell what you were staring at. It looked like you were–"

"I know." Katelyn laughed.

Ashley laughed as well. Then, Madelyn laughed.

"So? What now?" Katelyn asked when the laughter died down.

"I'd like you to stay," Ashley said. "But I don't think we should have sex tonight."

"You don't?" Katelyn asked.

"Let's just all hang out."

"Movie?" Maddie asked.

"I can order us something to eat," Katelyn offered.

"That sounds good," Ashley said.

"And when the movie's over, and the pizza is gone? What then?" Katelyn asked.

"Then, we both kiss you goodnight, and you go home."

"Oh."

"But Maddie goes home, too."

"I do?" Maddie asked.

"Yes, Maddie," Ashley told her. "We all have a date night tonight. Since it's technically our first, I think we should all stay at our own places."

Katelyn smiled at that idea, which made Ashley happy.

"Who's picking the movie, though?" Maddie asked.

***

"I got *you* a chocolate cupcake, I got *you* a blueberry scone, and I got *me* a fork so that I can steal from both of you," Katelyn announced, sitting down at the table. "And Chelsea is bringing over our drinks in a minute." She leaned over and kissed Ashley. "Hi." Then, she leaned over and kissed Madelyn. "And hi."

"Hi," Ashley said, chuckling. "You can steal whatever you want, but you didn't get anything for yourself?"

"No, I can't stay long; I have to head to a client location for a negotiation meeting. I'm this close to locking in a massive commission, and if I do, I will move up in the pecking order at work. That's especially true now that Ryan is leaving."

"Oh, yeah?" Maddie asked.

"She's starting her own company," Katelyn explained. "She told me yesterday." Katelyn stole a bite of Maddie's cupcake, winking at her, and said, "Thanks, babe."

"I like the icing more anyway," Maddie replied.

"Here are your drinks," Chelsea told them. "Yours was to-go, right, Katelyn?"

"Yup. Thank you."

"No problem." Chelsea placed the drinks and walked off, leaving them alone on the patio.

"So, I'll see you tonight?" Katelyn asked Ashley.

"Yeah, I'll pick you up at seven."

"Cool," she replied, stealing a bite of the blueberry scone she'd gotten for Ashley. "And I'll see *both* of you tomorrow night." Katelyn leaned over and kissed Madelyn a little longer than she probably should be doing in public. "And I can't wait for you to do that thing you do to me sometimes."

"That thing?" Madelyn checked, lifting her eyebrow.

"The one where you make me scream every time you do it."

"Oh, *that* thing," Maddie replied.

"As for you," Katelyn leaned over to Ashley. "I'll be wearing something special for tonight."

She kissed her long and slow until Ashley heard someone clearing their throat. Ashley expected it to be Madelyn, but when she pulled back, she saw Anna and Troy standing there.

"Oh, hey," Ashley said, wiping her mouth, knowing Katelyn's lipstick was likely all over her lips, as it was on Madelyn's.

"Hey," Anna said. "What's…"

"Yeah, I should probably fill you in."

So, she did.

Katelyn left first, and then Maddie left for work almost right after. That left Ashley to explain what was going on between them to her friend and her friend's girlfriend.

"So, you're *all* together now?" Anna asked.

"We're dating. I mean, Maddie and I are still together, but we're both dating Kate, too."

"How does that work?" Troy asked.

"It's only been a couple of weeks, but so far, so good."

"So, you have sex with both of them?" Troy asked.

"Yes."

"And they have sex with each other?" Anna asked.

"Yes."

"Do you all have sex together?" Troy asked.

"Yes," Ashley said again.

"Damn," Troy replied. "That sounds complicated and confusing to me."

"Good answer," Anna told her, running her hand through Troy's messy short hair.

"No judgement here – whatever works for you, Ash – but I'm a one-woman woman."

"She's full of good answers today," Anna joked. Then, she turned to Ashley. "Are you sure this is what you want? You and Madelyn seemed so happy."

"We were. We still are. I know it's hard to understand – and, trust me, it's hard to explain, too – but when we first saw Katelyn, we were both totally into her right away. In the beginning, it was just sex, and it seemed to make Maddie and I want each other even more. I came home from work earlier just to be with Maddie, and she put more effort into planning our date nights when it was her turn. She also sees how ambitious Kate is and got a second job so she could pay off her student loans faster, and she's actually going to try to find a job she really wants, too. Katelyn is good for me, too. She's more assertive and direct and just tells me what she's thinking, what she wants. She encourages me to do the same thing, and – I don't know – I just feel better recently."

"And you don't think the sex has anything to do with that?" Troy teased.

"I'm sure it does," Ashley replied, laughing. "But it's more than that, too. We don't just sleep together now; we go on dates. Kate and I have one tonight. She went out with Maddie last night. It's like she's just opened things up for us; and I don't just mean in bed. She, strangely enough, is what we both need at the same time. And those needs are different, so it's crazy, but it seems to be working."

"Well, if you're happy, I'm happy for you," Anna told her.

"Thank you," Ashley replied, smiling at her friend.

***

Things had been good. They'd also been interesting. They'd made a few more rules to try to make things clear. For example, they weren't allowed to interfere in the relationship the other two women had – there would be no Madelyn and Ashley versus Katelyn or any other possible combination. It had only been a couple of weeks, but they'd had two dates out with all three of them, and they'd had two separate dates as well.

Madelyn and Ashley had gone to dinner and a walk on the beach. Ashley and Katelyn had gone to a movie and then an art show. Madelyn and Katelyn had gone to the Saturday night performances here at the café and then back to Katelyn's place for a movie. It took a lot of conscious scheduling now that Maddie was working late three nights a week and Katelyn's job meant she didn't always have a normal nine-to-five schedule, but they had a group text going and then separate texts as well, and they just promised to over-communicate with each other as much as possible. That meant a lot of work, but so far, Ashley thought it had been worth it.

"Hey, beautiful," Ashley greeted when Katelyn opened her front door later that night.

"Hi there," Katelyn replied, smiling a little shyly at Ashley.

Ashley had noticed that Katelyn could go from sexy and assertive to shy when given a compliment pretty quickly.

"I thought we could–"

"Hold that thought," Katelyn interrupted, letting her in. "I have to make a quick call to a client. The meeting today didn't go as well as I'd hoped, and she said if I don't call her tonight to lock this in, she might not go with the number we discussed, after all."

"Oh, no problem," Ashley replied, walking into the apartment. "We can just hang out here until you're done."

"Thank you," Katelyn said, kissing Ashley on the cheek.

Katelyn made her first call in the office of her two-bedroom apartment. The second call came later when they were making out on the sofa.

"Shit. Sorry," she said.

Ashley didn't mind; she just watched TV while Katelyn talked to her client on the other end of the sofa. Eventually, Katelyn took Ashley's legs in her lap and rubbed Ashley's calves while she talked. When that call ended, Ashley was already invested in the episode she was watching, so Katelyn ordered them food and moved to lie behind Ashley on the sofa, wrapping her arm around Ashley's waist and pulling her back against herself.

"I might pass out before the food gets here," she admitted. "Long week."

"Babe, it's fine. I can wake you when it gets here."

"But I wore a thing for you."

Ashley laughed and kissed Katelyn's hand, pulling it up between her breasts to rest there.

"You can wear it again another time. Tomorrow night maybe, when we're all together."

"No, this one is just for you," Katelyn said softly, kissing the back of Ashley's neck.

"Do you have one just for Maddie?"

"Yes," she said.

"I wore that thong just for you that night," Ashley shared.

"Yeah?"

"Yeah. Maddie's not really a fan."

"And I am *definitely* a fan," Katelyn replied. "Now, we have to stop talking about this; I'm getting turned on, and I'm so tired."

Ashley turned in Katelyn's arms and looked at the woman who had her eyes closed. She cupped Katelyn's cheek and kissed her lips. Then, she slid that hand down between them.

"What are you doing?"

"Unbuttoning your jeans," Ashley replied.

She unbuttoned and unzipped them, slipping her hand inside Katelyn's panties a second later.

"Oh, you're killing me. Please don't be a tease."

Ashley chuckled and said, "I won't. Just let me take care of you, okay?"

"Yes, please," Katelyn replied against Ashley's lips.

***

"How would it even work? Do we get three bedrooms? Four bedrooms?" Ashley asked.

"I don't know. We could do three and see how that goes. Four would be nice, though – one bedroom for the three of us when we all want to sleep together, but then we'd each have our own that would be our space," Katelyn said, straddling Ashley's hips and wrapping her arms around Ashley's neck.

"I don't think there are a lot of four-bedroom apartments around here."

"We could get one with three for now, and later, we can find a house."

"A house?" Ashley asked, kissing between Katelyn's breasts over her shirt.

"Yeah. Why not?"

"Who gets the master bedroom?" Maddie asked, coming into the living room after taking a shower.

"We could make the master the room we all share. Also, hi," Katelyn said.

After work, Maddie had gone straight to the shower, and Katelyn had let herself into Ashley's apartment with her key a few minutes later.

"Hi, love," Maddie replied, leaning down and kissing her. Then, she kissed Ashley. "Hi, love. So, we're thinking a three-bedroom place?" she asked, sitting next to them on the sofa, only wearing a towel around her body and running her hand through her long red hair.

"We can sign a one-year lease and see how it goes. My lease isn't up for another six months," Katelyn said. "But with that nice commission I just made, I can afford to keep it."

"You want to keep your place?" Ashley asked, moving her hands under Katelyn's flowy skirt.

"Not because of what you're thinking," Katelyn said. "Just because we should. Your lease is up in two months. Mads doesn't want to live with her roommate anymore, and her lease is up next month. We can move in together, and if something happens, there's still my old place. I don't want a backup plan, Ash, but I think it's smart. It's not like any of us thought we'd be with two people; it just happened."

"I think it's smart," Maddie agreed, nodding.

"I just don't like the idea of having a place *just in case*," Ashley replied, running her hands up and down Katelyn's thighs. "I like that we're making plans for the future."

"I know; I've seen the spreadsheet," Maddie said, reaching over and placing her hand on the back of Ashley's neck, rubbing the tension out of it. "And I love you for it."

"Think of it like this," Katelyn suggested, reaching for the top of Maddie's towel and pulling it apart. "If we get a three-bedroom place, I'll still need an office when I work from home. I can use my old place for that, and you can, too, if you want; you work from home sometimes. There are two bedrooms there, and one can be your office." She glanced down at Maddie's body. "And you can feel free to visit either of us at work anytime, Mads. Towels are optional."

"We were supposed to be getting ready for dinner," Ashley noted, watching Katelyn's gray eyes darken when she stared greedily at Maddie's body.

"I still have to shower. We can take advantage of that," Katelyn replied, looking down at Ashley and reaching for the buttons on her own shirt. "Your thumbs are already playing with my clit over my panties, babe."

They were? That was news to her. Madelyn smiled at Ashley and then lifted Katelyn's skirt up. Sure enough, both of Ashley's thumbs were moving against and around Katelyn's clit.

"And now that you've got me all worked up, you two will have to do something about it," Katelyn added.

"What do you want?" Maddie asked, her eyes darkening as she watched Ashley work their girlfriend up.

"You... from behind... while I..." Katelyn's hips began to move. "Suck on Ash's clit... until she screams."

"Fuck," Ashley whispered and pressed against Katelyn's clit harder.

"And then..." Katelyn said, rolling those sexy hips against Ashley. "I want to use that toy I got for you, Mads, while you're inside Ash."

Madelyn stood up, leaving the damp towel on the sofa, and said, "Let's go."

***

They'd been together for nine months before they actually made the move. The three-bedroom apartment allowed them each to have their own room, for them to have space when it was just two of them, and a king-sized bed in Katelyn's room was for when it was all three of them. It was crazy to a lot of people, but it worked for them. Katelyn was like this missing piece they hadn't known they'd needed.

"Are you sure we have to do this? We can just keep on letting them think we're all just roommates," Maddie said.

"Babe, we're not just roommates. You were on your knees in front of me this morning in our kitchen while Kate was behind me; I don't think roommates do that."

"I know I never did with my roommates," Katelyn remarked, moving hair out of Maddie's face before she placed her other hand in Ashley's lap. "But if you're not ready,

Mads, we can wait. I know my parents coming to town wasn't planned, and they're not going to understand this at all, but that's too bad. I love you both, and I want them to know."

"It happened," Anna told them, running over to the table.

"What happened?" Ashley asked.

Anna held up her hand. Then, Ashley saw Troy walking up behind her, smiling wide.

"Oh, *that*? You're engaged?" Ashley asked.

"Troy asked me last night. I said yes."

"About time, Troy. What took so long?" Madelyn chimed in.

"Hey, I wanted to wait until after my dad retired and things got settled. Now, we can plan a wedding."

"That's great, guys. Congrats," Katelyn told the two of them.

They all stood up from their table at *The Meet Cute* and hugged the women in turn. Then, Anna and Troy went to get drinks before they'd come back to join them.

"Ryan asked me to join her company," Katelyn blurted out of nowhere.

"What?" Ashley asked.

"Last week. I've been thinking about it since, but it means starting over. It's residential and much smaller, so I won't be making as much as I am now."

"Do you want to do it?" Maddie asked her.

"Actually, I think I do. It's weird. I worked pretty much all hours of the day before, and I loved it, but then I met you two, and this thing with us started, and I found myself still loving my work but also wanting to be with you, guys. I don't want to work all day, every day anymore. I'd like to still work hard and make good money – I mean, I want that house for us."

Ashley took Katelyn's hand and entwined their fingers.

"We don't need it tomorrow; the apartment is fine."

"Yeah," Maddie added. "And I have a bunch of interviews lined up, so I'm bound to get one of them, and then I can quit my jobs and make more money. I've got my student loans on a payment plan, so anything extra I make can go toward the house."

"You should take the job if you want it. If not, that's fine, too, but it's your career, Kate," Ashley said.

"I'll talk to Ryan tomorrow. I think I need more information before I decide officially, but I know that I'm always so tired these days, and that's because of work. If I can slow things down just a bit, I think I'll be happier. Plus, I'll be in residential, so… I'll know about all the good listings." She winked at Maddie and then turned to Ashley. "I love you." She kissed her. "And I love you." She turned and kissed Maddie.

"I love you, too," Maddie said.

"Come on. Before you have to run off to work, let's all take a walk on the beach," Ashley suggested.

"What about Anna and Troy?" Maddie asked.

"They'll still be here when we get back. I want time with my two loves right now," Ashley replied, smiling at each of them in turn.

FIRST LOVE

Georgia was nervous. She knew her parents would be upset, but they'd told her to go out and get a job, and that was what she'd done. Now, she had to tell them that it was as a barista. No, they wouldn't have a problem with that; they'd actually suggested she try to find something like that. But at sixteen, she couldn't get hired at most coffee houses. She could, however, get a job at *The Meet Cute Café*. They hired baristas at sixteen. So, she'd filled out the application, had the interview with Shelby, and had gotten her very first job. She didn't *need* the money – her parents had enough money – but they wanted to teach her a valuable life lesson and make her work for a car. Technically, they'd bought it for her already, but the conditions of their agreement meant that she paid them monthly for the car and had to pay for the gas on top of that, and they'd take care of the insurance payments. Georgia liked her car, and she wanted to be able to afford it, so that was what had brought her to the café.

No, her parents wouldn't mind her slinging coffee at a beachside café. They just wouldn't like that it was *The Meet Cute*; the café predominantly frequented by women who loved women and other people along the spectrum of gender and sexuality. As conservative Christians, they also probably wouldn't like having a gay daughter, but she wasn't planning on telling them that any time soon.

"Another new person?" Georgia asked. "I thought you were just hiring me."

"That was the plan," Shelby replied. "But Chelsea is leaving me now."

"Sorry, Aunt Shelby," Chelsea said as she put dishes into the dishwasher.

"It's okay. I always knew you'd be moving on at some point. You've worked here since you were sixteen, and it's crazy that you're twenty-two now."

"You got a new job?" Georgia asked.

"I got *a* job, period. I just graduated from college. I'm going to be working about thirty minutes away, and I'm moving in with my girlfriend. Well, we basically already live together, but I stay at her place all the time and technically still live at home with my parents. She's in law school about an hour away from here, so we're getting our own place, finally."

"Finally? How long have you been together?"

"About three years. We met when I was a freshman. *Here*, actually; we met here. You'll see her. She comes in all the time to hang out with me, and even though I'm moving a little far away to come in every day, I'll still come by for open mic nights and coffee on the weekends when I can."

"Three years? Wow," Georgia said, stacking mugs on the shelf in the back room.

"Yeah. Crazy, huh? She's gorgeous, smart, funny, and so sweet. I still can't believe she wants me sometimes."

"You're all of those things, too," Shelby remarked.

"You have to say that; we're related," Chelsea waved her off. "Oh. Customer. Want me to walk you through it?" she asked Georgia.

"Sure," Georgia replied.

Chelsea had been training her, and while Georgia was picking it up quickly, she still had a lot to learn. She'd burned the milk yesterday and overcharged a customer accidentally because she hit the wrong button.

"Kelsey, hey," Chelsea said to the customer who was standing next to another woman. "Ryan, how's business?"

"Good. I finally got Katelyn to join the dark side. Took a while, but she's on the team now, so we've got five agents and me now."

"She's a superstar," the other woman Georgia now knew to be Kelsey said, taking Ryan's hand and winking at her. "She just sold a massive five-bedroom place on the water, so I brought her here for a treat. Well, I gave her a treat before we left the house, but–"

"Kels!" Ryan exclaimed.

"What? Did you not like your treat?"

"Okay… I'll have a large iced latte," Ryan said. "And she'll have a–"

"Large coffee to-go," Kelsey finished for her. "And can we get two croissants, too?"

"Chocolate or plain?" Chelsea asked.

"One of each," Ryan replied.

Chelsea took care of the register, and Georgia got the croissants into a paper bag and then watched Chelsea make the latte after Georgia poured the coffee into the cup. They placed everything on the bar and watched the women leave toward the patio.

"So, they're together?"

"Yeah, for a while now," Chelsea replied. "Actually, they met here, too, I think."

"They did," Shelby said, coming out of the back room with bottles of hazelnut syrup.

"You'll see them a lot, too. Kelsey performs here almost every week, and they just bought a place together a few blocks from here, so they're usually in at least a few times a week. They don't have usual drinks, or I'd tell you what to make for them; they switch things up a lot."

"Okay," Georgia said, cataloging the information for later.

"Georgia, can you go clean up the table on the patio for me, please?" Shelby asked.

"Sure," she replied.

"Erica, haven't seen you in here in a while," Shelby said to a woman who walked into the café hand in hand with another woman and a boy who looked to be about thirteen or fourteen standing next to them.

"We just got back from Deacon's indoor league," Erica replied. "It's a month-long thing, and I cannot wait to have a decent cup of coffee."

"Deac, can you get us a table? Your mom and I will get you a hot chocolate," the woman next to Erica told him.

"I'm old enough for coffee now," Deacon argued.

"Hot chocolate or nothing, buddy," Erica stated.

"Fine."

The boy walked off to find an empty table, and Georgia grabbed a wet rag to wipe down the table she'd been told to clean.

"How was it?"

"Way too much baseball," Erica replied to Shelby.

"I liked it," the other woman said.

"*You're* the coach," Erica noted, smiling at her.

"That's Erica," Chelsea whispered to Georgia. "She and my aunt went out a long time ago. They were together for a while, but they broke up. Then, Aunt Shelby met Aunt Maria, and Erica met Melissa. They got married, like, two months ago. That's their son, Deacon. He's, apparently, a baseball phenom or something. I don't know; not a big baseball fan. Anyway, Melissa typically drinks just a black coffee when she comes in. But if she's with Erica and Deacon, they get him hot chocolate with extra whip, and Erica will get a latte of some kind. Though, sometimes, she goes iced or asks for whatever's new on the menu."

"Thanks," Georgia replied, trying to catalog everything Chelsea was telling her in her mind again but knowing it was no use.

"Oh, Lucy's here," Chelsea added.

"Lucy?"

"I tutor her in algebra. She's a sophomore in high school, like you. She was interested in a job, and I suggested she come in and meet with my aunt."

Georgia turned to see a beautiful girl about her age standing there looking around the café as if she were lost. She had big brown eyes, deep caramel skin, and long, dark, wavy hair. The girl also looked to be a little shorter than Georgia, but not by much. She seemed so overwhelmed; or maybe that was just Georgia's impression of her, and Lucy was just nervous about having a job interview.

"Does she go to my school? I don't recognize her," Georgia said, wanting to add that she'd *definitely* recognize Lucy if she'd seen her before.

"No, she's at Sacred Heart, the Catholic school," Chelsea replied. "I put an ad up there offering my tutoring services to help with extra cash before I got my new day job – I wanted to make sure I had enough saved up for the security deposit for my new place with Taylor."

Georgia nodded, forced herself to look away from Lucy, and walked to the table that needed to be cleaned.

***

"Lucy is only fifteen, so she's not allowed to make the drinks with the espresso machine, but she can do everything else. Would you mind showing her how to run the cash register?" Shelby asked.

"Sure," Georgia replied.

It had only been two weeks since Georgia had started at the café, and she was already training the new girl. Chelsea's last day had been yesterday, which meant she was at her new job and unable to help. Lucy's first day was today, and Shelby would be there to help out, but it really would be just the two of them trying to figure this out together. Georgia prayed they didn't get a rush of customers.

"So, you press the drink, add another if you have to, and then just hit subtotal; it's pretty easy," she told Lucy. "Most people pay by a credit card or their phones, so the screen will tell them what to do; like, if they want to tip or something. If they pay with cash, though, just enter the bill they give you, like a twenty, and then the drawer will open. It'll tell you the change."

"Okay," Lucy replied.

"It's taken me about two weeks, but I've pretty much memorized now where all the drinks are on the menu, so it won't take you long to get the hang of it. Just remember, if they add espresso or syrups or something, you have to click here and then find the button you need on the next screen. I've forgotten a few times. Shelby's great about mistakes but try not to forget."

"Okay," Lucy said again.

This girl didn't talk much. Since she'd gotten to work that morning, Georgia had only heard her say a few words, and mainly to Shelby. She wasn't sure if Lucy was just shy or was still nervous about her first day.

"So, you go to Sacred Heart?" Georgia asked after she helped the next customer.

"Yeah," Lucy replied.

"Nice school."

"Yeah, I guess."

"You don't like it?"

"It's fine." Lucy shrugged. "Where do you go?"

"Kennedy," she said of JFK High School, the public high school.

"What year?"

"Sophomore. You?"

"Same," Lucy said.

Another customer approached.

"Hi. What can I get for you?" Georgia asked.

"Hi. You're new," the woman said.

"Yes," Georgia replied.

"Babe, what do you want?" the woman asked another woman who followed her in.

"Iced latte. Can you get it with caramel?"

"Large one of those, please, and I'll have a blueberry scone, vanilla cupcake, and a large cappuccino," the woman said to Georgia. "Babe, what do you want?"

Georgia looked up from the register, confused since this woman had already asked her *babe* what she'd wanted.

"Are *you* an option?" another woman said as she

wrapped her arms around the first one from behind and kissed the woman's neck.

"Kate," the first woman said, blushing a little.

"Just a coffee for me and a bite of Maddie's cupcake," the woman named Kate said, looking at the second woman who leaned over and kissed the third woman.

"You wish," the woman named Maddie said to her. "I'll get us a table."

Georgia rang them up and went to make their drinks. She watched as they walked back to a table on the patio.

"Are they…" Lucy didn't finish her sentence.

"I think so, yeah," Georgia said, staring at the three women who were putting on all sorts of public displays.

"All three of them?"

"First time I've seen that," Georgia said.

"Me too," Lucy replied.

"Does it bother you?"

"Three people together?" Lucy checked.

"Yeah?"

"I don't know. I've never really thought about it."

"Me neither," Georgia said.

"It's a lot, though, huh? Working here?"

Georgia wasn't sure what she meant by that, so she didn't say anything.

"I mean, the women being together," Lucy added.

Georgia turned to her and said, "The gay thing? You have a problem with the gay thing?"

"No, I don't. I just–"

Another customer approached and said, "Hi."

"Hi. What can I get for you?" Georgia asked her.

***

"I think I didn't explain myself right the other day."

"What do you mean?" Georgia asked as she clocked in for her shift.

It had been three days since she'd seen Lucy. Their

shifts didn't always overlap, but they both seemed to work on Saturdays. While Lucy had gotten there earlier and had opened with Shelby and Brendon, the lone guy who worked at *The Meet Cute*, Georgia was working the swing shift and would be there until the event that was every Saturday. Neither she nor Lucy could actually work Saturday nights since *The Meet Cute* had gotten its liquor license and served alcohol from six until close on Friday and Saturday nights now. Shelby had just decided it was easier to hire two part-time people who were over twenty-one instead of having Lucy and Georgia there.

"I said something, and I think you took it the wrong way. I don't have a problem with the gay thing," Lucy said.

"No? You *do* go to Catholic school."

"I'm on scholarship there. It's a good school, and I want to get into a good college. My parents are very religious, yes, and I believe in *some* of what the church teaches, but I don't have a problem with gay people. I wouldn't work here if I did."

"What about your parents?" Georgia asked.

"They think I'm working at a coffee shop; they don't know anything else about it."

Georgia smiled and said, "Mine too."

"Really?" Lucy smiled.

"Yeah, conservative Christian upbringing. My parents are one step away from evangelical."

"Not you?"

"No, not me," Georgia replied. "I…" She looked down at her hands that were pressed to the counter. "Never mind."

"Hey, you two," Shelby addressed both of them. "We're out of peppermint syrup if anyone asks. More coming tomorrow, so I'm not going to run out and get more today."

"Okay," Georgia replied.

She turned to see Lucy staring at her and caught Lucy's shy smile. She liked it.

***

"No… Really?" Lucy asked, laughing.

"Yes, really. I play softball, *and* I'm a cheerleader," Georgia replied. "Why is that so funny?"

"I don't know. I can barely focus on school and my academic clubs. Chelsea helped me get my algebra grade up from a B to an A."

"You got a tutor to help you improve a B? God, I have three Bs right now, and I'm celebrating."

"Well, I don't do anything other than school. You seem to have a ton of activities going on."

"Just two," Georgia replied, wiping down the milk steamer wand. "And they're not at the same time. Cheerleading is during football and basketball season. Then, I start softball. I should make varsity this year, which will be cool. I play third base, and our third base woman was a senior last year."

"I've never played a sport," Lucy shared.

"Not athletic or just don't like them?"

"They're expensive," the girl said, shrugging. "And I know I'm not good enough to get an athletic scholarship anyway, so academics will be the way I might get into a decent college."

"I'm not even thinking about college yet," Georgia replied.

"I'm hoping to get in somewhere at least a few hours away," Lucy added.

"Why?"

"I'm just ready to not be at home."

Georgia turned to her and asked, "Is something going on there?"

"No, my parents just kind of run my life. I'm actually surprised they haven't shown up here yet. I've managed to keep my checks hidden so that they can't see the name or address of *The Meet Cute*. If they came here, they'd want me to quit."

"I think my parents would, too, but they pretty much leave me alone most of the time, so I doubt they'll just show up."

"What made you want to work here?" Lucy asked, wiping down the counter.

Georgia wasn't sure how honest she should be.

"My car," she replied. "My parents bought it for me, but I have to pay them back, and I've got to cover gas, so I need money."

"You have a car?" Lucy asked.

"Yeah. You don't?"

"No," Lucy said. "I take the bus everywhere."

"Where do you live?" Georgia asked.

"About fifteen minutes away from here, off of Silver and Kern."

"That's on my way. If you want, whenever we have the same shift, I can pick you up or take you home when we're done," Georgia offered.

"No, that's okay. I'm used to it," Lucy replied.

"It's not a big deal. And it's not even out of my way. It would be, like, once or twice a week, anyway."

Lucy looked around the relatively empty café. They were in their mid-afternoon lull, which was a nice break from the long lines.

"Okay," she finally said.

***

"You can just drop me off here," Lucy told her.

"Silver is up another block," Georgia pointed out.

"I know. I can walk the rest of the way."

"It's another block, and I have to go that direction anyway, Lucy. Just—"

"Georgia, I don't want you to see where I live," Lucy said.

"What? Why?"

"Your car is brand-new; you have nice clothes, and

your bag looks designer. I live on the fifth floor of a walk-up, in a tiny apartment with my parents and younger sister. I share a room with a nine-year-old."

"So?" Georgia asked.

"So, it's embarrassing. I'm going to get out here," Lucy stated. "Can you pull over?"

"No," Georgia replied, stopping at the light instead. "Lucy, I don't care about your house."

"My apartment; it's not a house."

"So? Plenty of people live in apartments, and plenty of people share rooms with their sisters – there's nothing wrong with that," Georgia argued, turning toward her now that they were waiting for the light. "You have nothing to be embarrassed about."

"Fine," Lucy replied, crossing her arms over her chest. "It's up on the left."

Georgia nodded, and when the light turned green, she drove to the building Lucy had indicated, which looked fine as far as Georgia was concerned.

"Thanks for the ride," Lucy said, climbing out of the car quickly.

"Yeah, sure," Georgia replied as the door slammed.

**

"Can I ask you something?" Georgia asked.

"Sure," Shelby replied, looking up from the computer in the back room. "What's up?"

"Is everything okay with Lucy? She hasn't been in this week."

"Oh, I think so. She's just been sick," Shelby replied. "She called me the other day to let me know she'd be out the whole week. I guess she came down with a pretty bad cold."

"That sucks," Georgia said.

"She'll be back when she's better, though. Why do you ask?"

Georgia sat in the empty chair next to Shelby and said, "I don't know. I dropped her off at home one night, since she doesn't have a car, and she seemed to not want me to see where she lives. I just worried that I'd said something, and she quit."

"No." Shelby patted Georgia's leg. "I'm sure it's not that. She's just not feeling well."

"Okay. Thanks," she replied. "I'll get clocked in and get to work."

Georgia hadn't seen Lucy in a week, and she'd been worrying every time she'd see Lucy's name on the schedule and then not see Lucy at work. Brendon was fine to work with, and Makayla, who had worked at *The Meet Cute* before and had left for a while, had also returned recently. She was fine, too; she was just a few years older than Lucy and Georgia. Brendon was in his early twenties, so that left just Georgia and Lucy still in high school. It was more than that, though. The two of them had fun when they worked together. Lucy had just begun to open up to Georgia. She was kind and good with the customers, but she was also focused on school and driven to succeed. Georgia had been focused on making varsity and passing chemistry this year.

Lucy was also really cute. She usually wore her long, wavy hair back under their uniform hat, but when she clocked out for the day, she let the hair down and shook it out, and Georgia found herself swallowing every time she saw it happen. This was a problem, but it wasn't one she could fix. She'd had many crushes on girls since she'd first figured out she was interested in them and not boys; Georgia just had to wait it out. Eventually, she'd find a new girl to crush on, and one day, she hoped, she'd find a girl who crushed on her, too, and she'd get her first girlfriend.

***

"Hi. I was glad you asked me to pick you up. Are you feeling better?" Georgia asked when Lucy climbed into her car.

"I'm fine, yeah," Lucy replied.

"*Are* you?" Georgia asked.

"I just have a ton of homework to catch up on and a test I'm not ready for, and I have to go to work when I should be studying."

"Oh," Georgia uttered.

"I need the job, but I need to keep my grades up more," Lucy added.

"Don't you have As?"

"In everything but geometry. Math is my downfall. Chelsea helped with Algebra, but I haven't found a tutor I can afford who will help me get my geometry grade up."

Georgia smiled and said, "Do you know the one class I'm actually getting an A in this semester?"

"What?"

"Geometry. I'm really good at it. I have no idea why. I'm typically a B or C student, but in geometry, I'm getting an A. I can help."

"You don't have to," Lucy replied. "You're already picking me up and dropping me off and not letting me pay for gas."

"Because I literally have to drive down this street to get home," Georgia reasoned. "Let me tutor you."

"How much?"

"How much?" Georgia checked.

"Yeah, how much per hour?"

"Oh, I wouldn't charge you."

"Georgia, I don't need charity. I have a job; I can pay you."

"And I don't want your money."

"That's not fair, Georgia."

Georgia sighed and said, "Okay. What about we go to a movie after our shift tonight, and you buy the tickets and get me a huge bucket of popcorn and a large Cherry Coke?"

"What?"

Georgia hadn't planned to make that suggestion, but

she had, and now it was out there.

"You seem like you could use a friend hang-out session," she said, covering her intentions. "It's two hours, at most. Then, I'll drop you off. We can talk about our first tutoring session."

"I barely have time to study as is, Georgia," Lucy told her. "I don't have time for a movie."

"It's two hours," Georgia said, laughing.

Lucy looked over at her with those big brown eyes that seemed to pull Georgia into her. She looked like she was considering Georgia's offer, and she also looked like she wanted to say yes and no at the same time. Then, Lucy licked her full lips, and Georgia wanted to kiss them. She'd kissed two boys in her life, and she hadn't really wanted to kiss either of them. She *did* want to kiss Lucy, though.

"You get a box of candy, too. Final offer," Lucy said.

Later that night, after a long shift of slinging coffee and cleaning tables, Georgia went to the back room to take off her apron and hat. Moving into the employee bathroom, she took a look in the mirror. She hadn't planned on a movie tonight, so she'd worn only a black V-neck shirt and a pair of jeans. She checked for coffee stains and didn't see any, but there was nothing she could do about the fact that she smelled like the stuff.

"It's not a date; it doesn't matter," she said to her reflection in the mirror.

"Are you ready?" Lucy asked when Georgia got out of the bathroom.

Georgia watched the girl shake her hair out and swallowed.

"Yeah. You?"

"I just clocked out," Lucy said.

"Cool. Let's go."

Minutes later, they were in Georgia's car, driving to the nearby theater. When they walked inside, Lucy headed to the ticket counter. They'd spent their break earlier that day figuring out which movie they wanted to see, and they'd both agreed right away on the new romantic comedy. Lucy paid for their tickets while Georgia waited. Then, they went farther into the theater and waited in line.

"Butter or no butter?" Georgia asked.

"Butter," Lucy replied.

"Good call," Georgia said, laughing. "And will you share the Milk Duds with me?"

"I prefer chocolate-covered raisins," Lucy replied.

"I can get down with that," Georgia said.

"*You* can get Milk Duds, Georgia." Lucy looked over at her and laughed.

"No, I'm good with the raisins. At least, they used to be grapes, right? A little healthier."

"I don't think it works like that." Lucy pulled on the short sleeve of Georgia's T-shirt when it was time for them to move up in the line.

Then, Georgia watched as Lucy's hand fell to her side again. They carried their items into the theater and found seats. They sat in silence and snacked on their food while the previews went on. The movie started, and neither said much. When the two lead characters kissed for the first time, Georgia noticed Lucy shift in her seat. The characters didn't have sex on screen – the movie wasn't rated R – but the scene did insinuate that was what they'd done, and Georgia noticed Lucy shift again. When Georgia looked over at her and found Lucy staring at her, she saw the girl look from her eyes to Georgia's lips. She thought she'd imagined it, but then Lucy did it again, and Georgia knew it was real. She turned back to the screen, trying to pretend that hadn't just happened.

Her heart raced, and when Lucy shifted a little closer to her, Georgia wondered what was happening. She moved closer to Lucy, picking the cup up from the middle cup holder and moving it to her right side. Then, she waited. It seemed like forever, but Lucy's hand moved to the armrest between them. Georgia continued to stare at the screen, but she couldn't help flitting her eyes down to that hand that was now palm-up. Lucy's hand was resting between them, palm-up… That was a sign, right? Georgia waited another long minute. Then, she lifted her own hand and placed it on top of Lucy's. Neither of them moved at first. A minute later, Georgia licked her lips and decided to be brave: she entwined their fingers. Lucy gasped. Georgia looked over at her, but Lucy wouldn't meet her eyes, though. Then, her hand slipped out of Georgia's and ended up in her own lap. Georgia turned back to the screen and dropped her own hand in her lap. She shifted away from Lucy and closed her eyes. She'd just messed up big time.

"Are we going to talk about it?" Georgia asked when she dropped Lucy off at her apartment.

"Talk about what?"

"Lucy…" Georgia replied, turning to her.

"Don't, Georgia." Lucy stared at the passenger's side window. "I can't."

"Can't what?"

"Be this way."

"What way?"

"I just can't. Thanks for the ride. I'll see you at work."

"I'll pick you up—"

"No, I can take the bus." Lucy opened the car door, adding, "And I think I can find another tutor for geometry, so don't worry about it."

"Lucy, come on."

But Lucy slammed the car door.

***

"You like Lucy?" Chelsea asked.

"Shh!" Georgia looked around the café. "Not so loud."

"She's not here," Chelsea argued.

"Babe," Taylor replied. "You like a girl. That's great," she said to Georgia then.

"I think she likes me, too," Georgia said softly as she

sat down next to the couple on her fifteen-minute break. "She looks at me like she does, and ever since the movie incident, she looks at me like – I don't know – like she wishes things would've been different."

"The movie incident?" Taylor asked.

Georgia filled them both in. It had been two weeks since the movie, and while Lucy and Georgia had had five shared shifts since then, Lucy had insisted on taking the bus. She'd also not brought up the tutoring thing again.

Chelsea had stopped by the café with her girlfriend, Taylor, that morning to check in on the place and get a good cup of coffee, and since the woman knew Lucy, Georgia was hoping she could maybe get some advice.

"Well, she's only fifteen," Chelsea replied. "Maybe she's still trying to figure things out for herself."

"Yeah, it takes some people longer than others," Taylor echoed.

"But she put her hand there, and she didn't pull it away right away."

"Maybe that was her first step, but she wasn't ready for the next one," Chelsea suggested.

"Yeah, I guess," Georgia sighed. "I think her family might have something to do with it, too."

"Yeah, they're pretty religious; I remember," Chelsea said.

"You met them?"

"Once. I went over to her place to tutor her because the bus she normally took wasn't running. She hated me being there; I could tell. Her parents were nice until Taylor texted me, and I mentioned she was my girlfriend. I don't know what happened, but I never went back, and Lucy made it seem like things were fine. I got the impression they didn't want my gayness to rub off on their daughter."

"As if that's how it works," Taylor said, shaking her head.

"What should I do?" Georgia asked.

"Nothing," Chelsea stated. "She might not be ready to

do anything about how she feels yet, assuming she *does* feel something. She might not, you know?"

"Yeah, I know," Georgia replied.

***

Near the end of Georgia's shift, she stocked the back room and counted down her drawer. Then, she removed her hat and apron, hanging them on the hook, and left out the back door.

"Hi."

Georgia looked to her left and saw Lucy standing there, clasping her hands tightly in front of herself.

"Hi," Georgia replied.

"Can we talk?" Lucy asked.

"Now?"

"Or not. Do you have to go?"

"No, I just… It's packed in there," Georgia replied. "We can talk in my car if you want."

"There's the beach," Lucy suggested, nodding toward the sound of the waves.

"Yeah, okay."

The night was a chilly one, but Georgia had worn a sweater today, so she hugged it to herself as they walked down the path and into the sand. She'd have to clean it out of her shoes later, but since this was Lucy talking to her for the first time in two weeks, it would be worth it.

"Want to sit?" Lucy asked.

"Sure."

They sat in the sand about twenty yards from the water they could only see because of the lights coming from the buildings.

"So," Georgia said after a few minutes.

"Yeah," Lucy echoed.

"You wanted to talk, Lucy," Georgia reminded.

"I know." The girl sighed loudly enough for Georgia to hear it over the sound of the waves. "It's hard."

"I know. It's hard for me, too."

"What's hard for *you*?" Lucy asked.

"I know you think I'm some rich, popular girl, but things aren't just easy, Lucy. My parents are religious and conservative, too. I'm lucky they haven't asked a bunch of questions about where I work. I'm not out anywhere. I had a boyfriend last year, and I've been on three dates with boys from my church this year just so that no one gets suspicious, but I don't want to go out with boys."

"You don't?"

"No, I like girls," Georgia stated. "I've known for a while, but I can't tell my parents because they'd freak out. No one at school knows, either. I only just told Chelsea and her girlfriend because I knew I could trust them."

"So, you're gay?" Lucy asked, turning her face to Georgia.

"Yeah," Georgia said with a nod.

"Do you know that today is my sixteenth birthday?" Lucy shared.

"What?" Georgia asked, smiling at her. "Why didn't you tell me?"

"In Mexican culture, the fifteenth birthday is the one that matters; sixteen isn't a big deal. My parents got me a cake and a new backpack for school, but there's not a big party or anything at sixteen."

"So? It's still your birthday, Lucy. I would have gotten you something."

"Like what?" Lucy asked.

"I don't know; free geometry tutoring for life."

Lucy laughed.

"Maybe something else, too," Georgia added. "I don't know; like, dinner and a movie."

"Dinner and a movie?"

"Yeah, one where we call it a date," Georgia said. "A date on your birthday."

"I've never been on a date," Lucy replied.

"If you *did* go on one, though, would you consider going on one with a girl?" Georgia asked.

Lucy turned to the waves and said, "I'd *only* consider going on a date with a girl."

Georgia smiled softly and said, "Yeah?"

"I can't, though."

"Parents?"

"They'd disown me if they found out."

"Do they *have* to find out?" Georgia asked.

"My plan was to go away to school, Georgia. Once I hit eighteen, and I'm in college on scholarship, I don't have to worry about what they think. I love my parents; they want what's best for me. But I can't change this. I've prayed; I tried. I've wished that I could just be interested in boys, but I'm not. It's just easier if I get through high school first, go away, and then see what happens."

Georgia nodded and said, "So, you don't want to go on a date with me?"

"I do," Lucy replied with a shy smile. "I held your hand, Georgia."

"I know."

"I had to pull away, though."

Georgia nodded and held out her hand.

"No one can see now," she said.

"Georgia…"

"Just for a minute. Just while we're here. I get what you're saying. I'll drop it after this, but I just want to hold your hand out here for a few minutes. Then, I'll go."

Lucy slowly placed her hand on top of Georgia's, and they stayed that way for those few minutes. Instead of leaving or pulling away, though, Lucy stayed. She stayed, and she moved closer to Georgia. She also rested her head on Georgia's shoulder, and Georgia let go of Lucy's hand to wrap her arm around her.

Lucy tucked her face into Georgia's neck then.

"I wish I would've met you two years from now," she murmured.

"But you didn't," Georgia replied.

"I like you," Lucy whispered into her ear. "You make me feel special."

Georgia smiled and placed her free hand on Lucy's thigh.

"You make me feel special, too."

Lucy lifted her head and connected their eyes.

"I know what you can get me for my birthday," she said softly.

"Anything," Georgia replied, hoping Lucy wouldn't ask her to go right now.

Lucy leaned in and placed her lips tentatively to Georgia's. Georgia pulled back for a second, surprised. Then, she smiled and leaned in again, reconnecting their lips and cupping Lucy's cheek. They shared sweet kisses for a few minutes as the waves drowned out everything around them. Then, Lucy opened her mouth, and Georgia slipped her tongue inside. Lucy gave her a soft moan that Georgia almost hadn't heard. They kissed for several more minutes until Lucy finally pulled back, and they just stared at one another.

"That was my first kiss," Lucy shared.

"Mine too," Georgia replied. "Well, the first one I really wanted and the first one that matters."

"What do we do now?" Lucy asked.

"I think we have two options," Georgia began. "Go on that date in secret, or make tonight our first and last kiss and be friends."

Lucy nodded and said, "I don't know that I can do either of those things."

Georgia nodded as well and asked, "Do you want to think about it?"

"Can I?" Lucy checked.

"Can I kiss you again before I drive you home?" Georgia asked her instead.

Lucy smiled and leaned back in.

***

"We can't keep making out in your car," Lucy said.

"We're teenagers; we're *supposed* to make out in cars," Georgia replied, kissing Lucy's neck.

"I have a curfew," Lucy told her, moving Georgia's hand into her lap. "But I love your lips."

"*I* love my lips on *your* skin," Georgia replied.

Lucy pulled Georgia's face to hers and said, "Happy anniversary."

"Happy anniversary, baby," Georgia replied, kissing her softly. "One day, we won't have to make out in cars."

"One day, like when we move out of our parents' places?" Lucy asked.

"We only have two more years," Georgia said, kissing her nose.

"Do you think about that?"

"What?"

"The two years part? I mean, it's been three months. Do you think about us in two years?"

Georgia wrapped her arm around Lucy's shoulders and pulled her even closer. They were in the back seat of Georgia's car, parked at an overlook. They'd come to this particular spot many times now – it was one of the few places they went to spend time alone together. They also went to movies regularly and only sometimes watched the movie. And they sat on the beach outside the café late at night when they could, watching the tide change, but most of their time alone was spent in Georgia's car.

"Yeah, I do," Georgia said. "I know it's only been three months, and people will say that we're young, but I think about what happens after we graduate all the time. You'll end up at some super-genius school, and I'll be at the state school, but we can figure out how to make it work."

Lucy lifted up her head to smile at her and said, "You're really sweet."

"Do you think about that stuff?" Georgia asked this time, cupping Lucy's cheek.

"Yeah," Lucy replied. "I never thought I'd have to. I

thought I'd go to college, and maybe I'd get lucky enough to find a girlfriend there."

"I came a little early, huh?" Georgia smiled.

"Yes, but I want you to stick around," Lucy smiled back.

"Me too," Georgia agreed. Then, she bit her lower lip and added, "You have the academic decathlon tournament this weekend…"

"I know. I'll miss you."

"It's only about two hours away from here," Georgia said. "I could maybe go."

"You want to watch the tournament?"

"No, I want to support my girlfriend," Georgia replied, laughing a little. "And you'll be there for two nights. I was thinking, maybe I could get a room there for one of those nights. My parents wouldn't even know I'm gone, but I can tell them I'm sleeping over with a friend, which wouldn't be a lie, exactly – you *are* technically a friend." She smiled at Lucy.

"You want to stay over?"

"Saturday night," Georgia said. "Could you get away from whatever roommate they stick you with? We could wake up before you have to be at breakfast; no one will know."

"Oh. You want us to…" Lucy swallowed. "You want us to sleep…"

"Not like that. I was just thinking we could sleep to-gether. Sleep, Luce."

"Sleep?" Lucy checked.

"Yeah," Georgia replied.

"But it's been three months," Lucy said. "And we've never really talked about *not* sleeping."

"You want to talk about that?"

Lucy shrugged and said, "I know I want that with you."

Georgia took a deep breath and said, "You do?"

Lucy nodded and asked, "Do you want that with me?"

"Yes," Georgia replied instantly.

Lucy smiled shyly and said, "I've never…"

"Me neither," Georgia admitted.

"This weekend?" Lucy asked.

"You know I'd never pressure you, right? We can wait as long as we want. I'm not in any hurry."

"I know," Lucy said, leaning in and kissing Georgia. "You should come this weekend. We can just see."

"Okay," Georgia replied. "I should take you home; I don't want you to miss your curfew."

"We can do this, right? Just another couple of years; we'll be in college, and we won't have to be so secretive."

"Just a couple more years, baby," Georgia replied, kissing her once more.

***

"I told her I loved her," Georgia said.

"You did?" Shelby asked.

"And she said it back." She smiled.

"That's great, Georgia," Shelby replied.

Georgia hadn't stopped smiling since Lucy had said those three words back to her. Lucy had gotten away from her roommate and had spent the night in Georgia's room. They'd woken up together after, and Georgia was certain she'd never been so happy in her life. She loved Lucy, and Lucy loved her.

Shelby had known they were a couple since the beginning. Georgia and Lucy both trusted her and her wife, Maria. Chelsea had also been by the café a couple of times, and Lucy had been the one to tell her they were officially together. Outside of them and Chelsea's girlfriend, Taylor, no one else knew. They'd managed to keep it a secret, and now all they had to do was keep that up until both of them moved away from home. It would be hard, but they were in love, so it would be worth it. Georgia smiled at the thought. Then, she turned around when she heard someone coming into the room.

"Babe?" she asked, seeing her girlfriend rushing toward her in tears.

"They found out," Lucy said as she crashed into Georgia and pulled her in for a hard hug. "They found out."

"*Who* found out?" Georgia asked, hugging her back.

"They... My roommate..."

Lucy was sobbing uncontrollably against her.

"Sweetie, sit down. What's wrong?" Shelby asked, moving to Lucy and rubbing her back as Lucy clung to Georgia.

"Roommate... saw us kiss. She told... the chaperone. He... told... my–"

Georgia's face fell.

"Your parents?"

"Yes," Lucy said, clutching her harder now. "I ran... out with my... stuff."

Georgia looked down at the floor and noticed a duffel bag and a backpack behind Lucy.

"You ran away?" Shelby asked.

"No, they..." Lucy pulled back to look at Georgia, who tried to wipe the tears from her cheeks. "They told me... not to come... home."

"What?" Georgia asked.

"They're going to call... your parents. They took my phone, found our messages, and got your number. They... want them to know."

"Oh, shit," Georgia said.

"You should... go home," Lucy told her.

"I'm not leaving you," Georgia replied, pulling Lucy back against herself, never wanting to let her go.

"Lucy, let me get you some water, okay?" Shelby offered, walking over to the sink.

"They don't want me anymore," Lucy said through tears. "They told me I wasn't their daughter."

"They don't mean it," Georgia said. "They were just in shock or something. They need time to cool down."

"Yes, I'm sure that's it," Shelby echoed, walking back over to them.

"Excuse me? Where's my daughter?"

Georgia recognized that voice even though she couldn't see her mother yet.

"That's my mom," she whispered.

"She knows," Lucy replied.

"Let's go," Georgia stated. "We'll leave out the back, figure this out."

"You can't run from your mom, Georgia," Shelby said, handing Lucy the water.

"I love you," Lucy told her. "No matter what happens, I love you."

"Nothing's going to happen," Georgia said, pressing her lips to Lucy's. "And I love you, too."

"Georgia," her mother said, walking into the back room. "Is this her?"

"Mom, let me explain," Georgia said.

"You will. Let's go." The woman motioned for Georgia to go with her.

"Mom, I can't leave Lucy here."

"Lucy isn't my concern. *You* are."

"She's my girlfriend, and I love her. That makes her your concern," Georgia argued.

"Georgia, get in the car. We will talk about this at home."

"I'm not leaving her here."

"Georgia, let me take care of her," Shelby offered. "I'll take her upstairs. Maria's working from home today. She'll be fine."

Georgia held on to Lucy's hand, tears in her own eyes now, and said, "I can't. Mom, please, don't make me."

"You lied to your father and me about this job. You lied to us about being…" She looked away from her daughter. "And you've been doing… I don't even know what with another girl. You don't get to make requests right now, Georgia. Get in the car."

"It's okay," Lucy told her. "It'll be okay." She pressed her forehead to Georgia's. "I love you. Two years from now, I'll find you."

"What? No, I–"

"Georgia! I came here, but your father wanted to. Do you want me to call him and get him over here instead?"

"Mom!" Georgia kissed Lucy quickly. "I love you." She looked at Shelby. "You'll make sure she's okay?"

"Of course."

"I'll call you as soon as I can," Georgia said to Lucy. "I promise; I'll get away if I have to," she added in a whisper.

Lucy pulled her in for a long hug. Georgia kissed her neck, feeling her own tears fall into Lucy's skin. Then, she let go. It was the hardest thing she'd ever done.

***

There was the initial shock that took her parents more than a week to get over. They hadn't let Georgia out of their sight. They'd taken her phone, and her laptop could only be used for homework, but she'd managed to contact Shelby and check on her girlfriend. Shelby had been kind enough to take Lucy in since Lucy's parents still weren't talking to her. Shelby told her Lucy was crying a lot but had put her focus on school, asking if Shelby knew anything about Georgia. And since Lucy was on scholarship, she wouldn't have to leave school, which was good because Georgia didn't think Lucy could handle losing her parents, her little sister, her school, and potentially, her girlfriend all in one week.

They'd been so careful that weekend, but when Georgia was leaving to drive home, Lucy had followed her to the parking lot. They thought no one was around, so Lucy had leaned in to kiss her. They'd shared a long hug and whispered that they loved each other over and over. That weekend had changed their entire life. They'd both been so happy that morning; they hadn't paid enough attention. Lucy's horrible roommate had seen them together, though, and now, everything was ruined.

In the second week, when the shock had worn off, her parents had questions. Georgia did the best she could to answer them as honestly as she could. In the meantime, they'd asked the pastor to come to the house to talk to her and try to convince her to reconsider her attraction to girls. As if that was even possible. Georgia had stood her ground and told him she was gay; she couldn't change that. He'd left defeated. Then, during the third week, her parents asked more questions. They also suggested she couldn't be sure; she couldn't be in love. She was only sixteen. She'd argued that she loved Lucy, knew it to be true, and nothing they said would change that. By the end of that third week, they gave Georgia her phone back.

"Baby?" she asked.

"I missed your voice," Lucy said.

Lucy no longer had a cell phone, but Shelby had lent her hers so that they could talk.

"How are you? Are you okay?"

"I'm still with Shelby and Maria. They've been so amazing. How are you? Are *you* okay?"

"They gave me my phone back knowing I'd call you right away, so I think I'm okay for now."

"I miss you."

"I miss you, too," Georgia replied, lying in her bed, staring up at the ceiling.

"Can I see you?"

"I don't know. I'm still grounded."

"No, I mean right now. Can we FaceTime?"

"Shit. Why didn't I think of that?"

She quickly made the FaceTime call.

"Oh, you're so pretty," Georgia said when she saw Lucy's face.

"*You're* so pretty." Lucy smiled at her.

"I love you."

"I love you, too."

"We'll figure this out, okay? I'll ask my parents if you can stay here; I just need a little more time. They're finally talking to me about something *other* than me being gay, so I think they'll come around, and we have the room. Your parents will come to their senses, too."

"Your parents aren't going to let me stay there," Lucy told her.

"I'll convince them," Georgia argued.

"Shelby and Maria both said I can stay here as long as I need to," Lucy replied. "They're actually going to buy me a phone this weekend. I'm still working at the café, so I'll pay them back for it."

"No, you won't," Shelby's voice came from behind Lucy.

"I have a bedroom here and everything," Lucy said. "They've been so nice to me."

"I'm glad," Georgia replied, smiling back at her and rolling onto her side to get more comfortable. "Text me your new number?"

"Of course," Lucy said with her sweet smile. "How are you, really?" Lucy was moving. "I'm going into my room. One sec."

Georgia heard the door close behind her.

"I miss your lips," she said.

"I miss yours, too," Lucy replied, lying down on the bed in her new room. "I miss your hugs, too. You give such great hugs, babe."

"Do I give great other things?" Georgia asked, laughing at her joke.

"Babe!"

Georgia laughed more. God, she'd needed that. She'd needed to see Lucy's face and to laugh with her.

"I'm working on my parents," she said.

"I know."

"Have yours reached out at all?" Georgia asked.

"Shelby called them for me, but they didn't want to talk to me. Maria went over to pick up more of my stuff for me and tried to convince them to take some time to think about losing me, but they seemed pretty certain that I'm an abomination."

"You're beautiful. They're assholes," Georgia stated. "God, I'm so sorry, Luce. I shouldn't have gone to that hotel with you. I should've stayed home. This is my fault."

"If you hadn't gone, we wouldn't have had the best night of my entire life," Lucy replied. "I don't regret that at all, Georgia. I never will. I know what this is. This is real; it *has* been since we met."

"I know," Georgia said.

"I hope they come around," Lucy added, "but I know no matter what, I want to be with you."

Georgia smiled and said, "I want that, too. I'll try to see you as soon as I can."

"Don't push them too hard. They gave you the phone; that's a big step. I'll be here. Don't make them want to keep you locked up there forever, okay?"

"I won't," Georgia replied. "I love you."

"I love you, too," Lucy said, blowing her a kiss.

By the end of week four, Georgia had her computer back to use however she wanted. By the end of week six, the pastor had made three more trips to the house, but her parents let her have her car to go to and from school. Every time she climbed inside, Georgia was tempted to drive to Lucy, but her girlfriend was a good influence on her, telling her to bide her time and not to risk a setback.

By week eight, Georgia was allowed to look for another job, but not at the café. She didn't try to find one right away, hoping that if she gave it a little more time, they'd let her go back to *The Meet Cute*. By the end of that week, her parents surprised her, asking if Lucy could come over for dinner. Shelby and Maria drove her over. Georgia hadn't seen her girlfriend in person in two months, but with her parents standing right behind them, all she could do was hug the girl tightly and whisper that she loved her. At dinner, she'd held Lucy's hand whenever she could. Her parents had asked Lucy the same questions they'd asked Georgia, and some new ones, too. At the end of the night, Georgia had been allowed to walk Lucy outside to Maria's car. Maria had been kind enough to look away, and Georgia had pressed her lips to her girlfriend's for the first time in two months. It was short, but it was enough.

"Call me when you get home," she said.

"I will," Lucy replied. "I think tonight went okay." She put her hands on Georgia's hips.

"Me too," Georgia replied. "Love you."

"Love you, too."

Another peck on the lips, and Lucy was gone.

By week ten, Georgia was allowed to have Lucy over to study in the living room, but only when her parents were home. By week twelve, she was allowed to go to the café to visit Lucy. The next week, she was allowed to take her out on a date. The pastor stopped by again to talk to her about how sex before marriage was a sin. Georgia pointed out that he already thought she was sinning by dating a girl, but he continued with his lecture anyway. Her parents gave her a strict curfew, which she made sure not to miss. Lucy was still staying with Shelby and Maria, and her parents had made no attempt to contact her. Since Georgia's parents seemed to be dealing better, she asked if they'd be willing to talk to Lucy's parents, but they told her they weren't ready for that. Georgia understood, but she wanted her girlfriend to have her family back.

"Hello," she said.

"May I help you?"

"I'm Georgia," she introduced herself to Lucy's mother. "Lucy's girlfriend."

***

"You did the best you could," Lucy told her. "And I love you for trying."

"I just don't understand how they could stop talking

to you; you're their daughter," Georgia said, placing Lucy's legs in her lap on the sofa.

"I miss them so much. I miss my sister. I don't even know what they've told her about me, but it's not good, and they won't let me see her to talk to her."

"They will. If not, she'll be old enough soon. You can call her or take my car and visit her when she's at school."

"I don't want to confuse her, and I don't want to make them any angrier than they already are."

"I get it." Georgia leaned over and kissed her.

"Hey, you two," Shelby said as she opened the door.

"Hi," Georgia greeted.

"Hey, Shelby," Lucy said. "Maria just ran out to get something for dinner. She said she'd be right back."

"And you two are behaving, right?" Shelby checked. "I've never had a teenager live with me before, so I'm not sure what rules we should have now that Georgia's allowed over." Shelby dropped some paperwork onto the kitchen table.

"We're behaving," Georgia replied. "We've just been sitting here, talking."

"I think if you're in the bedroom, the door should be open," Shelby said, sitting down next to them. "Is that fair?"

"I think that's fair," Lucy replied.

***

By the beginning of their junior year, Georgia was back working at *The Meet Cute*. Her parents had nearly accepted her sexuality, though sometimes, they made comments or suggested she'd figure something out when she got older.

Lucy's parents had dropped all of her things off at Shelby and Maria's, and Lucy worked with them to get emancipated since she didn't want to have to go into the system. It made Georgia want to punch those parents, but Lucy was doing what she had to do to survive. Shelby and Maria had taken her in, and now, Lucy had decorated her room there and seemed to be adjusting as well as she could.

"Babe, we can't here," Lucy told her.

"Why not?" Georgia asked, running her hand up Lucy's thigh under her plaid uniform skirt. "We haven't since that night. That was forever ago."

"I know, but this is Maria and Shelby's place; I'm a guest here. I want to respect their rules."

Georgia stopped her hand but continued to kiss Lucy's neck.

"The door is open," she pointed out between kisses.

"You're not even supposed to be up here when one of them isn't here," Lucy replied.

"I was on a break from work." Georgia kissed her lips.

"And I was studying."

"Fine, I'll go. But it's not like we can do this at my house: my dad works from home, and my mom is there whenever he isn't."

"I have another decathlon coming up, but I doubt they'll be as lax as they were before, given the scandal we caused."

"Do we really have to wait until we're in college to have sex again?" Georgia asked, rolling off of her.

Lucy laughed and said, "No, we'll figure something out."

"How? All my money goes to pay off my car, and all your money goes to pay for the things you need. And we can't exactly get a hotel even if we could afford it – we're too young."

"Well," Lucy climbed on top of her, straddling her hips. "If you remember correctly, we seemed to have no trouble having some alone time in your car."

Georgia laughed and said, "Tomorrow night?"

Lucy nodded. Then, there was the sound of a key in the front door.

"Shit," Georgia said.

They hurried out of the room and landed onto the sofa in a huff.

"Georgia?" Maria asked, dropping groceries on the table. "I just saw my wife downstairs, so…"

"I had a break. I just came up to make plans with Lucy for tomorrow night. I'm on my way back down, though."

"You might want to consider buttoning up your jeans before you go back to work," Maria pointed out.

Georgia looked down and saw that her button was undone. She hadn't even noticed and had no idea if she'd been the one to undo it or if Lucy had.

"We were just—"

"I won't tell Shelby if you don't," Maria said. "But if you're going to be doing that in this house, you're going to have to sit through a lecture about emotions and hormones and how sex changes things. I've never had to give it before, so give me some time to prepare it, yeah?"

"We weren't. We didn't do anything," Lucy spoke.

"I've been a teenager before," Maria replied, pulling bread out of one of the reusable grocery bags. "And I've been madly in love with that woman downstairs for years. I know what it's all like, but I'm the adult, so you get to sit through the lecture. Deal?"

"Deal," Georgia said hopefully.

"Babe!" Lucy laughed.

Georgia kissed her quickly, stood up, and said, "I've got to go. I love you like crazy."

"I know. I love you, too."

"Tomorrow night?" Georgia asked, winking at her.

Lucy nodded, and Georgia practically skipped down the stairs.

THE BEGINNING

After Erica left, Shelby wondered if she'd ever fall in love again. Things had been hard for them toward the end. Erica was insistent; she wanted a child. Shelby didn't. She had no problems with kids, but she didn't see herself having one. She'd never looked at babies and got that maternal biological clock ticking. Sure, they were cute, but they also took a lot of time and energy, and Shelby just didn't have it in her. She loved Erica, though; that hadn't changed. So when they'd finally decided it had to end for them both to be happy, Shelby had cried night after night, after night.

There had been moments when she'd thought about calling Erica and begging her to come back – they could have a baby together; Shelby could be a mom, and things would be fine then. But she'd known enough to stop herself from making that call, and eventually, she hurt less. Then, though the hurt was still there, she was able to think about dating again. Finally, she felt ready enough to attempt a new relationship.

"Whoa!" Shelby looked down and felt the heat before the sight even registered.

"Shit. I'm so sorry," the woman, who had just spilled her burning hot coffee all over Shelby after running into her, said. "Oh, shit. Are you okay?"

"I think I have mild first-degree burns," Shelby replied. "But that's what I get for wearing silk, right?"

Her beige silk button-down under her suit jacket was now mostly brown and covered in coffee.

"I didn't see you there. I was looking at my damn phone and not paying attention. I'm so sorry."

Shelby looked up and saw the big blue eyes, dark-brown curly hair, and lightly tan skin of the culprit.

"I have no idea what to do here," the woman added. "I can pay for your dry-cleaning. How much is a whole suit usually? Doesn't matter. Will twenty cover it? No, probably not. I only have twenty on me, but I can run to an ATM and get cash. Can you wait here? I think there's one down the street."

"It's fine," Shelby replied, smiling at her. "I don't live far from here. I can run back home and change."

"But I've ruined your clothes. Let me just give you cash for–" The woman pulled out her wallet. "And let me buy you a cup of coffee, at least. You were going into the café, right?"

"For a cup of mediocre coffee, yes," Shelby said, chuckling. "It's the closest place to my house, and I'm in court this morning, so I need to get my fix."

"Court?"

"Lawyer," Shelby explained, pointing at herself.

The woman nodded and said, "Here's twenty." She handed Shelby cash she didn't want or need. "And the largest coffee in the world is coming right up."

"I need to get home and change," Shelby replied. "But thank you." She held out the twenty-dollar bill back. "And I really don't need this. It was an accident."

"Please, just take it. It'll make me feel better," the woman said.

"Okay," Shelby agreed, smiling at her.

"You have a beautiful smile," the woman said as if she hadn't meant to.

"Oh," Shelby uttered. "Thank you."

"I'd love it if you tell me how much the dry-cleaning costs so that I can pay the difference. Maybe we could meet back here sometime, and I can get you that coffee, too?"

Shelby blushed. Was this woman asking her out or merely trying to pay her back for the damage she'd caused to Shelby's clothes?

"I come here most mornings that I'm in court," Shelby said. "Usually around this time."

"Okay," the woman said. "I'm usually in later. This is what I get for waking up early and trying to get a head start on my day. Actually, this is what *you* get for me trying to wake up early for once. I'm sorry."

"It's really okay."

"I'll be in tomorrow at this time," the woman told her.

"I don't think I'll have this back from the dry-cleaner by then."

"That's okay," she replied. "I'll still be here."

Shelby's blush crept down to her neck, and she nodded.

***

"Why wouldn't they open that back up?" Maria voiced her thoughts out loud.

Shelby followed her gaze toward the back wall and asked, "What do you mean?"

"That's the beach back there. The ocean is about forty yards from their back door, and there's just a brick wall there with a window. It's not even a big window."

"Are you an architect or something?" Shelby asked.

"What? Oh, no. I'm a copywriter by trade. I have a small company. I started at a large ad company just out of school, but I didn't like the corporate environment, so I went freelance, and I was pretty successful. Then, I started my own company, and I've got about five employees now. We do digital advertising, social media, copywriting, and other marketing. We actually just got a major client last week that should put us on the map."

"That's awesome. Congratulations," Shelby said.

"I think that my job means I'm usually pretty good at seeing the potential in things," Maria replied, smiling at Shelby.

"Like the potential for them to have better coffee than this?" Shelby asked, lifting the cup to her lips.

"Among other things." Maria smiled.

They'd met at the café the next morning before Shelby

had to get to court, and she'd learned the clumsy woman's name was Maria when they'd first arrived. Maria had bought Shelby coffee and a bagel that Shelby would take with her and eat later. Shelby had learned that Maria was five years older than her, single, and gay, all in the first ten minutes. Now, Shelby really needed to get going. She had some last-minute prep to do, but she couldn't seem to say goodbye to Maria.

"I have a meeting at nine, so I should really be going," Maria said, apparently not having the same problem Shelby was having.

"Oh, sure," Shelby replied.

"But I still don't know how much your dry-cleaning cost, so maybe we can do this again?" Maria suggested.

Shelby smiled and said, "You could give me your number. I can call you when I go to pick it up."

"Yes, that sounds perfect," Maria replied, holding out her hand for Shelby's phone. "There. I texted my phone from yours, so now I have your number, too. Wouldn't want to accidentally ignore a call from an unknown number or anything."

"Right." Shelby laughed and added, "Well, I have court, so…"

"I'll wait to hear back from you," Maria said.

***

"Oh, my God. So much better," Shelby said.

"Yeah? I thought so, too," Maria replied.

For their first date, Maria had taken Shelby to a local coffee roastery that was open to customers. The place was in an industrial part of town and had a giant garage-style door that they rolled back each morning, and if they got there early enough, they'd get one of the first cups of freshly brewed coffee. It was an odd first date, to say the least, but Shelby had woken at five on Sunday morning. Maria had picked her up. They'd driven and parked, yawning all the way there and not exchanging much conversation. The door rolled up, and they were met by the guy who owned the place. He had a cheery grin as he said good morning to the two of them and the other ten or so people that had gathered outside. The roastery smelled like heaven. Then again, coffee had always smelled like heaven to Shelby. This coffee smell, though, was different. It wasn't bitter or acidic; it was aromatic and strong, and Shelby loved it.

There were three or four small tables placed haphazardly around the place, but there was also a coffee bar right by the giant roaster. Shelby wanted to sit there but didn't want to say anything in case Maria wanted a table. Maria walked to the bar, though, and pulled out a chair for Shelby, who smiled and sat down. They sat there and drank several cups of amazing coffee while people milled about.

"God, I'm highly caffeinated, but I feel like I need a nap," Maria said around eight in the morning.

"Not used to waking up early?"

"No, I like to sleep in when I can."

"Then, why did you ask me out on a date at five in the morning?" Shelby laughed.

"You like coffee. And I heard this place has amazing coffee."

"It does," Shelby confirmed, taking her final sip.

"What do you say we walk around for a bit?" Maria offered. "It's a nice day out."

"I'd like that," Shelby replied.

Minutes later, Maria had paid for their coffee and left a generous tip. She'd also bought Shelby a bag of the stuff to take home. It was sweet. They walked around the city, block after block, and talked.

Shelby told Maria about law school, coming out, and about some parts of her relationship with Erica. Maria talked about her family, starting her own business, and an ex-girlfriend of her own. By eleven, they'd been walking for hours, but Shelby's feet didn't feel tired. Eventually, they ended up at a diner where they stopped for lunch. Shelby paid this time. As they walked back to Maria's car, Shelby wasn't surprised when Maria took her hand and entwined their fingers. It was one in the afternoon before they arrived back at Shelby's apartment with their hands still joined over the center console.

"Do you want to come up?" Shelby asked.

Maria turned to her.

"For that nap," Shelby added.

"Yeah, that would be nice," Maria said.

Up in Shelby's apartment, she got them both a bottle of water and placed it on her bedside tables. Maria changed into something of Shelby's in the bathroom while Shelby changed in the bedroom. Then, they slid into bed. Maria was lying on her back, and Shelby wasted no time in moving into her and placing her head on Maria's chest. Maria put her arm around Shelby, and this was way more amazing than the coffee they'd just had.

"Do you want to go out again?" Maria asked.

"Name the time and place," Shelby replied, wrapping an arm tightly around Maria's waist.

"Tonight. Here," Maria said softly, running her hand through Shelby's blonde hair.

Shelby nodded against her chest.

***

"You don't really like your job, do you?" Maria asked later that night.

"What? Of course, I do," Shelby replied, chuckling. "Why do you say that?"

"I know a few lawyers. You don't seem like you're like them."

"How so?" she asked, sipping her wine at her dining room table.

"Well, you're a litigator at a major firm – you're an associate, and you're not putting in hundred-hour weeks."

"How do you know that?"

"Because you've been with me all day, and I haven't heard you once talk about billable hours or trying to make partner."

Maria poured Shelby another glass of wine and then added a bit to her own glass.

"I'm taking the day off to be with you."

"I don't think associates in high-powered firms get days off," Maria replied, laughing.

Shelby sighed and said, "I'd be lying if I said I was totally happy."

"Yeah?"

"I guess I thought it would be different; that I'd want it more than I do now. I put three years into law school, made law review, graduated near the top of my class, passed the Bar on my first try, got a job right out of school at a major firm in the city, and… I don't know. I thought I'd want all the things you just mentioned. I thought I'd find the ambition and drive along the way."

"You haven't yet?"

"No," Shelby said honestly.

"Do you think you will?"

"I don't know," Shelby replied. "Maybe."

Maria nodded and said, "Dinner was amazing. Thank you for cooking."

"Thank *you* for providing the company."

"Well, I should…"

"No, don't," Shelby interrupted. "Don't make up some excuse to go because you think you've been here all day and need to. I don't want you to go. You just topped off your wine. Let's just move to the couch and talk."

"Okay." Maria smiled warmly at her. "What about the dishes?"

"Those can wait."

They sat on the couch that night and talked for hours. Even though they'd already spent the entire day together, Shelby didn't want Maria to go. Tomorrow was Monday. Shelby had to be in the office by seven. Maria had work, too. They really should call it a night so that Maria could get home and they could both get some sleep. But as Shelby lay with her head in Maria's lap, she knew she didn't want Maria going home for the night.

"Stay," Shelby said, looking up at her.

Maria nodded.

***

"Hey," Erica greeted.

"Hi," Shelby replied, looking down at the table.

"I've never been here," Erica said.

"I come here in the mornings now."

"*I* used to make your coffee," Erica replied, taking a sip. "This isn't as good as mine."

"No, it's not." Shelby laughed. "I'm due in a client meeting at nine, Erica. What did you want to meet about?"

"Hey," Maria greeted, walking up to the table. "I thought you had an early meeting today."

Shelby looked from Erica to Maria and then back to Erica.

"Oh," Maria said, looking at Erica, too, now. "Sorry, I just interrupted you and…" She met Shelby's gaze. "I'll just grab my coffee and go."

"You said you were working from home today," Shelby replied.

"I was, but a client asked for a meeting at the office, so I'm on my way in," she explained.

Shelby nodded and said, "This is Erica."

"Erica?" Maria asked, looking at Shelby's companion again. "*The* Erica?"

"I'm guessing that's a yes," Erica said.

"Erica called and asked me to meet her."

"Got it," Maria said. "Well, I'll leave you to that, then."

The woman nodded and gave Shelby a forced smile. When she turned to walk to the counter, Shelby stood and followed her there.

"It's not what you think. She just called me last night, said she wanted to tell me something, and asked to meet. I *did* have an early client meeting when I told you I did. I pushed it back thirty minutes last night after Erica called."

"You don't owe me an explanation; we've been on one date."

"Two."

"What?"

"Two dates. We had two dates in one day, and you stayed the night," Shelby corrected.

"Still, we haven't exactly made any promises. You can do–"

"Maria, it's just a meeting; I haven't seen Erica in a while. We haven't talked in forever, either, so when she called, I thought it might be important."

"You just told me the only reason you two broke up was because of the kid thing."

They got in the line.

"It is. And my opinion on that hasn't changed."

"Maybe *hers* has," Maria argued.

"Can you just come by my place tonight like we'd planned? I'm going to the store later to buy ingredients for dinner."

"Yeah, sure," Maria replied, kissing her cheek and moving up in the line. "But I really did just stop in for a coffee to-go." She looked to the barista, who was ready to take her order now.

"Okay," Shelby said.

She waited for Maria to order. Then, she walked back over to the table and sat down.

"Girlfriend?" Erica asked.

"No, but we've been on a couple of dates, and we're going out tonight," Shelby replied.

"Sorry, Shell."

"It's not your fault. I shouldn't have asked you to meet me here. I just… You said it was important."

"I just wanted you to know that I'm pregnant."

"What?" Shelby asked.

"Yeah. I'm fourteen weeks along. I'll find out soon if I'm having a boy or a girl," she said with a wide smile on her face.

"That's great, Erica. Congratulations!"

"Thanks," the woman replied. "I don't know why, but I thought you should know."

"I'm really happy for you," Shelby told her. "I know how much you want this."

"I think I wanted you to know because I *needed* you to know."

"What do you mean?"

"Just that we ended because I wanted something you didn't want. I needed you to know that I went through with it."

"You didn't have to tell me that; I knew you would. We were together for five years, Erica. I know how much you want to be a mom."

Erica nodded and said, "Well, I'll have a baby shower, and I'd like to send you a birth announcement, but I don't know if I should invite you or–"

Shelby wasn't exactly sure what the protocol was for something like this, either.

"Maybe just the birth announcement," she suggested.

Erica nodded and took a drink of her coffee.

"Okay," she said after a second. "I'll let you get to your meeting."

"Erica, seriously, I really am happy for you. You're going to be an amazing mom," Shelby said, smiling at the woman she'd once thought she'd spend the rest of her life with.

***

"You really don't have to explain, Shell," Maria said.

"We're not getting back together."

"Okay. Good. If you were, it would really be cruel of you to have me over tonight," Maria replied.

Shelby sat down next to Maria on the couch, holding out a beer for Maria to take.

"She just wanted to tell me that she's pregnant," she said.

"Oh." Maria took a quick drink. "And she wants you to do *what*, exactly?"

"Nothing. She just wanted me to know that she'd gone through with the insemination. She's wanted to do it for years, and I didn't want to be a mom. So, I'm glad that she did it and that it worked. She's going to make a great mother."

"So, there are no, I don't know, residual feelings I should be worried about?" Maria asked, placing the beer bottle on the coffee table. "I mean, if this goes beyond tonight."

"*If?*" Shelby asked, lifting an eyebrow at her.

"I like you," Maria stated honestly. "I'd like this to continue, but I'm not interested in someone who isn't–"

Shelby placed her own bottle on the table, halting Maria's words. Then, she moved into Maria's lap, straddling her hips.

"I'm not still in love with my ex-girlfriend. It's taken me a long time to get here, but I'm ready to be with someone else. And I'd like that someone else to be you."

Maria's hands moved to Shelby's thighs, under the dress she'd put on after the trip to the grocery store.

"I'm so glad I spilled coffee all over you," she said, laughing.

Shelby leaned down, smiling until she connected their lips and the smile wouldn't allow her to kiss Maria how she'd wanted to since the moment she first laid eyes on her.

"Me too," Shelby said, reconnecting their lips right after.

Minutes later, Shelby was still in Maria's lap. Maria's lips were on Shelby's neck, and Shelby was ready to take things to the bedroom. Maria's mouth was molten heat on Shelby's already hot skin. She knew they clicked, but she had no idea if they'd really *click*. The way Maria's hands were running up and down her inner thighs, though, getting dangerously close to where Shelby needed her, told Shelby that Maria would have no trouble giving Shelby her first non-self-induced orgasm since Erica.

Sex with Erica had been great, but Shelby had realized after their break-up that they'd both needed the same thing, and it was something neither of them could give the other entirely.

"I want you," Maria said, sucking on Shelby's collarbone.

Shelby began to roll her hips.

"Shell, I want you now. Let me have you, please," Maria added.

Yes, that was what Shelby had wanted. She'd wanted someone to take the lead. Then, the timer on the damn chicken went off.

"Fuck," Shelby said.

"I don't mind dry chicken. Leave it," Maria told her, covering Shelby's breast with her hand and squeezing it.

"I need to turn… the oven… off," Shelby managed out as she felt Maria's hand on her back, sliding down the zipper of her dress.

"Do you want to stop?" Maria asked, looking into Shelby's eyes.

"No," Shelby replied. "Just pause. Maybe we can go into the bedroom?"

Maria nodded, and her eyes had grown darker since Shelby had sat down next to her.

"Just give me one minute," Shelby said, quickly kissing Maria and standing up.

She'd forgotten, though, that Maria had just unzipped her dress, and it fell instantly to the floor.

"You…" Maria's jaw fell. "That…"

Shelby had worn a strapless black bra and a matching thong, secretly hoping they'd take this step tonight.

"Do you like it?" she asked.

Maria nodded slowly and reached for her, leaning forward on the sofa and pulling Shelby against herself. Then, Maria kissed her stomach and ran her hands up and down Shelby's bare ass.

"I need to turn the oven off," Shelby said when Maria's fingers slipped beneath the thong and began pulling it down.

"Don't move," Maria told her.

Quickly, she jumped up and over the sofa, rushed into the kitchen, and pressed the button on the oven, turning it off. Shelby laughed as the woman practically lunged back to her seat.

"Where was I?" Maria asked, kissing around Shelby's belly button.

"Bedroom," Shelby said, running her fingers through Maria's long curls.

"But we're already here, and you feel so good," Maria replied, her fingers slipping back inside the thong to slide it down Shelby's legs. "Can I have you here first?"

Shelby couldn't do anything but nod as Maria looked up at her at the same time the thong fell to the floor.

"I'll take my time in there, but right now, I just want…" She leaned forward and pressed her lips to the short curls between Shelby's legs.

Shelby twitched and shifted on her feet.

"Is this okay?" Maria checked. "I know it's our first time, but I wanted you the other day in bed, and I–"

"Do whatever you want to me," Shelby said. "I'll come."

Maria smirked up at her, causing Shelby to swallow hard. Then, she lifted Shelby's leg and placed it next to herself on the sofa. Shelby was fully exposed to her now, and Maria was staring at her. As nervous as she thought she should be, Shelby wasn't nervous right now. Previously, she'd always had slow first times with women, and they'd taken their time to get to this point and then took a long time to work up to the part where one or both of them came. There was always foreplay involved. Tonight, though,

Shelby didn't want foreplay. Well, she might want it later, but right now, she wanted Maria to touch her and make her come for the first time. Shelby reached behind her back and unclasped the strapless bra, letting it fall off her body.

"Good God, woman, you're so fucking sexy," Maria said, running one hand up the inside of Shelby's thigh and the other up between her breasts.

Then, Maria leaned forward more, and her tongue slipped between Shelby's folds. Shelby closed her eyes and just tried to hold on. Maria licked her a few more times before she grabbed on to Shelby's ass with both hands and sucked.

"God," Shelby gasped out, holding Maria as close as she could.

When Maria slipped two fingers inside her, Shelby nearly fell over, but she managed to keep herself upright. It didn't take long. Within minutes, Shelby's hips were rocking against Maria's face while Maria's fingers curled inside her before they thrust deep, taking her over the edge. Shelby yelled Maria's name over and over until she finally slowed her rocking, and Maria moved her mouth to kiss Shelby's stomach and the inside of her thighs.

"That was…"

"What?" Maria asked, sliding her fingers out of Shelby and sitting back against the sofa, looking sexy with a satisfied smirk on her face.

"You're still wearing all your clothes," Shelby noted, realizing it at the same time.

"Would you like to do something about that?" Maria asked.

Shelby nodded.

***

"Try that," Shelby said.

"It's good, Shell. It's just as good as the other three drinks you've made for me. Are you trying to kill me by caffeine?" Maria laughed.

"No, I just got this new cappuccino maker, so I thought I'd try all the drink possibilities with the coffee *you* bought me."

"You don't have to do it all at once." Maria smiled, pushing a latte back toward Shelby. "You'll run *out* of that coffee I bought you."

"We can just go back to the roastery and pick up more. Want to go this weekend?"

"Do we have to wake up at five again?" Maria asked, moving to Shelby and wrapping her arms around her from behind. "You know I'm not good at waking up early." She kissed Shelby's neck.

"I do," she replied. "I tried to wake you up for sex before work yesterday, and you kind of growled at me, and not in the sexy way you usually do."

"Oh, no." Maria kissed her neck again. "I made you go without?"

"Yes, you did," Shelby replied playfully. "And you stayed at your place last night, so you've left me without twice now."

Maria unbuttoned Shelby's jeans and slipped her hand inside.

"Well, we can't have that, can we?"

"We're supposed to have coffee and then... Oh," Shelby said when Maria found her clit and began stroking.

"I don't like leaving my girl wanting. I want her fully satisfied at all times."

"Never stop doing that, then," Shelby replied, closing her eyes and leaning back against her girlfriend. "That leaves me... totally... satisfied." She gripped the counter in front of her.

"What *else* leaves you totally satisfied?"

"When I get to touch you," Shelby said softly as Maria dipped a little lower, gathering wetness and bringing it up to Shelby's clit to stroke faster. "I love touching you."

"I love when you touch me," Maria said, sucking on

Shelby's earlobe. "If you come for me now, there's time for you to touch me, too."

"Yeah?" Shelby checked.

"Yeah."

Shelby turned around then, confusing her girlfriend. When she unbuttoned and unzipped Maria's jeans and slid her hand inside, Maria looked down and smirked.

"If we both come now, we'd have time to come again before we have to go," Shelby reasoned, stroking Maria's clit as Maria stroked her. "I got a head start, so I might need to get you caught up."

"Oh, fuck," Maria gasped out when Shelby stroked hard and fast.

"You're so hard, so wet," Shelby said into Maria's ear.

"I wanted sex when I got here. Oh, there. Yes!" She nipped at Shelby's shoulder. "You kept putting… coffee in… front of– Fuck, Shell! I'm–"

Shelby came when Maria's hips rocked uncontrollably into her.

"Me too," she replied.

When they both came down, they kissed slowly until Maria began walking Shelby backward toward the bedroom.

"We can be late," Maria said.

"God, I love you," Shelby replied.

Maria pulled back to look at her in surprise.

"Do you mean that, or is that the lust talking?" she asked.

They'd never said those words to one another before, but Shelby knew she felt them. She had felt them all along, but it had been a month of dating, three months of being Maria's girlfriend, and she'd wanted to say it from the beginning.

"I love you," she repeated honestly.

Maria smiled and said, "I love you, too. God, Shell… I can't believe I get to say that to you now. I've wanted to say it for–"

"I know. Me too." Shelby pulled Maria in for another

kiss. "Show me," she requested.

Maria walked Shelby backward more, kissing Shelby's neck in the process. They loved each other. Shelby hadn't ever thought she'd love someone how she loved Erica. And maybe she never would because Erica had been her first love, but, God, she loved Maria. And as Maria slowly removed all the barriers between them and climbed on top of her, Shelby knew that this was one of those kinds of love that just made sense in the most amazing way. When Maria slipped inside her and rocked while she kissed her, Shelby thought about all the times they'd done this and how perfect it always seemed.

"I love you," Maria whispered after Shelby came at her touch.

"We're canceling on your friends for brunch; we're not leaving this bed today," Shelby replied, smiling up at her. "And, God, I love you, too."

***

"Where do you want this?" Maria asked.

"In the bedroom for now," Shelby told her.

"You said you hated this lamp," Maria pointed out, laughing.

"I do," Shelby said.

"So, you want it in the bedroom?"

"No, I want it in the garbage, but you insisted on bringing it here," Shelby replied. "So, it can go on your table if you want, or it can go in the walk-in closet behind the boxes."

Maria laughed again and said, "You love me enough to accept my lamp?"

"I love you enough to *tolerate* your lamp."

Maria placed the lamp on the kitchen counter and pulled Shelby into her.

"Is this crazy?"

"Moving in together this early? Yes, it's crazy," Shelby

replied. "But I want to. I want you here all the time."

"I know. I want to be here all the time. I still have my lease, though, so if–"

"No backup plans, babe. This is it – this is *the* plan," she said.

"Yeah?" Maria wrapped her arms around Shelby's waist. "Forever?"

Shelby smiled and said, "Forever."

***

Later that day, after they'd moved most of Maria's stuff into Shelby's apartment, Shelby checked the mail and was surprised to find a letter from Erica. Then, it dawned on her. She tore the envelope open quickly at her kitchen table and smiled when she saw the sleeping baby on the left of the birth announcement and his information on the right. Erica had a little boy named Deacon.

"What are you smiling at?" Maria asked her, moving out of the bedroom.

"Erica had her baby," she replied, holding up the card. "It's a boy named Deacon."

"That's a nice name," Maria said, moving to Shelby's side. "How are you doing with all of that?"

"What? Her having a baby?"

"You were together for five years, Shell."

"I know." Shelby stared down at the announcement again. "But she always wanted this. She wanted the two AM feedings, the diaper changing, the nursery, the dropping them off at pre-school, and buying the car seats that have to constantly be changed as they grow. I never did. I just don't have that in me." Shelby looked up at her girlfriend then. "You're sure, right? Erica and I were fine for a while until her clock started that tick-tick-tick, and it was–"

"I have no desire to be pregnant myself," Maria interrupted. "I don't want the two AM feedings, and I know you don't, either – I knew what I was signing up for when we met, and I know I only need you. I don't need a baby. Honestly, they're cute and all, but they're so much work. I mean, I want to go on vacations with you to beaches and private villas where we can be naked in our chairs, sip adult beverages, and then do other adult things."

"Oh, yeah?" Shelby teased.

"Whenever we want, we can just pack our things and go." Maria pressed her lips to the underside of Shelby's jaw. "We don't have to worry about a babysitter or having to put money away for college."

"So, private beachside villas, huh?"

"With clear water," Maria added. "And my body pressed up against your body."

"Let's go christen the bed," Shelby suggested.

"Babe, we've more than christened that bed."

"Now, it's *our* bed; it's different."

***

"You're exhausted," Maria said.

"I'm fine," Shelby replied.

"Babe, I love you, and I know this is going to get me in trouble, but you have bags under your eyes; you're so tired."

"I just have to finish typing up this motion," she replied.

"It's after two in the morning. Can't a paralegal do that, or someone else from your office? We're going on vacation tomorrow. It's a long flight."

"Think of it like this: I'm much more likely to fall asleep on the plane," Shelby replied. "I'll be in soon, okay? Go back to sleep."

Maria leaned down over the sofa and kissed her forehead.

"I love you."

"I know. I love you, too."

Shelby was beyond exhausted; her girlfriend was absolutely right about that. Work had gotten a lot busier just in time for their first real vacation as a couple. They'd done a few weekends away already, but now, they were flying to Fiji. They had one of those tiny houses over the water rented for an entire week, and Shelby could not wait to only see Maria and room service for seven full days. Maria had planned the whole thing, and now that it was upon them, Shelby just wanted to finish the last thing she needed to for work so that she could leave it all behind.

The next morning, they hopped on their plane, and within minutes, Shelby was asleep. Hours upon hours later, they were on the island and headed to their villa. Once their escort left them alone, Maria was on top of Shelby on the bed in an instant, kissing her neck and chest until Shelby finally stopped laughing and relented. She pulled off Maria's shirt, and Maria did the same to Shelby's. Minutes later, Maria's head was between Shelby's legs, and Shelby finally released all the tension she'd been holding in her body for weeks.

Later that night, they swam in the clear water, holding on to one another so tightly until they finally went back inside for dinner, which was delivered and set up for them. They'd decided to dress up as if they were going out, and Shelby had put on a soft pink sundress while Maria had chosen nice black pants and a light blouse. When they got to dessert and coffee, Shelby had been prepared to skip it because she wanted her girlfriend back in bed and naked beneath her. They only had seven days here, and she'd planned on taking advantage of every moment.

"I wanted to talk to you about something," Maria said.

"Does it involve *that* bed over there or *that* hot tub in the corner?" Shelby asked.

"No, it involves a question."

"A question about?" she asked.

Maria stood up from the table and moved to the big suitcase, which they'd yet to unpack. She turned back around to Shelby after pulling something out of it, and then she knelt in front of her.

"Our life together," Maria said. "I was kind of hoping you'd say yes to marrying me."

Shelby looked down in shock as Maria opened the ring box she was holding.

"Oh, my God," she said. "Really?" Her eyes welled with tears.

"I am so glad I'm klutzy and paid more attention to my phone than my surroundings that day," Maria told her. "I fell in love with you then. And every day since, I've fallen more and more. I want to spend the rest of my life with you, Shell. Will you marry me?"

***

"You're crazy," Shelby said.

"I must be; I married *you*," Maria replied.

"And, apparently, you want to sleep on the couch to-night." Shelby laughed at her wife.

"Babe, I'm serious."

"Maria, I can't just quit my job."

"Why not? You hate it."

"I don't hate it."

"You don't *like* it," Maria argued. "Plus, you've been working a million hours a week because everyone else does, and I hardly get to see you these days."

"It's just this case; it's a big deal."

"And the last case, and the one before that."

"I'm getting put on the big ones. That's a good thing," Shelby replied.

"Shell, I love you. If you can honestly tell me you love being a lawyer, I'll leave it alone. But ever since we met, I've had this feeling like you're just doing it because you went to law school, and you don't want to waste that. Maybe that's the wrong way to put it."

"Everyone in my family is a lawyer."

"So?" Maria asked.

"So, they love it. I'm supposed to work my way up to partner," Shelby replied.

"Babe, we don't need the money. We don't need you to make partner. We don't need you to hold on to a job you don't like. If your family loves it, great. If it's not for you, that's great, too."

"But a coffee shop? That's risky, Maria." Shelby closed the computer in her lap and turned to her wife. "I have a law degree, not a business degree."

"Hello," Maria said, waving. "I own a business already; I know what to do."

"And you're going to wake up at five to open the place with me?"

"Hell, no." Maria laughed. "I mean, I would if you needed me to, but this would be your place. I'll help with whatever else you might need, of course, but, Shell, it's for sale – the place where we met is for sale, and we could tear out that stupid wall. We could put a deck out there so that people could have their coffee while staring at the ocean. We could have the roastery as our supplier and make better coffee. You could run the place and staff it however you want. It would be ours. It's fate, babe."

"You're really serious about this?" Shelby checked.

"Yes, I am." Maria took the computer from her and placed it on the table. Then, she straddled Shelby. "Babe, I'm totally serious. This place is special; we met there. We went there all the time before they closed it down." She wrapped her arms around Shelby's neck. "We could own it, Shell." Maria smiled wide. "We could buy the building; we can afford it. And there's a huge apartment upstairs; I already checked it out. It's two bedrooms, but we can make a third one if you want an office up there. The other one could be a guest room or something. We could build a balcony off the master so we could look out at the ocean each night."

"You want to *live* there, too?"

"Why not? It's closer to my office, and you'd have a really short commute. We could take the time to build it all how we want it. There could be a space for performers in the café. We could have open mic nights or something. I can market the hell out of the place. That would be my main contribution."

"Oh, I think you'll contribute in other ways, too," Shelby said teasingly as she peered down Maria's V-neck T-shirt.

"Oh, yeah?"

"Yeah, you'll be my eye candy," Shelby smirked up at her wife. "And you can contribute in other ways as well."

"Other ways?" Maria asked.

Shelby lifted Maria's shirt up and off.

"I'm thinking, there will be many long days for me where I come home and just need some stress relief from customers who are rude, or when something breaks and I have to fix it."

"Stress relief? You mean, like, yoga or meditation?" Maria asked, unclasping her own bra and letting it fall aside.

"Those help sometimes, but there's something that *always* works." Shelby pressed her lips between Maria's breasts.

"Always? What do you mean?"

"Well, if I'm busy all day being the big boss downstairs, and you're waiting for me upstairs, I might need you to…"

"Boss you around?" Maria said, smiling down at her.

Shelby nodded.

"So, is that a yes? Are we doing this?"

"Your shirt's already off, so—"

"Shell," Maria said.

"Yes, we're doing this." Shelby laughed. "I'll put my notice in at work and become a café owner with you."

Maria pulled her in for a hug, and Shelby laughed more. Then, she dipped her hands into her wife's shorts and underwear, cupping her ass.

"Let's celebrate," Maria said. "You; naked; on your back on our bed. I'm getting a little something." She stood up quickly and ran to their bedroom.

"Get the *big* something; I don't want a *little* something."

Maria laughed from the bedroom.

***

"Chels, are you sure you want to work here?"

"Why wouldn't I?" Chelsea asked.

"Your mom told me you're tutoring a lot right now," Shelby said to her niece.

"Oh, I was, but not anymore. I will again, but I don't make much doing that since I'm still a student myself. I'd like to make some extra cash for a car, but I also want to work here."

"Here, specifically? You love coffee or something?"

"Can I talk to you about something and you won't tell my parents until I'm ready for them to know?"

"That depends… Are you in some sort of trouble? I can't–"

"No, it's not that." Chelsea paused and looked down at her hands. "I wanted to talk to you about this anyway because I think you'll understand."

"Chels, you can tell me anything, you know that," Shelby said.

"I think I might be…" Chelsea looked up then. "Gay."

"Oh," Shelby uttered. "I see."

"Yeah. I've known for a while, I think. I want to tell my parents, but I don't know how they'll react. And you're gay, and you're married to Aunt Maria, so I thought you'd be a good person to tell first."

"Well, thank you for trusting me with this, Chels," she replied, smiling at her niece.

"You're not going to ask me how I know?" Chelsea asked.

"No. Why would I do that?"

"I don't know. I'm sixteen; adults usually love telling kids that they don't know things yet."

"Chels, I'm gay. I know what it feels like to know that at sixteen. Besides, no one asks people how they know they're straight, right?"

Chelsea laughed and said, "I guess not."

"Sweetie, I won't say anything, but your parents love and support me and your Aunt Maria. They love you more than life."

"But I'm their kid. They might not want–"

"I know your Mom and Dad, Chels. When you're ready to tell them, they'll be fine with it. Hell, your dad will probably celebrate it. He just wants you to be happy."

"You think?"

"I do." Shelby smiled wider. "Maria will be home soon. Are you okay with her knowing, or is this our secret for now?"

"No, she can know." Chelsea shrugged a shoulder.

"And the reason you wanted to work at the café…"

"It's in gay town," Chelsea replied, smiling. "Your café will be on the same block as a bunch of other gay-owned businesses. I know because I… Well, I know. Anyway, I just thought it would be nice to work where my people might be."

"Your people?" Shelby said, laughing.

"Yeah. Who knows? Maybe I'll meet a nice girl there how you met Aunt Maria."

"Maybe," Shelby replied.

"Hey, babe. I brought dinner," Maria said, walking through the door. "Oh. Hey, Chels."

"Hi, Aunt Maria."

"I have enough if you're staying for dinner," Maria said.

"No, I'm just here asking Aunt Shelby for a job."

"You want to work at the café?" Maria asked, placing the bag of food on the kitchen table.

"She does," Shelby said, walking over to her wife and giving her a quick kiss. "Hi, babe."

"Hey," Maria replied, winking at her.

That wink still did things to Shelby. Now years later, after they met in the café, whenever her wife winked at her, Shelby got weak in the knees. She leaned in and kissed Maria once more because she just had to.

"Gross," Chelsea commented.

Maria laughed and said, "No one is making you watch, Chels."

"Did you get pizza?" Chelsea asked.

"No, I got pasta."

"Oh, bummer." Chelsea walked over to the bag and rifled through it. "But you got Alfredo sauce with the bread-sticks, right?"

Shelby rolled her eyes at her niece in Maria's direction, and Maria pulled out plates.

"Oh, Aunt Maria?"

"Yes?"

"I'm gay," Chelsea told her.

***

"Spread your legs, babe," Maria said.

"We can't do this down here," Shelby replied.

"Yes, we can. We have before."

"We weren't open before," Shelby argued.

"We're not open now; the doors are locked." Maria pushed Shelby's legs apart. "Chels went home." She moved between Shelby's legs. "And you were sitting on top of your desk when I got here, wearing this dress that I love so much. What was I supposed to do?" Maria leaned in and kissed Shelby's neck.

"Well, when you put it that way." Shelby wrapped her arms around Maria.

"I'm wearing something for you," Maria whispered into her ear.

"I know. I can feel it," Shelby said.

"Do you *want* it?"

"Yes," she replied.

Maria undid the button on her jeans and unzipped them, pulling out the toy she'd worn and watching Shelby's reaction to it. Then, she reached for Shelby's panties as Shelby lifted up off the table to allow her to take them off.

"You might have to warm me up first. I *was* working before you came downstairs, all strapped on."

"Oh, that's not a problem," Maria replied, kneeling in front of her.

She took Shelby with her mouth first, making her come slowly, which she knew Shelby loved. Then, she stood back up and moved into her, slipping inside.

"Warm enough?"

"Yes," Shelby said softly, lying down on her desk.

Maria thrust into her slowly at first until Shelby was begging her to move faster and make her come. They hadn't done this since the café had opened, but they'd done it once while it was still under construction. The last time they'd done this, though, Maria had been behind her. As much as Shelby had loved that, she loved watching her wife take her even more. Maria was everything Shelby ever wanted and, somehow, still more. Now that *The Meet Cute Café* was open for business and doing seemingly well, Shelby felt totally fulfilled in her life. She had a gorgeous wife who made love to her just how she liked, supported her in every way, and loved her completely, and she now had a career she loved, too.

"Yes, there."

"You like it there?" Maria asked, thrusting harder.

"You know I do," Shelby replied with a smirk.

Then, she rolled her head back and let the orgasm take her away.

"Fuck, I love you," Maria said, crashing down on top of her on the desk.

"Did you just–"

"Yes," Maria said, kissing Shelby's shoulder.

"I love you. Thank you."

Maria laughed, lifting her head back up to look at her.

"You're welcome?" she said, laughing. "Anytime."

"I didn't mean for that, but thank you for that, too," Shelby said.

"What did you mean, love?" Maria asked, kissing her lips.

"Thank you for recognizing that I was unhappy before and that I needed this place."

"You're doing an amazing job, Shell. People are coming back every day. The coffee's great. The service is great. Personally, I have the hots for the owner, so I plan on being a regular."

Shelby laughed and said, "Oh, yeah? Should I be worried?"

"I'm still inside you, so I think it's safe to say I'm sticking around for a while."

"Is that a promise?" Shelby asked, lifting her hips.

"Yeah?" Maria checked, looking down and lifting Shelby's dress in order to see under it. "You need me again, babe?"

Shelby nodded and said, "One more time here."

"And then?" Maria asked, rolling into her.

"One more time in our shower; I smell like coffee."

"I know. It's a big turn-on for me now."

***

"So, Chels and Taylor?" Maria asked.

"She wanted to know if she could invite Taylor over for dinner. She wants her to spend time with us. It's cute," Shelby said as she rested against Maria's chest. "They're cute together, and I like Taylor. Plus, it's been going on for a while now – I think they're serious. Chels is basically living at Taylor's place, and her parents are… adjusting."

"And Erica and this Melissa?"

"She seems happy," Shelby replied. "Melissa seems to get her, but she also gets Deacon, which is huge."

"Yeah, I know," Maria said, running her hand through

Shelby's hair.

"That's two couples that met at our café."

"I guess that's true," Maria agreed. "Well, three, if you count us," she added.

"Do you remember Troy, Courtney's kind of, sort of adopted daughter?"

"I think so, yeah," Maria said.

"She's dating someone she met here, too."

"She is?"

"Yeah."

"How do you know that?"

"I see things," Shelby said, shrugging into her wife.

"You see things?"

"I hear things, too," Shelby said, smiling.

"You eavesdrop?"

"No, but people don't always pay attention to the barista behind the counter or the one dropping off their drinks. Chelsea and I hear things all the time. We may or may not share those things with each other from time to time. In fact, Kelsey has been flirting with our favorite realtor."

"Ryan?"

"Yeah," Shelby said. "It wouldn't surprise me if that turns into something."

"Ryan knows we're not selling, right?" Maria checked.

"She does. She gave up, but she said someone else would be coming in someday, so I'm just waiting for that."

"So, you basically watch couples fall in love all day at work while I slave away behind my desk?" Maria joked.

"Yup; that's pretty much all I do. Still love me?"

Maria kissed the top of her head and said, "Forever."

***

"They're all here," Shelby said, turning to Maria and smiling wide.

"Well, you *did* invite them all," Maria replied.

"Not like that. It's Kelsey's last performance before she and Ryan move to LA. I put up signs, and you blasted social media. I didn't think they'd *all* show up, though."

"They all met here. Maybe some of them came to Kelsey's performances before, and so they want to see the last one together."

Shelby looked out at the café. There were at least a hundred people out there now. Kelsey was still setting up. Anna was playing the keyboard for her tonight. Troy and Ryan, their wives, were talking off-stage as they drank their beers.

"What happens to Ryan's business when she moves?" Maria asked.

"Nothing. She's just going to work from there and maybe open an office in LA. I'm sure Katelyn will do just fine taking over being in charge here," Shelby said, nodding to Katelyn.

She was sitting between Madelyn and Ashley. The three of them couldn't legally get married, but they all wore rings, indicating that they were more than just girlfriends. Ashley had her head on Katelyn's shoulder, and Madelyn had her arm around Katelyn's chair.

"I guess that's good. Katelyn's been wanting to move up."

"Yeah, she's ambitious," Shelby said, laughing. "And Andrea and Courtney are here with Taylor and Chels."

"God, I can't believe they're getting married," Maria replied.

"Chels is all grown up, isn't she?" Shelby said, wiping down the counter.

"Hey, can I get you guys a drink? On the house?" Lucy offered, winking at them.

"On the house, huh?" Maria laughed.

"Where's Georgia?" Shelby asked, wrapping an arm around Maria's waist.

"She's on the patio, wiping down a few tables."

"You two don't work here anymore; you don't have to

serve drinks or clean tables," Shelby reminded.

"Please, I owe you two basically everything. I can make a few drinks, and Georgia can clean a few tables when we're home and you're busy." She handed them each a beer. "We're moving in together."

"Really?" Shelby asked.

"Yeah, finally," Lucy said.

Over the years, she'd gone from being a shy fifteen-year-old who wasn't completely comfortable with herself to a young woman who had a girlfriend she loved and had no problem showing off. Lucy was smart and beautiful and still madly in love with the girl she met on her first day of work. Georgia, her girlfriend, had gone to state school next to the private university Lucy had gotten into. Lucy's parents still weren't involved in her life, but she'd been able to connect with her sister, and they had a relationship, at least. Georgia had turned into a good student, likely because of Lucy's influence, and they'd been together for years now.

"Hi," Georgia greeted, walking up and dropping the rag and tray of dirty dishes on the counter.

"You don't have to do that," Shelby replied.

"You took care of the love of my life for two years; I can clean–"

"A few tables; we know. We know," Maria said jokingly. "And we're glad to have you both home. We miss you two when you're gone."

"We miss you guys, too," Georgia replied, moving behind the counter and to Lucy's side. "Did you tell them?"

"Yeah." Lucy smiled.

"It's a small place, but it's ours," Georgia said. "I mean, it's the landlord's, but we'll pay rent, so it's ours."

"We're proud of you both," Shelby told them.

"What do your parents think?" Maria asked.

"My dad wanted us to get someplace he deemed to be safer, but we like this place, and it's pretty safe."

"Should we be worried?" Shelby asked Georgia.

"No, we're good."

"Hey, Chels wanted me to ask you guys if you were joining us or not." Taylor approached, placing her palms on the counter. "You're not going to work tonight, are you? We were thinking about doing a little wedding-planning since everyone's here."

"We'll be over in a minute," Shelby said.

"Hey, isn't that your mom's friend?" Maria asked, nodding toward the front door.

Taylor turned to see who Maria was looking at and said, "Yeah, that's her. My mother has decided that Stephanie has been single long enough and set her up with someone from the school. How a principal is allowed to set up one of their teachers with one of their friends is beyond me, but, apparently, that's not an HR violation."

"Another one?" Shelby whispered into her wife's ear.

"Maybe," Maria said.

"Hey, Aunt Shelby? Can I get a hot chocolate?" Deacon asked.

"*You* want a hot chocolate?" she asked him.

"No, it's for Daniel," he replied, chuckling. "Mom sent me over."

Shelby looked beyond him to Erica and Melissa, who were sitting at a table with their younger son, Daniel.

"How's school, Deacon?" Shelby asked as she watched Georgia get to work on his hot chocolate.

"Fine. Baseball is going great, though."

"I bet." Maria laughed at the boy who had practically grown up in this café, prioritizing baseball over school.

"People are saying I'm going to be drafted in the first round. I could even go two or three," he added.

"That's amazing, Deac," Shelby said, knowing this information already because Erica and Melissa had always bragged about their oldest son non-stop.

"Hello, everyone. Thanks for coming out tonight," Kelsey said into the microphone. "Well, most of you came out *before* tonight, but thanks for coming to see me perform tonight."

The crowd quieted and then laughed at the joke.

"Look at what you made, babe," Maria whispered, wrapping her arms around Shelby from behind.

"What?"

"Shell, you did all this."

"*We* did all this."

"Babe, all I did was suggest we buy this place. You put the hard work in." She kissed Shelby's neck. "You made a place where people like you and me can be themselves, where they can meet people and fall in love, and where they can feel safe and supported. You did all of this, Shell. And now look at all of them – they're happy, love."

"I'm happy, too," Shelby replied, smiling.

"Happy anniversary, baby," Maria whispered. "I love you so much."

"I love you, too. Happy anniversary."

"To the couple that started it all," Maria said in a whispered mock-toast.

"To *The Meet Cute Café*," Shelby replied, looking around her coffee shop.

EPILOGUE

Now, I wasn't there for it all, obviously. You'll just have to trust me on what happened, but some of the details might not be one-hundred-percent accurate.

When Maria and I first started noticing women coupling off in *The Meet Cute*, she suggested I keep a journal of the things I see and hear in the café. It was supposed to just be for me. Well, maybe for *her*, too. It was something fun we could talk about over dinner; how our niece met and fell in love with a girl named Taylor; or how Anna, the quiet woman who had been raised to believe she had to be perfect or she wouldn't be loved, met her wife in our café.

I could write about how my very own ex-girlfriend, the woman I thought I'd marry one day, met her future wife on an app but then met her in person at *The Meet Cute*. Melissa had turned out to be exactly what Erica had needed, and they'd had another son together, giving Erica the family she'd always wanted and that I could never give her.

Then, there was Ryan, the woman who had only stopped by because she wanted to convince us to sell the café, and she'd ended up meeting Kelsey and moving to LA with her. The last I heard from them, Kelsey was working with an independent label and writing her dissertation at the same time, while Ryan had opened another office for her real estate business, and they were planning on trying for a kid someday soon.

Andrea and Courtney had a house on the water now. They'd talked about getting married but hadn't made things official yet. Courtney's business got even more successful, and Andrea had been a school principal for quite some time now. Her friend, Stephanie, had met someone new, and they'd become regulars of the café recently.

Madelyn, Katelyn, and Ashley still came into the shop together at least once a week. Katelyn had taken over Ryan's main office here, and Ashley had gotten a few promotions at work. Madelyn had gotten into the career she'd wanted all along, and they owned a giant five-bedroom house on the outskirts of the city. Ashley had only recently told Shelby that she couldn't drink coffee right now and would need to switch to decaf tea because she was pregnant.

And then, there was Lucy and Georgia.

***

"Is it okay?" Lucy asked.

"It's beautiful, sweetie," Shelby said.

"Do you think she'll say yes?"

"I can't imagine she'd say no," Maria replied.

"It's small," Lucy said, looking down at the modest ring.

"Georgia doesn't care about how big a diamond is. She loves you, Luce."

"When you asked Shelby, were you nervous?" Lucy asked Maria.

"I was incredibly nervous," Maria replied honestly, laughing lightly.

"You were?" Shelby asked.

"Babe, I was asking you to marry me – of course, I was nervous."

"I want it to be perfect," Lucy said.

"It will be. However you do it, it will be perfect," Maria assured her. "Just trust me. I had this whole thing planned, and I got so nervous, I just grabbed the ring and got down on one knee."

"What are you talking about?" Shelby said. "We had a romantic dinner. We were in Fiji."

"I know. And there was more. I had a whole speech, but I only got through part of it."

Shelby smiled at her wife and kissed her on the cheek.

"I'm thinking about doing it this weekend," Lucy said.

"I can't wait to hear the good news. We can celebrate with dinner here. Champagne, and I'll make Maria bake that cherry pie you love."

"Hey, don't sign me up for baking," Maria joked. Then, she winked at Lucy. "Whatever you want."

***

So, Lucy and Georgia got engaged the following weekend, and Maria baked that pie. I picked up the champagne, and we all celebrated. When the girls… *women* left for home, Maria and I cleaned up and went to bed. My wife gave me the rest of her speech that night, the one she'd planned to give me all those years ago when she'd gotten down on one knee, and I knew how I've always known that Maria was my soulmate. As I held back my tears, she kissed my cheeks and my lips, telling me over and over again how much she loved me, and I told her the same.

When I think back about the day we met, it always makes me think about the magic of *The Meet Cute Café*. It was never a dream of mine to run a coffee shop. I'd had a plan for myself that involved law school, becoming partner, and marrying Erica. Recognizing I was wrong for her was important because it led me to Maria, and Maria helped me realize that I hated my job. She led me to *The Meet Cute.*

My love led me to my dreams, helped me fulfill them, and then I got to watch as the people in my café fell in love day after day and year after year. There's not much better than that, is there?

This journal, which Maria got me, is almost full now, so I asked her to pick out another one for me. She grabbed one just yesterday, and now, I have another book to fill with stories of love at *The Meet Cute Café.*

Printed in Great Britain
by Amazon